# A NECESSARY EVIL

Daniel Borrachero Tamame

# A NECESSARY EVIL

EDITORIAL
**Letra Minúscula**

First edition: March 2025
ISBN: 978-84-1090-184-1
Legal deposit: MU 81-2025
Copyright © 2025 Daniel Borrachero Tamame
Translated by Garrett Leatherman
Published by Editorial Letra Minúscula
www.letraminuscula.com
contacto@letraminuscula.com

# CHAPTER I

Harry had been told that it never rained in his new city. An umbrella there would be another decorative object, like a plant, a vase, or an ashtray in a home of non-smokers. Since Harry wasn't the kind of person who generally trusted people by habit, he looked it up on Google and, indeed, Google confirmed those claims. It may rain sometimes, even quite heavily, but it wasn't normal. In the two months he was in his new city, many locals referred to it as a desert. They would say, "It's a desert here; we're in the driest year on record." All of this made Harry think: "Maybe I should trust people for once." In the end, people trust others and carry on. If people say it doesn't rain, perhaps it's true. "If it's like a desert, maybe it's like Las Vegas, which is an actual desert where it barely ever rains," he repeated to himself on the plane before arriving to his new home. Right when he got off the train in his new city, after his flight landed in Madrid, everything seemed to fit, weather-wise, with what they had told him. Indeed, it wasn't raining; it was 6 p.m. on March 14th, and the thermometer on his phone showed 87 degrees Fahrenheit. The heat was suffocating for that time of year, exactly as they had already told him (a claim that Harry, of course, had double checked with Google), but with his stubbornness, Harry had remained skeptical and had taken those claims with some reservation. As he was walking to his new house, he realized that perhaps his New York Knicks sweatshirt with his jeans and Adidas sneakers were a bit excessive for the weather. In the short ten minutes it took to get to his house (Google Maps had told him eleven minutes, but Harry hurried to get there to avoid getting a heat stroke) he noticed that many people were already wearing summer clothes, or at least what seemed to Harry to be summer clothes. Many of them had on shorts, short-sleeved shirts, and some even had flip-flops or sandals. What seemed evident was that it didn't seem like it rained much in his new home. At least that's what Harry thought then.

Today, May 12th, as he was looking for the key to the entrance of his apartment building, soaked from head to toe, and hearing thunder, he remembered with resignation that first sunny day living in his new city. If he was a believer, he would think that God was somehow punishing him or laughing at him. But since he wasn't a believer and didn't believe in fate either, he simply cursed inwardly as he was still looking for the key. He finally found it and managed to open the heavy iron and glass entrance door to his building. He turned around to look at the street now that he was under cover, but he could hardly see anything with the amount of rain that was falling. "Fuck me," he thought to himself as he walked towards the elevator. This reinforced his belief that people can't be trusted, at least not entirely, especially people who make categorical assertions. How could it never rain?

It has to rain no matter what, fifty times a year, twenty times, five times, one time. It may rain more or less than that, but never? Are we on Venus or something? Those people, by definition, lied. And Harry didn't like liars. Google, however, gave information, not absolute claims. It would tell you, for instance, that the average precipitation was 0.4 inches per month. That's very little (only about .01 inches per day), from which you could deduce that it didn't rain much there. But not that it never rained. Google one, people zero.

Harry was by no means antisocial. He liked being with people, laughing with them, chatting.… Sometimes he needed to tell things to someone; it wasn't enough to tell them to Alexa or his pet (when he had one), or to look them up on the internet. He liked human contact. But life and work had taught him in large part that you have to take everything you're told with a grain of salt, especially when people claim that something is what it is no matter what, all the time, and that there's no other option. As he waited for the elevator to go up to his apartment, a neighbor was coming down the stairs. Harry had seen him three or four times in those two months.

"Hello," the neighbor said as he walked by him.

"See you later," Harry replied.

Those were all the words they had exchanged during those two months, the four or five times that they saw each other at the entrance or in the elevator. Harry didn't even know the guy's name or which apartment he lived in, though he looked to be about twenty-five years old. Once, he saw him coming in through the entrance as Harry was leaving. He was with another guy who looked to be around thirty years old, but he didn't know if he lived with him or if he was visiting. He hadn't seen him since. To tell the truth, he didn't care all that much. Harry didn't believe it was necessary to be friends with all his neighbors. Neighbors are in principle just that: neighbors. They're useful for giving you salt if you don't have it, holding the elevator door for you, calling the fire department if it smells like smoke in your apartment, those types of things. And it wasn't a problem to reciprocate those things, of course. That was a duty in the life of a good neighbor. At least that's what Harry thought before arriving in his new city.

That new city was called Murcia, a beautiful city in the southeast of Spain. Harry Fernández, as he was named, was the son of a Spanish father and an American mother. Both had already passed away. He had lived in the US his entire life. His father had always spoken to him in Spanish; thus, it was a very familiar language for him that he had no trouble speaking and understanding, even though his native language was English. When a job opportunity from across the pond arose for him, at thirty-six years old and single, he didn't think twice and accepted it. Plus, they provided him housing, the salary wasn't an issue, and the work was the same that he had a passion for then and that he had already been doing in the US. Moreover, in Spain, as he had learned, he didn't have to worry about medical bills and things of that sort. Even though Harry was in good health, not having that worry seemed like a plus to him. So, there he was in Murcia, and after a couple of months, he practically felt at home.

Harry pushed the button in the elevator for the third floor even though he lived on the fourth. When the elevator stopped, Harry got out and knocked on the door with the letter A that had a Homer Simpson doormat. A couple of seconds later, his neighbor and friend Alfonso opened the door.

"Dude, Harry, you look like a mop with that hair," Alfonso said as he contained his laughter.

"Fuck off, asshole. Grab me a towel and a beer," Harry blurted out, smiling as he walked into Alfonso's apartment without waiting for an invitation.

He didn't need it. Since the day he met Alfonso, the second day after he moved in, they were inseparable. It was that day that Harry knocked on his door and introduced himself:

"Hey, I'm the new neighbor in 4C. My name's Harry."

"Hey Harry, I'm Alfonso. Welcome to Murcia. You're not from around here, right? Do you need anything?

"Well, I wanted to know how internet works around here, what's the best deal, and just get to know the neighborhood a little bit."

"Of course. I'm a little busy right now; how about we meet up in an hour at Bar Chema right downstairs, and I'll give you the rundown?"

"Perfect. It's 7:30 now, so I'll see you downstairs at 8:30. Thanks, Alfonso."

At 8:20, Harry went down to Bar Chema, which was right next to the entrance of his building, and ordered a beer while he waited. It was very different from a typical American bar. It didn't look like a diner either. It had a medium-sized bar, four tables inside, and an outdoor patio with about eight to ten more tables. There were paintings on the walls of what seemed to be the city long ago; behind the bar there were bottles of alcohol, many of which Harry had never seen. Moreover, there was a glass display case at the bar with trays of food as though it were self-serve, but you couldn't access it; it opened on the side from behind the bar. There was a very thick Spanish omelet, some peanuts, and a couple of other things he didn't recognize. He decided he would start asking and learning about the local food, but perhaps that day wasn't the day to start. However, since he was hungry, he also ordered some French fries. He thought they would give him normal fries, but they gave him some potato chips on a plate with a slice of lemon and a pepper shaker. "These people are crazy," he thought. However, since Harry was someone who liked to try new things, with an open mind, he put lemon and pepper on the chips, and he actually liked it[1].

At 8:35, Alfonso walked through the door and towards Harry and shook his hand:

"Sorry about earlier—you caught me at a bad time," he said to him.

Naturally, Harry forgave him, since he had been the one who knocked on his door and interrupted him. Then, he started to ask about the neighborhood, the city, internet providers, and the way they ate "French fries" with lemon. From that day on, Alfonso and Harry were great friends. Alfonso would often go up to Harry's apartment to watch soccer with him, since Harry, despite being American, was a staunch follower of European soccer, or meet up at the bar downstairs to have a beer in the evening, or go to the supermarket together from time to time. Alfonso was thirty-seven years old and single. He had no formal relationship, but that didn't mean he wasn't successful with

---

1   In Murcia, many people eat bagged potato chips with a slice of lemon and a bit a pepper.

women—quite the contrary. In fact, on one occasion, Alfonso didn't show up when he and Harry had planned to meet at the bar downstairs. The next day, Alfonso called him, and it turned out that, in his own words, "an opportunity had come up that he couldn't pass up," and he said he was very sorry. Harry didn't get upset, but Alfonso nonetheless invited him for some beers the following day to formally apologize. Apart from that time, Alfonso had always been there. Plus, he was a fun guy and was always willing to do you a favor. If they were in the US, Alfonso would be the typical neighbor who welcomes you by bringing you an apple pie to introduce himself.

As Alfonso gave Harry a towel to dry his hair, Harry realized that Alfonso had unwashed dishes in the kitchen. There were at least five plates and five glasses, even though Alfonso lived alone and didn't always eat at home.

"Sorry for the mess. I've been busy the past few days and haven't even been able to wash the dishes," Alfonso said as he gave him the towel and left a recently opened bottle of beer on the table.

It seemed a bit strange to Harry. Alfonso worked as an official in the City Council of Murcia from Monday to Friday from 8 a.m. to 3 p.m. He didn't know what exactly he did, but it was a job that didn't require any extra hours or that he would get fired from for poor performance. Thus, Harry ruled out the idea that Alfonso was busy with matters at work. Moreover, Alfonso didn't have a family. He was an only child, and his parents had died in a car accident four years prior. He had a cousin but had no relationship with him. So, it seemed like it probably wasn't a family matter. From what he knew about Alfonso, and applying the logic of Occam's razor, it must have been some girl-related issue. Maybe he was juggling two girls, or three, and his plans were getting all mixed up. Who knows. For now, Harry only wanted to propose something to his friend.

"Well, aren't you going to ask me why I've been so busy?" Alfonso shouted from the kitchen as he grabbed him a beer.

"Do I dare?" Harry responded.

"Come on, Harry, ask me—sheesh."

"Okay. Why have you been so busy that you haven't washed your dishes these past few days, Alfonso?"

Alfonso laughed and pointed at the couch for Harry to sit down as he sat in his armchair. Harry took a sip of his beer and sat down. Alfonso started to talk:

"Remember Barbara, the brunette who I talked to you about before who works at the supermarket a block over?"

Of course Harry remembered her. He had gone to that supermarket several times and had always been captivated by one of the cashiers. She was gorgeous. Barbara was her name, according to the nametag that the workers wore there. She was a twenty-something-year-old girl, with short brown hair and a nice figure. Harry certainly found her quite attractive. Later, it turned out that she was a romantic interest for Alfonso, and that was a line that Harry was never going to cross. He would never get in between a friend's relationship with a girl, as beautiful as she was to Harry. After Alfonso talked to Harry about it, they both went to the supermarket together to get groceries at one point. Harry noticed how they greeted each other with a certain complicity, which suggested that the relationship, whatever its nature, formal or not, was going well.

"Yeah, I remember her. What's going on with her?"

"Well, she introduced me to her little sister and..."

"And what, Alfonso?"

"I'm hooking up with her."

"What? How much younger is she?"

"Two years younger than her; she's twenty-seven. Damn, who do you take me for, Harry?"

"Oh, okay." Harry feared that he had made a friend who was, in reality, a pedophile.

He went on to ask: "And how did that happen?"

"Well, one day, she was there at the supermarket, and Barbara introduced me to her. I greeted her and then left with my bags to go home. When I opened the door to our building, she suddenly showed up and asked me if I needed help with the bags. I told her it wasn't necessary, but thanks. And you know what she said to me?"

"What did she say to you, Alfonso?"

"If I needed help with anything else at that moment, she was there to help…"

"And, of course, it seemed like a good idea to you to tell her that any help was welcome. It didn't seem reasonable to you to stop and think for a second that you were hooking up with her sister and that she didn't even know."

"That's right."

"And that's what's had you so busy recently, right?"

"Damn, you have no idea—she really wants it. I have her here every night, and she leaves me exhausted."

"Right, but you're not a kid anymore." Harry took another sip of beer; he had already almost finished it.

He felt like he was going to need another one soon.

"But, dude, I mean, what do I do now? I can't be with two sisters at the same time."

Once again, Occam's razor had been victorious. Harry didn't quite know what to say to his friend. He had gotten himself into a problematic situation on his own, a situation which (this time you could truly say) wouldn't end well with one hundred percent certainty. And the less he got involved, the better. He had no intention of having to stop getting his groceries at that supermarket.

"You have to drop one of the two before one finds out that you're also going out with her sister." Quite basic, shitty advice Harry just gave his friend, but nothing else came to his mind.

"Some shitty advice you're giving me, don't you think?"

"What else would you want to do, you moron?"

"Fine, you're right. But we're not going out; we just fuck."

"Barbara or her sister?"

"Both. It's not like one is going to catch me going to the movies with the other."

"Well, Alfonso, do whatever you want. What do you want me to say, man."

Harry downed one last gulp of beer and got up to leave. He decided that he no longer wanted to talk to his friend about what he had gone to tell him. Alfonso had enough trouble as it was without putting other things in his head. It was better to wait for his friend to get his affairs in order before telling him, or at least wait until the following day. At that point he was mentally and physically exhausted from the whole day.

"Thanks for the beer, Alfonso, but I'm going home. I've been tired all day. Plus, I'm sure you're busy now, so I'll let you relax a bit," said Harry heading towards the door.

"You're leaving already? Okay, as you wish. I'll think about what you said. Maybe you're right. There's a saying here in Spain: '*quien mucho abarca, poco aprieta*[2].' Maybe I should apply that to myself. Thanks, Harry."

Harry left Alfonso's apartment thinking about how he hadn't understood the last thing Alfonso had told him. He understood Spanish perfectly, but sayings were still difficult for him. Though in this instance, he didn't care. He was tired and simply wanted to go home; he didn't care at all about the saying. He was going to use the stairs since it was just one floor up, but the elevator opened, and out came Barbara and another girl, who looked quite like her but with darker hair and a somewhat shorter stature. Harry deduced that she was the protagonist sister from the story he had just heard.

---

2 Translator's note: Literally, "He who takes on much, grips little," meaning that undertaking more things than you can manage leads to not being able to adequately handle any of them. An English equivalent would be "biting off more than you can chew."

"Is your friend home, Harry?" Barbara asked. Since it didn't make sense to lie, Harry said yes.

"Thanks. Now please leave." Harry deduced from Barbara's face that it was a very good idea to follow that order. So, he went upstairs to his apartment, opened the door, and looked at the dry umbrella that he had in the umbrella stand and thought: "You were fine here. At least I don't have to put you out to dry."

He immediately grabbed a beer and sat on the couch, exhausted. It was already 9 p.m. In the US, he would almost be asleep, but he had already adapted to Spanish time. He turned on the TV and put on the channel that aired CSI, his favorite show in the US, to relax a little while he thought about Alfonso. It must have been quite the situation going on right below him. At ten, he got up from the couch and took out a prepared dish of pork with tomato from the fridge and warmed it up in the microwave for dinner. It was a dish with slices of pork with tomato sauce and peppers, all fried together. In Murcia, it was in all the bars as a small dish, called a *tapa* in Spain. Harry tried it one day at the bar downstairs and liked it. Since he saw that they sold it premade in the supermarket and he didn't have time or desire to cook, he bought it every now and then, mainly for dinner. When the microwave made its characteristic sound that it had finished, he heard a door slam from the floor downstairs. "The conversation must have already ended. They probably told Alfonso to go to hell and then left." He leaned out of his living room window that faced the street, but it was still pouring out, so he couldn't see anything.

Thus, he couldn't tell if someone was coming out of the entrance.

"Well, Alfonso will tell me what happened."

He sat on the couch with the pork with tomato and ate it in a couple of minutes. Then, he grabbed a book and went to bed, prepared to read a little before sleeping. It was a spy novel that he was halfway through, one by Agatha Christie. He liked novels about spies, mysteries, intrigues; he found them interesting.  They even made him laugh. At 10:45, his phone went off. It was a WhatsApp message from a girl that he had met at a bar one night a couple of weeks prior. That night had ended well for them, so they met up a couple of times for drinks or coffee, but it was nothing serious at that point. Nonetheless, Harry liked her and felt comfortable with her, so he had a feeling that she could become his official girlfriend soon.

Her name was Sofia, a forty-year-old Italian teacher who taught classes in the Official Language School of Murcia for two years, though she had lived there for several years. She was another foreigner like him, but she had ended up making Murcia her home.

"What are you doing? Are you asleep?" Sofia texted him on WhatsApp.

"No, I was reading, but I was about to finish."

"I had a really good time on Wednesday."

"Yeah, me too, it was nice. How about I call you tomorrow when I'm done work to hang out?"

"Sounds great, I'm looking forward to it J."

"Perfect, *buonanotte, bambina*[3]."

"Goodnight, handsome."

Harry then put the book on his nightstand and went to take a shower. He liked showering before sleeping; that way, he could wake up ten minutes later than he would have to if he showered in the mornings. Moreover, if he was stressed, like almost always, he masturbated in the shower which would leave him relaxed before bed. That day wasn't going to be an exception.

At 11:30, Harry got in bed to go to sleep. It had been a rough day, but it was coming to an end. Harry fell asleep in less than five minutes with the sound of the Murcia rain in the background.

---

3   "Goodnight, babe" in Italian.

# CHAPTER II

Harry's phone alarm woke him up at seven in the morning, like every day. And, as he normally did, he turned it off right away without delay, stretched in bed, and got up. At 7:10, he was already in the kitchen whisking a couple of eggs. Every morning, Harry had a nice, strong coffee with milk, some scrambled eggs with bacon, and fresh-squeezed orange juice. The American in him was robust in some regards, and breakfast was one of them. He always had that for breakfast. He still hadn't been convinced of having toast with some other thing for breakfast as nearly everyone he knew in Murcia did.

As he ate, he asked Alexa for the day's news. She began announcing them: *The Nasdaq index closed yesterday with the biggest gain of the week.... The Taliban execute four women accused of dancing in the streets of Kabul.... The Spanish national football team faces a decisive match tonight for qualification to the final phase of the next World Cup....*

At 7:50, Harry was ready to leave his apartment and head to work. It was beautifully sunny, so an umbrella wasn't necessary. Good: he hated walking with an umbrella when it didn't rain and lugging around a useless object. He walked out of his building to the left towards the bridge that crossed the river and reached the City Hall Plaza. His building was in a beautiful area called Plaza Cama-chos, which was just a three-minute walk from City Hall and the city center, which Harry loved. The location allowed him to walk to work and to the city center to have a beer at any time. In many areas of the US, a car was necessary for everything, and Harry hated that since, though he likes to drive, he didn't want to have to depend on a car for absolutely everything. He liked being able to walk. He went behind the Town Hall toward the plaza where the city cathedral was with its majestic tower. He still hadn't had the chance to visit it inside and climb up the tower, but he would do it. After walking the streets for five minutes, he arrived at his destination. Harry thought the neighborhood was beautiful, certainly different from his birthplace of Arkansas.

Without drawing too much attention, he walked into a small entranceway of a three-floor building near Romea Theater, the biggest in the city. There was a black plaque with white lettering with "*Fernández Anticuarios Internacionales*[4], FAI" on it. That's where he was headed. He rang the bell, and a porter opened the entrance door of the building for him.

"Good morning, Harry," he cordially greeted him.

"Good morning, Pepe," Harry responded. "Is there anything for me?"

Pepe, the porter, grabbed the mail. "No, but someone is waiting for you upstairs."

Harry figured, after the last day he had at work. He went up to the second floor and opened the door with another plaque like the one in the entranceway but smaller.

"Good morning," he greeted Piotr and Angela, his colleagues who were already there. Upon entering, the place was open and spacious with two desks—one for Piotr and another for Angela. There was also a small couch at the entrance and a water machine. In the back was Harry's office and a small bathroom. Then, there was another room which, for the moment, was locked and had a "DO NOT ENTER" sign on it. Piotr and Angela looked at him, but they didn't say anything, as Angela pointed to his office. Apparently, his visitor

---

4   "Fernández International Antique Dealers."

was already inside. That could only mean it was one person, the only person that neither Piotr nor Angela would dare tell to wait on the couch outside. He opened the door, and, indeed, there she was.

"Martha, what a nice surprise," he said as he closed the door behind him and headed towards his desk.

"Harry, don't lie. You're not the only one who doesn't like liars."

"*Touché,*" Harry thought. "What can I do for you? Are you happy with my last job and coming to thank me in person?" Harry felt bold that morning.

Martha was in her late forties, black, and of medium height. She had purple-colored eyes, which Harry found quite attractive. She spoke Spanish perfectly, as well as English, French, Mandarin, and German. At first sight, she didn't have an intimidating appearance. But Harry had already known her for several years and, though he thought he could manage conversations with her, he knew she was a woman that could easily terrify anyone with her character.

Martha took out a cigarette along with her Zippo and lit it with a grimace of irony. She took the first drag and blew the smoke to the side.

"You don't have anything to say to me, Harry?"

Harry, in turn, took out one of his cigarettes and lit it.

"The job you requested is finished and what you wanted has been done. That's the important thing, don't you think?"

Then, Martha violently pushed the laptop on the desk to one side and screamed, "Stop bullshitting me, Harry!" Then, she added more calmly, "Tell me what happened yesterday from ten in the morning until you went home at the end of the day. Don't rush and don't omit details. We're not leaving here until you finish."

Harry thought about how long the day was going to be and how much he wanted to see Sofia. But he obeyed and began telling Martha how the day before had gone with as many details as he could, without being able to get out of his head how much he wanted the day to end, and he had only just started.

The previous day, at 10 a.m., Harry was sitting at his desk with his laptop, not doing anything, really, when his phone started to ring with the melody of the Imperial March from Star Wars. He set that melody as the ringtone for one person in particular.

"Hey, Martha. Good morning. What can I do for you? Need me to take care of an antique?"

At that moment, Piotr was in Harry's office looking for some documents on the shelf and noticed Harry's serious face, with an expression that was quite different from the one he had a minute before taking the call. When Harry hung up, Piotr uttered:

"Do we have work, boss?"

To that, Harry replied:

"You and Angela, on the third floor in three minutes."

On the third floor of *Fernández Anticuarios Internacionales* building (FAI, as Harry liked to abbreviate) was a room that had nothing to do with the floor below. It was locked, inaccessible to the public. Only the three FAI employees could access it. Not even Pepe had a key. It was a room with a large projector for video calls and a long, round table with six seats. At 10:15, Harry, Piotr, and Angela were sitting at the table. Angela was native to Murcia and still younger than thirty, with a strong complexion and short hair. She was an ambitious young woman who sought to do great things at that job. Piotr, in turn, was a Polish man based in Murcia already for several years, divorced, and in his forties. His physique gave him away; he couldn't hide his Eastern European origins. Both had received Harry with open arms, even though he came in as the boss, and he, admittedly, had grown fond of them.

Harry turned on the projector and pressed a button under the table. The table then opened, and three tablets came up where all three were seated. Martha appeared on the projected image and began telling them what the job that she had for them consisted of. It was a quick job that had to be done that same day which she would give them a good sum of money for. It was a job that strayed from the usual assignment given to antique dealers. But FAI, in reality, was not a company of real antique dealers.

Martha explained to them that an important transaction would take place that day in Murcia and that they were going to prevent it. According to what the client had told them (neither Harry nor his coworkers ever knew who hired them, whether governments, magnates, famous people, companies...), at exactly 4:30 p.m. that very day, an art dealer would deliver a highly valuable piece to them. It had been stolen a few months prior from the British Museum in London by a middleman, possibly for a private collector from the black market, in exchange for a briefcase full of money. It was the Royal Game of Ur, a piece of wood from 2600 BCE believed to be one of humanity's first boardgames. It had been found in Ancient Mesopotamia, and, though it had been stolen months ago, the news had not reached the public. Its spot in the museum had a sign for a week that said that it was undergoing minor restoration, and after a week, it returned to its spot, seemingly restored. In reality, it was a replica secretly developed in record time under the British government's orders. And, to date, it was still there in the museum, without anyone realizing that it wasn't the original. Perhaps due to British pride or perhaps to avoid a bad image in the eyes of the public for the museum and the entire city of London, with everything that it could entail politically, that didn't matter.

The place chosen for the transaction was the main auditorium of Murcia. The building was used for all types of events, from concerts to lectures, to conferences.... On that specific day, at that time, a meeting for metal companies from all eastern Spain would be held in the main hall of the venue. To be precise, by 4:30 p.m. the videoconference of the president of the Metal Association of Madrid would have already been going on for a half hour, with another half hour remaining. According to the tip, the dealer would meet with the buyer in the restroom where they would exchange briefcases. The job was to infiltrate into the event, get the piece, and then bring it to the FAI offices and await Martha's instructions.

The file with the information for the job showed up right away on the tablets in front of Harry, Piotr, and Angela. On paper, it didn't seem difficult. The person delivering the piece was an Argentinian dealer named Amadeo Perez. There was no information on the person who would deliver the money, but that wasn't relevant. The important thing was to keep Perez monitored, as he was the one with the object. According to the informants, Perez would have to wait in the restroom for ten minutes until the dealer arrived. The most noteworthy information from the file on Perez was that he was a well-known art dealer; even though he had been arrested and accused several times, he would always end up being released due to lack of evidence. He worked alone and wasn't exceedingly strong, so Harry wasn't too worried about the physical aspect. He could easily subdue him. Even though Harry had never been inside the building, he had the blueprint of the inside of the auditorium. It wasn't a very complicated venue where you could get lost easily. In theory, the job was a piece of cake. But there was something in Martha's expression that Harry didn't like. He knew her well and could tell she was hiding something. It wasn't because of Harry's innately skeptical character. This time he really knew. However, he decided to stay quiet so he wouldn't make the team nervous.

They were proper professionals, but he hadn't known them for too long and still didn't fully trust them for these jobs. He didn't know how they would react.

The information session ended at 11:20 a.m. Harry, Piotr, and Angela were looking at the file and discussing the plan until around noon. They decided, firstly, that Angela would go with Harry in a car and drop him off at the auditorium at 3:45 p.m. Piotr, for his part, would pose as an attendant at the event and be in the building at 2 p.m., which was when lunch would be served prior to the 4 p.m. conference. At the time of the conference, Piotr would position himself with the rest of the protocol staff upstairs (the auditorium sloped down toward the main stage, which was at the bottom, so the entrance was on an upper floor), and would have Perez located. He would communicate with Harry the whole time and let him know when Perez got up close to 4:30 to go to the restroom. Ten minutes later, Piotr would excuse himself for a moment and leave the auditorium through the main entrance exactly at 4:45. Angela would be waiting for him in a different car. They would drive around to the back entrance of the auditorium, where they would pick up Harry at 4:50 with the Royal Game of Ur.

Harry, meanwhile, would attend the business meeting as a participant. At 4:25, he would fake a phone call and use it as an excuse to leave the hall. He would go to the restroom and hide in one of the stalls. He would wait for Piotr's warning that Perez was coming and then go behind the door. When Perez walked in, he would drug him with the "needle jab" method with an off-market sedative that FAI had, which would instantly knock him unconscious. Then, he would place him in a stall and take the briefcase. Required time: just two minutes. Enough time to not cross paths with the buyer. He would leave through the back door, get in the car with his colleagues, and the mission would be accomplished. That was the plan.

At 12:05, everyone went to get ready. Piotr made a call to one of the assistants, telling him that he was from the temporary employment agency subcontracted for the event, and that a problem had come up, so it wasn't necessary for him to attend the event. To keep that assistant from complaining or calling the actual company, he told him that a deposit of double what he would have made that day working was being sent to him right then for the inconvenience caused. Then, he made another call to the auditorium, saying that they had changed one member of the event staff because he had gotten sick, and gave them the substitute worker's information.

Harry and Angela went up to the fourth and top floor of the building, also locked and inaccessible to the public. Only the three staff members of FAI could enter. The triple security lock resembled a regular door from the outside. It looked like an armored security door, but nothing extraordinary. However, when the lock was opened, a mechanism was activated that required you to remove the key from the lock and place the fingerprint of your right pinky on it. The door only opened for Harry, Angela, and Piotr.

Otherwise, a silent alarm would activate on their phones and automatic shackles would come out and clasp the hand of the person trying to get in. That amount of security was justified, since the door gave access to what they knew as "the storeroom." Everything they needed to carry out their missions was in there. The storeroom had a surface area of about one-thousand seventy-five square feet with several rooms. Upon entering, a dressing room to the left occupied a third of the room, with clothing and footwear for men and women. There was also a huge safe with cash, fake passports for the three of them, and some weapons. In Spain, firearms were prohibited for civilians. The police have guns, but apart from rare instances, they don't normally use them. Moreover, the anti-terrorist special police units also have weapons like machine guns and rifles for raid operations. At FAI, they had an automatic Glock for each person, as well as ammunition and some tasers for immobilization, but they rarely made use of them. And, of course, if they weren't on any missions, the weapons remained in the safe. On the other side of the storeroom, there was a mini-fridge next to a small locker. In the fridge, they kept different types of serums (sedatives, truth serum, adrenaline), many of them unavailable on the market. In the locker, there were syringes and other standard first-aid kit utensils. The rest of the storeroom had a table, a couple of chairs, and another small locker hanging on the wall. In that locker, there were keys to the vehicles that FAI had access to. At any moment, FAI had access to ten vehicles throughout the entire city. The locker with the keys to the vehicles had a small compartment with a screen that showed the GPS location of the corresponding vehicle. Every week, FAI received a closed package with the Amazon logo to avoid raising any suspicions. Pepe would take it and deliver it to Harry or one of his colleagues. In the package, there were ten new keys to other vehicles. Then, they had to take the ten keys they had, put them in a package, tape it shut, and leave it with Pepe. Later that same day, a person dressed as a courier would come by to pick it up, and so on every week. That doesn't mean that there were ten new vehicles each week; rather, they were the same ones. However, every now and then a car that was green would turn blue, another that was white would show up with black stripes…and, of course, with different registrations.

They grabbed two pairs of keys to two different vehicles—one for the way there and the other for pickup—prepared a syringe with a sedative, and grabbed the clothes they were going to wear. They grabbed Piotr's clothes too as he was getting his things in order.

Around 12:45, they went down to the office and ordered Chinese food from their favorite restaurant, which was open seven days a week. At precisely 1 p.m., Harry had the following conversation with Martha through the FAI messaging application (encrypted and secret— untraceable):

> Harry: All set.
> Martha: Thanks. I trust you, don't let me down.
> Martha: Do your colleagues have everything down?
> Harry: Yes, totally, they're professionals. We'll eat then head out right after.

At 1:10, Pepe brought the food up and each of the three ate in their place, as usual, each one with their pre-mission ritual. Angela put on her headphones with heavy metal at full volume on her phone. Piotr simply ate looking straight ahead in silence. Harry thought that may have been part of his Polish heritage: the coldness, the concentration, the discipline. In any case, Harry respected both his colleagues, and whatever they wanted to do before a job was fine for him. He had only been working with them for two months in Murcia, but up to that point they had responded quite well to everything. So, he didn't want to fix something that wasn't broken. Harry, meanwhile, watched an old episode of The Simpsons on his laptop while he ate. He had seen all of them an infinite number of times, but he still found them funny.

At 1:30, Piotr got changed and, at 1:35, left the office. He walked there; he liked walking, and the rain that started to fall then wasn't a problem for him. It was a twenty-minute walk, so he would get there at the scheduled time.

Angela and Harry stayed in their places until around 2 p.m. Harry got up to wash the dishes (they each took turns) in the bathroom sink. Meanwhile, Angela went and opened the door with the "DO NOT ENTER" sign, where there were three couches, a table, a small fridge, and a large coffee maker like the ones used in coffee shops. Harry joined her as soon as he finished washing the dishes, and they both had a coffee and lay down for a bit on the couches to relax before the job. Around 3 p.m., they got up. Piotr had texted in the group on the FAI messaging app: "Perez is here now, I have him located. All set. *Żegnajcie przyjaciele*[5]."

Harry threw on a black suit with a light blue shirt, grabbed a briefcase and the syringe loaded with sedatives, and left the office with Angela around 3:15. They headed to the car that Martha had assigned to them for the arrival to the auditorium, which was in a garage in the theater plaza, a two-minute walk away. It was a black automatic Audi A4 with a Madrid license plate. Harry liked stick shift, but since Angela was the one driving, she didn't care. They got in the car and, at 3:40, Angela stopped at the main entrance of the auditorium for Harry to get out. She drove away ignoring the unlicensed parking attendant coming towards the car to ask for money.

Harry headed towards the auditorium entrance where an attendant asked him his name and what company he was from. Harry said, "Javier Martín, from Metal Packaging of Europe SL." The

---

5   "Goodbye, friends" in Polish.

attendant, after verifying that he was on the list, handed him a credential and let him through without any trouble. Martha had said, when explaining the job to him, that the problem regarding entry was taken care of, and Harry knew that if Martha said so, it was true. She was one of the few people that Harry was sure did not lie. She may have many flaws, but Harry didn't think that being a liar was one of them.

Harry entered a large space that served as a lobby where there were several high tables with trays of food and drinks and people chatting. He immediately located Piotr, spotting him standing to one side of the lobby, right next to the stairs that led to the main hall of the auditorium, which was one floor above. Without having time for anything else, one of the attendants of the staff started to let everyone know to start heading to the main hall since the 4 p.m. conference would begin shortly. Right away, people started going up the stairs where Piotr was situated. Like a proper attendant, he was greeting them and indicating to them to go upstairs where the entrance would be on the left-hand side. Harry went upstairs as another attendee, but he didn't have time to locate Perez. Either way, he trusted Piotr to locate him; in the end, that was his job. Harry went upstairs and walked into the room. He went down four or five rows and sat in a free space. There were plenty of people. It was the main hall of the auditorium, with a capacity of more than seven-thousand people and superb acoustics. Harry thought he might want to come to the auditorium sometime to see a concert or something of the sort. It must be nice. One of these days he would tell Sofia about it.

The confirmed list of attendees was more than a thousand, unheard of for this kind of event. Before sitting down and making sure that no one saw him, he checked and already had the message from Piotr: "Located." Perfect—everything was going according to plan. At 4:25, his phone went off, as he had scheduled, and he left the hall pretending to take the call. He headed towards the only men's restroom on that floor that was open for the event (it was policy of the auditorium to not open more than one men's and one women's restroom per floor, unless there was more than one full room, and that day there was only that event). There were five urinals and five stalls in the restroom. He made sure that there was no one else and went behind the door. At 4:30, he received Piotr's message: "He's coming." Thus, he took out the syringe with the sedative and got ready. About a minute later, the restroom door opened, but it wasn't Perez who walked in. Harry realized it right as he jabbed the person with the sedative.

Two seconds later, a woman fell at his feet in a deep, unconscious state caused by the sedative.

"Wait a minute, Harry," Martha interrupted. "You mean a woman you don't know walked into the men's restroom right when Perez was supposed to walk in, and you jabbed her with the syringe?"

"Yes, that's right, Martha. Please, don't interrupt me. When I finish, ask me whatever you want, okay?"

Martha made a gesture to zip her lips shut, and Harry continued with the story.

# CHAPTER III

Harry delicately placed the woman on the ground and, right at that moment, the restroom door opened again. This time, it was Perez, with a briefcase in hand. When Perez saw the scene, he tried to run away, but Harry was able to trip him from where he was standing. Perez fell to the floor, hitting his head against the wall as the door closed. Harry stood up immediately and walked towards Perez, but he kicked Harry right in his private area. Harry was bent over in pain, while Perez was still a bit dazed and unable to get up. Harry, much burlier and stronger than Perez, recovered first since, luckily, even though the kick was in a sensitive area, it only grazed him. He grabbed the briefcase and hit him on the head with it to knock him unconscious. Unfortunately, Perez hit his head on one of the urinals and collapsed to the ground as blood poured from his head. Harry had killed him. After trying to check his pulse, he realized. He had killed him.

Clearly, this had no remedy. The woman, who was asleep on the ground, hadn't seen Harry, thus leaving no witnesses. But the attendees at the event had names, and the police, when they would investigate, would soon come across a Javier Martín that nobody knew and who came from a company that, apart from a website created specifically to look like a real company, had nothing else.

So, Harry knew there was only one thing he could do. He texted Martha a clear and simple message, one single word. After reading the message, Martha would activate the FAI protocol for these cases.

And that's what she did. After hiding Perez's body in one of the stalls and the woman's in another, at 4:48, he grabbed Perez's briefcase and walked out of the restroom towards the back entrance of the auditorium. No one saw him. The entire staff was in the main hall, and the door could only be opened from inside, so there was no security guard there. He left at 4:50, and Angela and Piotr were there with a 2015 Renault Megane, dark blue. They opened the back door for Harry to get in and then left.

"What the hell happened? Who was that woman?" Harry shouted once he was inside the car.

"What woman? What happened, Harry?" Piotr asked with an incredulous voice.

Harry told him, and Piotr swore up and down that no one else had walked out of the hall after Perez. However, he thought for a few seconds, and, indeed, a girl talking on the phone had walked out before, but at the time, Piotr didn't think much of it. Either way, they would deal with the matter later. Angela stopped the car at the entrance of FAI (you couldn't park and there were no garages, only a loading and unloading area). Harry and Piotr got out with the briefcase, and Angela went to leave the car at the designated spot, which, in this case, was a supermarket parking lot in the city.

Harry and Piotr went upstairs to the second floor and forced the lock on the briefcase open with a knife. And there was the Royal Game of Ur. Truth be told, it was beautiful. It was a board with some chips, all made of wood and, of course, clearly handcrafted. The board had twenty squares, each one painted with different illustrations, some with the same ones. The rules of the game weren't precisely known, but it seemed to be a primitive version of Game of the Goose. At least that's what it seemed like to Harry. It was wrapped in bubble wrap inside the briefcase, but it didn't seem like it would easily break from a hit or by accident. It was now 6:30 p.m., at which point it was pouring outside. Pepe went upstairs to say goodnight as he did every day when his shift was over. They thanked him and said goodbye for the night. At 6:43 p.m., Martha texted, "Leave briefcase with merchandise in the safe and then go home." And they did just that. Harry started on his way home under the torrential rain, and Piotr and Angela did the same in the other direction.

"Okay, great, Harry. Are you done?"

"Yes, Martha, regarding yesterday at work, I'm done."

"Do you want me to tell you what I did yesterday after 4:35, Harry?"

"Not really, Martha, but I suspect that you're going to tell me anyway, aren't you?

"That's right. And you're going to listen to me carefully from the first to the last fucking word. *Capisci*[6]?"

Harry agreed as he lit another cigarette and listened to Martha.

At 4:35 the previous day, Martha received a text from Harry on the FAI app. The text consisted of nothing more than one word, but it was devastating: "Rocket." Martha, who was in a private room in a high-end restaurant in Murcia eating with a few possible clients, excused herself for a moment. "I'm going to make a call, gentlemen. Give me a few minutes, please."

Martha called her contact at the Civil Guard Command of Murcia on a secret line and explained that she needed a rocket in the auditorium at that moment and that she sent them the necessary details, including the location inside the building. The rocket message always had the exact coordinates assigned.

"Harry, do you know what it means for me to have to make that call because you thought you worked for the fucking CIA and could just go around killing people?" Martha interrupted her story about the previous day.

---

6   "Do you understand?" in Italian.

Of course he knew. Harry had been working at FAI for two months, but he'd been working for his bosses (who owned FAI and thirteen other branches like FAI in the entire world) for more than five years. This group of mercenary agencies was known as The Conglomerate, and its various intervention protocols were the same in all the delegations in all the countries where they were found, broadly speaking. As far as the protocol regarding the rocket, a rocket meant that there was an unintended casualty during a job and that they needed a support team to arrive faster than a rocket. In other words, they were problem solvers—a Mr. Wolf, like in the movie Pulp Fiction. In every country and every area where the Conglomerate did jobs through one of their delegations, they relied on secret associates subcontracted as support teams in case of a rocket. If there was no rocket, they didn't intervene, barring a rare case. These teams weren't exactly cheap. They had to be elite professionals that would erase any trace that the members of the Conglomerate had been at the scene of the mission, and that they would be available at the agreed times in case they were needed. If, in addition to being available, they had to intervene, the extra fees could skyrocket depending on each case. And the Conglomerate didn't work for free, so any decrease in their earnings directly impacted certain decisions, as with any company or business. An intervention from a support team could lead to a mission being done at a loss, depending on the severity.

"Who was that woman, Martha? Because she wasn't in the information that you gave me about the mission. It wasn't our fault; no one was supposed to walk into the restroom at that time except for Perez, and no one left the hall. Piotr confirms it and I believe him. She wasn't the buyer because it wasn't the time. Or did your informants inform you wrong?"

"Harry, I'm asking, do you know what it means for me to have to make that call?" Harry gave up for the time being and went along with the conversation.

"We lose half of the reward in fees for the rocket?"

"I'm going to be very transparent with you, Harry. I think that, despite your gaffe, you're a very valuable guy for the Conglomerate and you're very much needed as the FAI director." Harry could tell that Martha seemed sincere. "So, you have to really be aware of the entire business, including the financial side and what happens when someone messes up. The FAI support team is led by a high-ranking officer from the Civil Guard of Murcia, who oversees two forensic police officers dismissed from the force due to corruption, and a private detective."

"*What a team*," Harry thought, though he didn't say anything.

"They're the best," Martha continued as if she were reading Harry's mind. "Obviously, I can't give you their names. Even I only know my contact's name. They talk to me about the rest as Athos, Porthos, and Aramis. Anyways, while my contact called the auditorium to give the order that they had received a bomb threat and that, even though it was most likely a prank, they had to evacuate following the security protocol, Athos, Porthos, and Aramis got dressed as bomb squad technicians and headed over there. My contact, who we can call D'Artagnan, to continue with the subject, also went over there with actual civil guards. Once he was there, he ordered the 'bomb technicians' to go inside and take a look with the explosive detectors that they brought, while the Civil Guard cordoned off the area without drawing too much attention, since it was probably a false alarm. One hour later, the bomb technicians came out and said that the building was clean and that it had been a false alarm. And, lo and behold, there was no longer a body in the restroom or an unconscious sedated woman. And everything ended up as an anecdote in a corner of today's local newspaper and a handful of messages on social media talking about the experience of evacuating the auditorium because of a false alarm."

Indeed, the way Martha had described it, Harry found it to be an impeccable and very professional job, even without knowing the details. And he knew that it wasn't cheap.

"That intervention, Harry, cost FAI sixty thousand euros," Martha added. "The agreed-upon fees for the job of recovering the piece were one hundred thousand euros, which the Conglomerate took fifty percent of, like with all jobs, and FAI, as the local division in charge of carrying it out, would take the other fifty percent. If we take the sixty thousand euros from that fifty thousand for the support team doing the rocket, how much is left for us, Harry? Because, in case you don't know, the support teams come at the expense of each delegation."

Harry didn't know the hard numbers, but he could imagine them before Martha said anything. During his time working at the delegation in El Paso, Texas, he became friends with the boss of the support team, who was a retired ex-Mossad spy based there, and the numbers they talked about were similar in percentage for each job. But it didn't seem like a big deal to Harry either. At the end of the day, it was normal for the support team to have to intervene in about one out of every twelve or thirteen jobs, so it was worth it. Why the hell was Martha so upset? "Damn, this woman. Why doesn't she go out more? She takes this job way too seriously," Harry thought. Martha was the officer for the European branch of the Conglomerate, which had FAI and a couple of other delegations: one in Cork (Ireland) and another in Corelone (Italy). She took her job seriously, which Harry found normal and had a lot of respect for, but he knew her, and something was off.

Harry got up from his desk, opened his office door and said, "Guys, you're off today. Go home and we'll see each other tomorrow," addressing Piotr and Angela. Then, he closed his door as Martha lit a cigarette and looked at Harry with an expression which, to Harry, seemed to say, "You know me too well, you bastard." Harry stood there looking out the window, where the beautiful pedestrian street that led to the back of the building was visible, in silence. A minute later, when he heard the office door close and they were alone, he sat back down.

"Martha, we messed up, and I'm asking for your forgiveness. But you know as well as I do that in this profession these things happen. And that's what I would tell you in any other circumstance, but I also know that you're not telling me the whole truth. You're hiding something from me. It's hard for me to fully trust people, but I do trust you. I ask you to have the same courtesy for me. I understand you may not be able to tell me everything because we're not at the same level in the chain of command, but here it's me and my colleagues who get our hands dirty and we deserve respect.

"Do you keep whisky in the office, Harry?"

"Martha, it's ten in the morning."

"Why aren't you answering my fucking questions?"

Harry opened his desk drawer and took out a half-empty bottle of Jack Daniels and two glasses. He poured it in both, no ice, and handed one to Martha. He wasn't going to play Martha's chaperone with alcohol by any means. She was old enough to know what she was doing.

"I like you, Harry, I really do. And if I wasn't married, I'd hit on you, I won't lie. I'm going to tell you everything I can, and don't ask me to tell you more because I won't, got it?"

It turned out that the woman in the restroom was Perez's "whore," in Martha's words. She knew from the beginning that, even though she'd attend the event, she wasn't going to make it known that she was with Perez, since he had to pose as a businessman. That's why Piotr didn't realize anything. When Maria (the name of the woman) walked out of the auditorium hall a few minutes before Perez, he didn't think much of it because, in theory, she was an attendee at the event who wasn't going to barge into the men's restroom.

Since Perez had to wait ten minutes for the buyer, apparently, Maria had decided to wait for him in the restroom to give him some pleasure in the form of pre-work fellatio. She knew that Perez would like that, and perhaps she could get a few euros off him. What she didn't account for was running into Harry. The rest is already known. When the bomb squad went in, they woke her up with a drug that they had and let her leave through the back entrance of the building. They knew she wasn't a threat; given that she was an accomplice of a smuggler, she wasn't exactly about to report his death to the authorities. They gave her some money to persuade her to forget about the matter.

"Why weren't we told that Perez was going to come with someone else, even if it wasn't officially, so we could have anticipated any risk?" Harry asked.

"Because they ordered me to not tell. They wanted to test you guys.

"Well tell them to go fuck themselves," Harry said, drinking what was left of the whiskey in his glass in one gulp.

"They wanted to see how you guys would react to an unforeseen event. You're a new team, and they wanted a real test. It didn't sit right with me, but I didn't think it was that crazy either, Harry. Anyways, losing money sucks, but I understand you. And since, in the end, they didn't let me give you all the information about the situation, I'll let it go, and I'll even tell them that it would be reasonable to split the cost of the rocket. Take the day off as well, and we'll talk tomorrow." Martha concluded, seemingly calmer.

Finally, some good news. He got up from his desk and, without looking at Martha in her face, said, "Lock up when you leave. See you tomorrow." He walked out the door. It was 10:30 in the morning on a Thursday, and he was free. He certainly needed it. He didn't at all like that the higher ups, with Martha's collaboration, put him and his team to the test. But he understood Martha's side. In the end, she fulfilled orders, and regarding the "intervention" that she had just done, he figured she had decided to play bad cop to see how Harry would respond, nothing else. Case closed: he didn't have to think about it anymore.

He wanted to see Sofia badly, but she didn't leave work until 7 p.m. He looked at his phone as he walked around the city center and saw two missed calls from Alfonso. He figured that he'd want to tell him how the situation ended from the night before with the two sisters. In truth, Harry was genuinely curious. He also had a pending conversation with him that he hadn't been able to finish, so he called him back, but it went straight to voicemail. "Weird," he thought without making much more of it. Surely, they'll talk later anyways. For now, he would go home and bum around a bit. He'd earned it. After the previous day, he wanted to relax, especially mentally. And that day, May 12th, when he left the office after the mission, from 6:43 p.m. to when he got to Alfonso's apartment around 8:15 p.m., the most impressive, unexpected thing of the day up until that point happened to him (without telling the story about Alfonso and the sisters which came after), despite how high the bar was.

# CHAPTER IV

May 12th at 6:44 p.m. Harry was in the rain for a minute and re-alized that the amount of rain that was falling was no joke. He also realized that if he continued walking without an umbrella, he would get drenched. He was in the city center of Murcia, surrounded by taverns and bars, so he decided to go in one of them. He observed and saw that there were more people that had thought of the same thing. He could tell by the looks on their faces. More precisely, their faces said, "I want to go home, but it's raining a lot and, since I'm from Murcia, I didn't bring an umbrella." Harry felt more and more like a native, without a doubt.

He sat at the bar and ordered a beer and a tapa of dry sausage with almonds. It was another one of the tapas he loved from the local cuisine, which paired well with a beer at that time of day. He would give the rain a moment to see if it would stop. He didn't rule out having another beer to give it more time, but he'd play it by ear without any hurry.

The place wasn't very big, and there weren't too many people, perhaps half-full. But the noise at the bar was substantial, so Harry decided to sit at a table to have his beer and his tapa. There was no need to be so close to the waiter and hear him shout at a man, who seemed like a regular patron, about those thieves in the government, how this was no way for someone to live, and how hopefully they would hang all politicians in the cathedral plaza for everyone to see or throw them from the bell tower.

Harry saw a thirty-something-year-old guy walking towards his table. He was very tall and had on jeans and a T-shirt with a drawing of a baby with an eyepatch and a wooden leg that said "baby pirate."

"Excuse me, can I sit down for a moment? I think I have something that might interest you," he asked Harry.

Harry hesitated for a second. He just wanted to relax and drink his beer and then go home when it stopped raining. He didn't want to put up with obnoxious people who asked him if he knew the Bible in depth, if he had thought about investing in cryptocurrency, or if he wanted to be his own boss. But clearly, he couldn't say no to someone with a baby pirate T-shirt, so he made a gesture for him to sit down.

"Thank you," the man said. "My name is Carlos." He reached out his hand, to which Harry responded in kind.

"How can I help you, Carlos?"

Carlos started talking, but Harry interrupted him mid-sentence.

"If you want me to listen to you, order another beer for me, on you."

Carlos raised his hand and told the waiter to get two more beers, one for Harry and another for him. With that, Harry found out that, whoever he may be, he had a genuine interest in telling him whatever it was, otherwise he wouldn't buy a beer for him. At least he, in his place, wouldn't do that; it awoke his interest to some degree.

Carlos started talking. It turned out that, apparently, he was the producer of a movie that would be filmed in Murcia soon. It was a movie like Star Wars: spaceships, aliens, fights...that sort of thing. Apparently, Carlos was working with people in the film industry for the production, but the idea was his. The script was already written by a scriptwriter from the Basque Country. They would begin casting, pending confirmation from the director, who, of course, Carlos didn't want to say who it was, but he did say that he was internationally famous, and that it would be a blockbuster. He didn't want to go into too much detail about the movie, but he said that just by looking at Harry, he knew he had a role for him. He couldn't explain it to him because it was something you either felt or didn't, like a kind of spark. But without a doubt, he had fallen in love artistically with Harry simply by looking at him. Harry was a bit flabbergasted. That day he had killed a man and had stolen (stolen from a thief, but stolen, nonetheless) a work of art of great value. But he certainly didn't expect someone to want to sign him up for a Star Wars-type movie in a bar in Murcia where he was taking refuge from the rain.

"Are you joking?" Harry inquired.

"Not at all…You didn't tell me your name before."

"Harry."

"Are *you* joking?"

They both started to laugh, and Harry made a gesture to the waiter to get two more beers. Carlos, however, declined since he had to go, but he left him his card with his information. He had to wait for the director to confirm his incorporation into the project before telling him about the role, the casting…. He told Harry to call him in a week and he would update him.

"Oh, one more thing, Harry. Do you know anyone else who'd like to be in this kind of movie?"

Of course he did. Alfonso loved Star Wars. It's what he liked most in this world, after women. Or even before, depending on the day. Harry liked it as well, but not at all to the same degree as Alfonso. If he asked Alfonso if he wanted to act in a movie like Star Wars, he knew he'd say yes.

"Yes, I do, but I don't know how well he'd act, or what role he'd do…"

"Don't worry about that, Harry. There's something about you that tells me I can trust you. Plus, we would have an audition beforehand. We're not going to blindly just take on anyone. But we want people who are passionate about these things and that world."

Carlos smiled. "Ask that person if he'd be interested in being an extra or in some other secondary role."

Harry agreed and said he'd call him in a week. Then, Carlos went to the waiter. Harry saw him give the waiter a fifty-euro bill and point at the table. He left without taking the change the waiter brought to him.

Harry sat there thinking for a moment about what had just happened. Of course, he thought there must have been a catch. A production like that, with a famous director who wants someone who's never acted or had any training in the field to be an actor in the movie? Who would offer to pay a stranger's fifteen- or twenty-euro bill and pay fifty euros without wanting the change? Had he run into him by chance?

Without a doubt, deep down he wanted to believe that it was all real. Of course he wanted to be an actor, even though it would mean he'd have to quit being a mercenary spy, something he liked and was good at. But he also knew that that life wasn't forever, and he already had more than enough money to retire. And, damn, why lie? Being an actor that could become famous in that kind of movie? Of course it sounded good.

For the time being, he wanted to tell Alfonso to see what he thought about the whole thing and if he wanted to take part. So, at 8 p.m., he decided to head out. It was still raining, but that didn't matter to him. What happened when he got to Alfonso's place is known.

# CHAPTER V

Harry got home on May 13th around 11:30 after stopping by the supermarket. Taking advantage of the day off, he went to buy some groceries he needed before going home. He didn't see Barbara and figured that she worked the evening shift that day or had the day off. After putting away the groceries, he lay down on his couch and grabbed the book he was reading the previous night. Before opening it, he checked his phone and saw that Alfonso hadn't called him back and was last on WhatsApp at 9:30, right before he had called him twice. He was probably busy working, so Harry texted him saying that they would talk later in the evening and that he had the day off. He also had some texts from Sofia telling him that she wanted to leave work already to see him. Harry replied right then: "Me too, I have the day off; if you get out early, let me know." Then, he opened the book where he had left off the night before to read for a bit. He enjoyed an hour of reading, then, since he got hungry, he paused and got ready to go to the bar downstairs to eat, as he sometimes did. They had a menu of the day with a first and second course and a dessert or coffee at a fair price. It was healthy, homemade food that they made for him, which was most important to him. The drink was paid for separately, but a mercenary like him didn't have money problems. Harry, like Piotr and Angela, received a paycheck every month as antique dealers: three thousand euros, before taxes, for him, and two thousand five hundred for his colleagues. But then, they additionally received envelopes of cash every month based on the jobs they had fulfilled. The month in which the envelope was smallest was five thousand euros for Harry as director of FAI; for his colleagues, about half of that. And, when he was in El Paso, Harry had once managed to get an envelope with three hundred thousand dollars. Harry's apartment was filled with boxes of cash, and in foreign bank accounts and safes, but he had to feign a lifestyle consistent with his paycheck. When he went out for lunch, dinner, or a drink, he normally paid in cash to avoid accumulating too much. As he went downstairs to go out, Sofia called him:

"Hey, you said you have the day off?" Sofia asked.

"Yes, I do. Yesterday we had a tough job, and the customer was happy, so I told my colleagues they have the day off; we'll see each other later, right?"

"That's why I'm calling. What if I tell work I have a few things to do and can't teach class this afternoon? Do you want to come take a nap at my place? Loretta isn't there."

"*Bambina*[7], I told you the other day I usually don't take naps."

"I know." Then, there was a few seconds of silence.

"I'll be there in about an hour and a half."

"Remember, first floor, door B. *Ciao*."

Well, Harry now had a plan for the day. Loretta was Sofia's roommate. Harry didn't know her and, truthfully, didn't care at all if she was there. They were all adults, and there was no reason to hide anything. But, if she wasn't there, they had the whole place to themselves, that was true.

He knew perfectly well what "take a nap" meant and thought it was a great plan. As he ate his first-course salad and his second-course of lentils (which were delicious, in Harry's opinion), he watched the TV at the bar that had on the local news for the region of Murcia. During the review of other news, images of the outside of the auditorium came up, along with about twenty-seconds of commentary,

---

7   "Babe" in Italian.

saying there was a false alarm of a bomb during the ceremony of a metal company meeting and that there were no injuries. Harry couldn't help but let out a laugh, though no one at the bar realized it was because of the news. It wasn't okay to kill people, though he wasn't sorry that a bastard like Perez was no longer with us.

The rules of FAI and the entire Conglomerate prohibited the killing of innocent people during jobs. Killing criminals in special situations, like accidents, was allowed. And since that's what had happened, Harry didn't have to fear any action taken against him, like being fired. However, it was also true that the concepts of "criminal" and "innocent," broadly speaking, were quite ambiguous and flexible for the Conglomerate, depending on the mission.

Harry finished eating, paid, and left a tip, then headed to his garage to get his car and drive to Sofia's place, who lived in a housing development on the outskirts, about a fifteen-minute drive from where Harry was. Her apartment was nice. It wasn't very big, but it had a community pool and common landscaped areas which were pleasant to take a walk in. However, being on the outskirts was something that had never interested Harry. But, for the moment, he wasn't going to marry her, so that potential discussion could be postponed. It certainly wasn't for that point in time. Harry grabbed his manual (he refused automatic) BMW Series 3 from his spot in the garage. If it was up to him, he'd have a Cadillac or a Mercedes Maybach, but as long as he was a mercenary, he had to keep up certain appearances. He started the car and headed to Sofia's place. There wasn't any traffic on the highway, so he got there quickly and didn't think he exceeded the speed limit. He parked at the entrance and rang the bell, which they opened without asking him anything. He got in the elevator and, after walking out, looked towards Sofia's door, which was at the end of the hall, and saw that it was ajar.

"Something's up here," he thought as he walked stealthily and put his hand in the back pocket of his pants where he carried his knife. As he got closer to the door, he saw that there wasn't much light coming from inside. It was clear that the shutters (one of the curious things he had encountered in Murcia—in the US, such shutters didn't exist), were halfway open.

"Sofia?" he asked as he put his hand on the ajar door and gently pushed it. He didn't receive a response. He walked in and closed the door behind him. He didn't know what he was going to find, but, if there was an intruder that tried to escape, he would have to waste five seconds opening the door, which would give Harry more of a chance to catch him. He walked down the hallway with the knife in his hand and heard a subtle noise from Sofia's room. He headed there. The door was open, and some light was visible, but not much.

"Sofia?" he asked again before entering.

"In here, Harry."

Harry walked in without quite knowing what he would encounter and saw Sofia lying on her side naked in the bed, as though she was the model from the painting The Nude Maja. Sofia smiled and made a gesture to Harry with her finger for him to come closer. Harry took a breath of relief as his entire libido suddenly surged. He dropped the knife and threw himself on the bed.

They had sex, then slept for a while. Harry woke up first, around 5 p.m. He stayed in bed without making any noise to avoid waking up Sofia, thinking. His soldier mentality (mercenary, soldier of fortune, but soldier, nonetheless) had made him imagine a dangerous situation when, in reality, it was the opposite. It may have been ridiculous, but did he really want to keep living that way, without fully trusting anyone? Seeing danger lurking in every corner even when it didn't exist? Being a soldier of fortune had to be that way. It was what kept you alive. He was good at the job, but clearly, there was more to life than that. Perhaps he'd have to start seriously thinking about how to leave the profession behind. This wasn't something as simple as turning in your resignation letter to your boss and telling him to fuck off. It wasn't that easy. Leaving the Conglomerate took time. You held their secret, but they also held yours, so the best thing was to present the idea and reach a mutual understanding. It wasn't like they would give you a letter of recommendation, although a peaceful exit was ideal and, in fact, happened in most cases; few people could hold up into old age. Perhaps the time had come. As he looked at Sofia, he thought about how at ease he felt at that moment. He had enjoyed a bit of reading, eaten very well, and just had amazing, wild sex, then took a nap with a woman he really liked. Knowing that money wasn't an issue, couldn't he have that every day? He got up to go to the bathroom, and when he came back, Sofia was waking up. He got back in bed, and they cuddled in silence for another fifteen minutes. Then, they had sex again and then took a shower together. Sofia's apartment had a shower big enough for two people to fit comfortably (even three would fit). They got out of the shower, and Sofia started to dry her hair. It was 7:15 p.m., and Harry's phone rang. It was Alfonso.

"Hey, Alfonso. What's up?"

"Hey, Harry, nothing much. Hey, I rang your doorbell. Where are you?"

"I'm at Sofia's place."

"Ah, got it, I won't interrupt you then, player."

"No, you're not interrupting at all. Hey, what happened last night? I ran into Barbara and her sister while they were heading to your place."

"Last night? Well, I guess what had to happen happened, as you can imagine."

"They told you off and said go fuck yourself?"

"Well, yeah, basically. You were right, I should think a little more before doing certain things."

"You want to meet up tomorrow for dinner and to talk? I have a proposition for you that you're going to love."

"Alright, yeah, tomorrow's Friday. Let's talk tomorrow afternoon to plan it. See you, man, take it easy."

"See you, Alfonso."

Harry wasn't one to say, "I told you so," someone who reproaches you when something happens and brags about knowing that it was going to happen instead of having some empathy. But, of course, if he was like that, this would have been the perfect moment to say it.

Sofia came out of the bathroom ready to go. They decided to go to a mall that wasn't far from the apartment to walk around and have dinner in one of the many chain restaurants to end their Thursday. They went in Harry's car and arrived in five minutes. There were a lot of people, but that was normal; there were always people in that mall. Harry thought that, if someone wanted to carry out an attack and kill as many people as possible, that would be the ideal place. Just thinking about it horrified him. "Damn, Harry, you're sick, man. Relax a little," he tried telling himself. They decided to have dinner at an Irish pub there that neither had ever been to. When they both had their pint of Guinness waiting for their burgers to arrive, Harry decided that he should keep trying to relax.

"Today has been amazing, don't you think, Sofia? And I'm not just talking about the sex."

"You didn't like the sex?"

"Yes, I did, it was incredible. What I meant to say was…"

"Hahaha. I know—I was just joking with you, silly. Yes, it was an incredible day. I like you, Harry, and I think what we have is moving along nicely. And I love it."

"Me too."

They gave each other a look of mutual understanding, and then the burgers came. Harry had ordered one with cheddar cheese, pickles, and lettuce, something simple. Sofia, on the other hand, had decided to get an Angus burger with bacon, mayonnaise, lettuce, and tomato. Each one came with deluxe French fries. They were hungry and wanted to replenish their energy. Harry asked her if she had plans for the weekend, and Sofia said that her parents were coming from Italy to see her, and she would show them around the city. They would arrive Friday and leave Sunday. She said she hadn't told him anything before because she knew it wasn't something for a couple that was getting to know each other to do; it was too soon. Harry couldn't agree more and took a breath of relief internally. Harry, for his part, told her that he didn't have plans then and would eventually find something to do.  Perhaps he'd have dinner with Alfonso in the neighborhood tomorrow, and Saturday he'd get up early to do some tourist activities, since he still hadn't been able to visit many places in the city like the cathedral and its tower, which were apparently quite nice. After spending Thursday together, being separated for the weekend wouldn't be an issue. Things had to move slowly, and they both understood that.   They planned to call each other Sunday afternoon and maybe meet up for dinner, but there was no pressure. They finished their burgers, and then Harry took Sofia home. They gave each other a kiss goodbye, then Harry left. The drive back was relatively smooth. At that time of day there weren't many people on that small stretch of highway. It was 10:30 p.m., and Harry wasn't too tired. He dropped by Alfonso's place and rang the doorbell. He opened the door in pajamas and one of his bathrobes.

"Shit, Harry, what the hell are you doing here?"

"How long does it take you to get dressed? Let's go get a drink—I'm in a good mood."

"Hell yeah, give me five minutes and let's go somewhere. It's Thursday, so I'm sure there's a good vibe downtown."

Thus, they walked towards the city center and went to a bar with music, which was quite full. There was an area with high tables, and they were lucky enough to find a free one. Alfonso explained what happened the previous night in more detail. Both Barbara and her sister said things like "who do you think you are sleeping with two sisters at the same time," and that he had made them feel completely humiliated.

Alfonso then apologized, saying that he had simply gotten carried away with the situation, but that he understood them and that he deserved all the insults they wanted to throw at him. However, he also insisted that he never had a formal relationship with either of them, and that since it was just sex, he didn't owe either of them any loyalty. They said he had a point, but emphasized that they were sisters, which he knew, and that he shouldn't be doing that. Alfonso reiterated his apology and told them that, if it made them feel better, they could hit him. Contrary to what Alfonso expected, they each slapped him.

"Dude, what? They hit you?"

"Yeah, man, these chicks slapped me. And there I was, thinking that that's something you say but doesn't actually happen. Like when you say, 'I'll call you some time to hang out,' and while you say it you know very well it's not going to happen."

Harry couldn't help but crack up. He was his friend, but, truthfully, he deserved it. Alfonso went to the bar to get two more gin tonics while Harry stayed at the table.

"Anyways, what was it you wanted to tell me? How's it going with the teacher?"

"Good, really good. But that wasn't what I wanted to talk to you about." Harry told him about Carlos and how he approached him, how he had agreed to call him next week, and asked Alfonso if he wanted to be in a Star Wars-like movie. Alfonso let out a scream:

"Shit, Harry, of course I do, man. Sign me up." Harry figured.

"But, Alfonso, doesn't the whole thing seem weird to you?"

"I mean, it's not something that happens every day, but coincidences do exist, so maybe this is one of them. Either way, when you call next week, we'll know more. For now, I'll choose to believe it's true, and that you're going to be the next Luke Skywalker, and me, the next musician playing guitar at the Mos Eisley cantina[8]."

They laughed for a bit and decided to get their last drink. It was almost 1 a.m., and they had work the next day. This time, Harry went to the bar to order the last round. The bar was full of people,

---

8   Reference to the movie *Star Wars: Episode IV – A New Hope*.

so it took a few minutes to order. When he did, he looked at the table and saw Alfonso talking and laughing with a girl. "Damn, that man does not waste time," Harry thought. Harry situated himself at a spot at the bar with the two drinks to see if he would come or not. As he took a sip of the gin tonic, the girl grabbed Alfonso by the hand, and they left. Alfonso turned his head and winked at Harry.

Apparently, Harry had to pay for two drinks and stay there by himself. He didn't feel like drinking alone at all, but he waited a few minutes. Sometimes, you could find some group or someone you knew and, if you're lucky, join them to continue the festivities. But it didn't seem like it would happen that night, so he left his half-finished drink and Alfonso's full drink at the bar and went to the restroom, since he couldn't hold it all the way home. Luckily, there wasn't a line at the men's or the women's restroom. As he peed, he thought about how nice it was that the restroom was so clean, though he left without touching anything, just in case; hygiene isn't only what you can see. To get to the door, he had to go through a crowd of people, so he gathered his patience and began walking towards the door. He was about thirty feet from the door when, looking to one side, he saw two girls making out near him. Something about one of them grabbed his attention, and in a second, he realized. "Holy shit, that's Sofia."

# CHAPTER VI

Harry went up and separated Sofia from the other girl, who scolded him: "What the fuck are you doing, you jerk?" Harry completely ignored her and looked at Sofia without saying anything. She lowered her head in shame and didn't say anything either. Harry then immediately walked out of the bar with a decisive step. When he started walking away, he felt a hand on his shoulder.

"Harry, wait, stop, please," Sofia begged him. "I can explain everything if you let me."

"I don't know what there is to explain, Sofia. What I saw has made everything pretty clear. Just tell me one thing: why did you lie to me today?" Harry said as he stopped and turned around.

"I didn't lie to you, Harry. Everything we talked about is true. That's Loretta. She's not just my roommate, she was also my girl-friend up until a few months ago." Harry looked at Loretta, who stayed several feet away from them on the sidewalk. Sofia continued her story.

"Earlier tonight, when I got home, I told her about how we're getting serious, that I was really happy, and she told me that she was super happy for me, and that I deserved it, and then she invited me for a drink to celebrate like old times."

"Well, as far as I can tell, it doesn't seem like you've forgotten about those old times," Harry responded in an angry tone.

Loretta then approached them and said, "It was my fault, Harry. She didn't want to, but in the heat of the moment, I told her that one last time wouldn't hurt anyone, and then, well, what you saw is what happened, but that's it. I'm sorry, and I'm really sorry to you, Sofia."

Harry was still furious, but he tried to understand the situation. However, at that moment, it didn't make any sense to him.

"Look, Sofia, I'm going home. I need to think. I'm not sure what's going to happen at this point. Enjoy your night." Then, Harry started to walk away.

"No, Harry, please, don't leave me like this. I'm really sorry. I really like you and…" Harry didn't hear anything else as he continued walking away without breaking stride. Along the way, a few teenagers stopped him to ask for a cigarette, but with the look he gave them, he got them to go away. When he got home, he looked at his phone and saw a message from FAI with one single word: "LUGGAGE." That was the code for them to bring a suitcase to work the next day to travel for a few days, indicating a mission outside of the region. "Good," Harry thought, "that way I can distract myself a bit and get away." How naïve he had been, thinking that someone wanted to try to get to know him better and establish a relationship beyond sex.

"That slut can go fuck herself. I don't need her," Harry said out loud, even though he was home alone. It was already 1:30 in the morning, but he decided to pack, take a shower (this time without masturbating since he wasn't in the mood), and go to the office to wait until the morning. He packed three pairs of underwear and socks, two shirts, a short-sleeved T-shirt, two pairs of pants, and a few pairs of moccasin-type shoes. At 2:30, he was at the office. He lay on a couch and cried until he fell asleep.

At 8 a.m., Angela came in and woke Harry up.

"Good morning, boss. What are you doing here already? You want a coffee?"

Harry slowly sat up on the couch.

"Morning, Angela. Yeah, some coffee, please," he replied to his colleague, ignoring her first question as he got up and headed to the restroom.

When he came out of the restroom, Piotr walked through the door, and at that very moment, the three of them received a message that said the explanatory meeting would begin in ten minutes. All three, coffee in hand, went up to the conference room on the next floor. They sat down, and Martha showed up right away on the screen in the room.

"Good morning, everyone. I hope you slept well last night and that you're ready for a job that may be the job of the year for FAI. At noon, we're going to Almería on a relocation mission."

The relocation mission was the one implied by the luggage code. That is, it entailed a relocation of several days.

Martha continued her explanation. "Before anything, I want you all to know that the clients are going to pay five million dollars for this mission, thus making it the highest paying mission in recent years of all the delegations. That's the good news."

It was very good news. Harry had never done a mission with such a high reward. Two and a half million dollars for FAI was what they might earn in several months of regular missions. With his corresponding share, Harry had even more reason to leave the job behind after the mission and be able to do essentially whatever he wanted for work, with or without Sofia. But with that reward for the mission, he imagined that the bad news, which was what Martha would talk about next, would more than live up to the adjective "bad."

"Regarding the bad news, this is a mission without a support team."

The Conglomerate or any of its divisions never carried out missions without a support team, apart from a rare case. This one had been catalogued as a rare case. That happened, in theory, (Harry had never done a mission without a support team) because the assignment was so dangerous that it was quite literally impossible to find anyone insane enough to be the support team if needed, but, at the same time, it was a mission that the Conglomerate couldn't refuse. Or perhaps it was because it had the maximum level of secrecy possible. All of this increased the price, so a five-million-dollar mission was likely, from the start, to be without a support team.

The team reacted differently when Martha revealed the bad news. Piotr sighed in his seat, as his face showed some concern. A certain degree of concern isn't bad, given that it makes you prudent, and, as one of those Spanish sayings that Harry struggled to understand goes, *hombre precavido vale por dos*[9]. It could mean the difference between success and failure in a mission, so it didn't bother Harry at all to appreciate his colleague's concern about the mission. Angela, for her part, smiled slightly. She was quite a courageous woman. Perhaps her youth made her daring, and that didn't bother Harry either. A certain degree of boldness, combined with common sense, could also be the difference between success and failure in a mission. She had to learn to better manage that boldness and combine it with common sense, but, given how young she was, Angela had room for that, Harry had no doubt. Harry, on the other hand, didn't show any reaction. He didn't care what kind of mission it was. Having heard the reward had made him consider retiring more seriously; he didn't think about anything else. "With everything I have plus this reward, Sofia and I are going to have fun traveling the world," Harry thought. Truth be told, he was missing Sofia already, even though he practically told her off. "Honestly, it's not like we were officially boyfriend and girlfriend yet, we just said we wanted to try for more, nothing else. Or am I trying to convince myself that what she did to me isn't that bad?" At that moment, he was all out of sorts. But it was clear that he missed her, and it didn't make sense to deny that to himself.

"Harry, do you have any problem with the mission being without a support team?" Martha interrupted his thoughts.

---

9  Translator's note: Literally, "a prudent man is worth two," meaning that knowledge beforehand of potential danger gives you a strategic advantage. An equivalent in English might be, "forewarned is forearmed."

Harry said there was no problem and apologized for being distracted.

"Excellent. I can continue, then. Okay, FAI team, we've located the one and only Abdul Akhbar living in Almería. The objective of our mission is to assassinate him and make it look like a suicide or an accident. I'll go off the premise that you all know who he is."

Of course they knew. He was the absolute leader of the most dangerous Islamist cell at the time. Under his command, thousands of murders of innocent people had been carried out in the name of Islam. He was at the top of the list of most wanted terrorists at Interpol and at most of the world's intelligence services. Educated in Switzerland, he was completely familiar with the western world. Besides his native language, he spoke English and Spanish. He aimed to establish radical Islamic laws against women and homosexuals throughout the world and kill the so-called infidels. Nearly one year prior, he had fallen off the radar in the mountains of Karakorum around India, while he was being pursued by the US Army and local authorities.

The client that was paying for the mission was probably a western government: perhaps the United States or any other country, or several of them together, or even the CIA. Abdul Akhbar could possibly have information about questionable actions by intelligence services that, if made public, could put any country involved in a predicament with public opinion. It could even initiate a diplomatic conflict if those actions occurred in foreign territory. And now that he was located, they couldn't risk Abdul suddenly wanting to squeal if the Spanish police arrested him.

On the other hand, committing this assassination with their own personnel, specifically on foreign soil, was quite risky.

That's why they sometimes considered it better to commission it, through whatever government, to professional mercenaries who would have no proof of a relation to the payer. That's where FAI came in for this case. And the money, at this point, wasn't a problem either. A few million dollars were nothing for the military budgets of some countries, which could easily be hidden in reserved funds or among other "legitimate" projects.

"He's been located in a villa in the middle of the mountains in the natural area of Sierra Alhamilla, on a twenty-five-acre plot of land that belongs to a company whose primary partner is another company from Pakistan. The satellite images that have aided us show a pool, lots of large trees covering most of the outside area, and the structure of the villa that appears to have two floors. I'll send all the information to your tablets for you to study until we leave. I'll be with you guys on the ground this time, but Harry will be the coordinator and director of the mission since he's more experienced than I am. We'll be there as long as it takes to complete the mission. Our information indicates that Abdul has no intention of leaving there for the time being. Okay, that's everything for now. You guys will update me in the car. At noon, I want you all at the office entrance. Goodbye, team."

Well then, Martha was coming on the mission as another participant. Harry was happy about that. He knew that she wouldn't cause any issues in the chain of command; she was a true professional. Before arriving at her current position, where her job didn't imply work on the ground, she had been in Harry's position at FAI for a couple of years and several more years in the Cambodia delegation, as well as in El Paso, where she met Harry. Harry knew that she had done great things; she was somewhat of a legend within the organization. But one day, she grew tired of the risk involved and considered quitting. In the end, the Conglomerate convinced her to stay in a less dangerous position, but she herself asked to be involved in a mission from time to time in a more hands-on way on the ground.

"So, guys, what do you think? A secret assassination, the boss coming to receive orders on the ground, one less son of a bitch in the world, and, on top of that, five million. Let's go," Angela said excitedly, doing a sort of celebratory dance.

Harry shared Angela's enthusiasm in some sense, though not to the same degree, perhaps since he wasn't so young. He knew it wasn't going to be a walk in the park. Even if they committed the files on Abdul Akhbar to memory, until they got to his hideout, they couldn't prepare for anything definitively.

"Alright, guys, we have a couple of hours. Let's study a little and then relax. I have a feeling we'll be quite busy the next few days," Harry commented.

According to the file, Abdul Akhbar apparently had a discreet life in the villa in Almería, at least outwardly discreet. That wasn't all that strange, given that the key for him to be located was precisely that. They had found him as they nearly always did in these cases: following the money. A Pakistani company that represented a company in a western country would sound the alarms, and the intelligence agency from one of those countries, with on-site verification, would visually confirm that it was Abdul. He normally wasn't in the same place for too long, so, if he was in Almería since the last time there was an update on him, they may not have much time to complete the mission. The information about the property was that it was enclosed by a typical barb-wired fence with "PRIVATE PROPERTY – NO TRESPASSING" signs. It didn't give off the clear impression of security, in order to avoid drawing the attention of the neighbors and the hikers in the area. It was just enough to prevent anyone from entering the property accidentally. A six-foot tall wall in the middle of the mountains or an electric fence would have drawn attention. Inside would be another story; Harry was convinced of that.

The pictures from the satellite seemed to indicate the presence of cameras on the roof of the villa and around the pool, but other than that, they were going in blind. That was the worst thing that could happen: initiating an attack on a property without knowing what they would encounter, or discovering something they hadn't foreseen, or having to replan the mission entirely. It was 11:30. Harry texted Alfonso saying he'd be gone for a few days for work and would let him know when he was back. He hesitated to text Sofia. In truth, he missed her, but he wasn't sure what was going to happen between them and, above all, what he wanted to happen. Who knows—perhaps she decided to get back with her ex-girlfriend after what happened last night. Ten minutes before noon, he made up his mind. Harry was one of those people that thought it was better to mess up by doing something than regret not having done it. He sent her a message saying that he was going out of town for a few days for work and that he was out of sorts, but that he hoped they could talk when he got back. He sent the message, and alongside Piotr and Angela, they went downstairs and directly into the car. Martha was already there at the entrance waiting anxiously.

# CHAPTER VII

When Harry caught Sofia kissing Loretta, Sofia's heart sank. It hadn't occurred to her to think about it until then, but at that moment, she could only think about what the chances were that Harry would catch her when he was supposed to go home to sleep. In any case, those thoughts were replaced by ones of remorse half a second later. She felt ashamed once she began to realize the actual situation. She tried explaining it to Harry outside of the bar, Loretta herself apologized and admitted that it was her fault, that she encouraged her, but it was all for nothing. Harry left, furious, and to be fair, Sofia couldn't blame him. Even though they were getting to know each other and it technically wasn't officially a formal relationship, they had both talked earlier that day about taking that next step, which should count for something. She messed up.

"Enjoy your night," Harry had said to her as he left. She didn't know whether it was the alcohol or not, but if she thought about it logically, there was no objective reason not to do it. She would try to resolve things with Harry before anything, but right now, he was too upset, so she had to give him some time and space. And, in the meantime, she couldn't complain either. She had already messed up, admitted it, and apologized.

"Fuck, Sofia, I'm so sorry. It's all my fault. What can I do to make you forgive me?" Loretta insisted, now at the entrance to the bar. At that point, Sofia was quite drunk and laughed.

"How about you buy me another drink? It wasn't your fault. I'm the one who fucked up. I'll fix it, but right now I can't do anything. So, I think I should listen to Harry and enjoy my night. You want to join?"

Loretta agreed, a bit incredulously, but went back up to the bar. The place did have a good vibe, and the music they played was from the 80s, Sofia's favorite. So, she let Loretta buy her another drink, and they hung out there for a little longer. Paradoxically, Loretta seemed to be in a worse mood than Sofia.

"Don't worry. We're all adults and are aware of our actions. Well, with the drinks, not that much, but still aware in the end," Sofia said in between laughing.

Loretta agreed but said she couldn't help but feel guilty. So, Sofia kissed her and whispered in her ear, "Let's go home—you can make it up to me there," as she slid her hand under her dress. Loretta looked at her and finally smiled. They both left the bar and got a taxi back home. They had sex and fell asleep in Sofia's bed.

At 8 a.m., the alarm went off. Loretta got up, showered, and went to work with a massive hangover, Sofia suspected, who barely moved in the bed. At 12:30 p.m., she got up. She had to work the evening shift that day, from four to seven, so she had time. Her parents would come directly from the airport and get to their hotel around 9 p.m., where Sofia had agreed to meet them and have dinner at a restaurant nearby. She didn't know how bad Loretta's hangover was, but hers was brutal, so she took some medicine for the headache along with a coffee with milk. As she stirred her coffee with a teaspoon at the table, she also stirred figuratively over the day before. It was quite an intense day with an equally intense night.

She had a lot of fun with Loretta, and the sex had been just like it used to be when they were together: fantastic. But with Harry, it did seem like there was a special chemistry. It would be a shame to lose that opportunity for a moment of sex with another person, because that's all it was. She knew that she and Loretta were a thing of the past and that it wouldn't work. They were too different and didn't get along well enough to be together. At the end of their relationship, there were continuous fights, so they decided to end it to try and salvage a friendship, which they had achieved up to that point. Then, she looked at her phone and saw that she had received a text from Harry a little while ago. He said he was leaving Murcia for a few days for work, that he hoped they could talk when he got back, and that he felt all out of sorts.

Leaving a few days for work wasn't abnormal, so it didn't seem to her like an excuse not to talk. According to what he had told her, he was a well-known antique dealer of certain prestige and sometimes had to travel to see rare objects in person to know if he would be interested in restoring them, selling them, or not at all. He had already done it several times, i.e., going away for a few days, so she assumed it was true and had nothing to do with what happened last night. It wouldn't make sense for him to lie to her about that. "Okay, I'll be waiting for you, I also want to talk. XO," Sofia responded.

She smiled. It seemed like Harry might forgive her, which is what she wanted. Surely, when he returned from his trip with a cornucopia or a canteen from the Civil War, they would talk and fix things, because she had sincere remorse and was sure that Harry would see that. Until then, she could only wait.

She could now focus on the rough family weekend that awaited her. She knew that her parents were coming with a suitcase full of complaints as luggage: about why she's so far away, her not coming to Italy anymore, when she thinks she'll settle down and have kids…. They were her parents, and she loved them, but she had already answered those questions many times and was tired of repeating herself. "Okay, I just have to put on a brave face for this one time that they're here," she thought.

Sofia took a shower and prepared herself some veal filets with a fried egg to regain some strength. Between that and the medicine she had taken before, she felt better. She didn't want to even think about poor Loretta, who had woken up early and was working at the clothing store in the mall where she was hired. She lay on the couch to relax for a half hour before heading to the language school to teach her class and fell asleep. Luckily, she had an alarm set. It was 3 p.m. when she left the house. She didn't start until 4 p.m., but she had to stop somewhere before. She got in the car and drove to a nearby park. She parked in one of the parallel spots that looked out onto an empty field. There was nobody there, except for a few teenagers sitting on a bench. They looked towards Sofia's car, and one of them came towards her. Sofia put the window down and took out an envelope.

"Hey, Pedro," Sofia said.

"Hey, Ana," the teen responded.

Sofia gave him the envelope, then Pedro in turn gave her a small, closed trash bag. Sofia put her window up, and, before driving away, her phone went off. "Sofia, I can't stop thinking about you, last night was a revelation, please call me when you're off work, I love you." It was Loretta.

# CHAPTER VIII

Harry, Piotr, and Angela got in a seven-seater Renault Grande Espace van that Martha was driving.

"Pepe, we're going on a trip. We have a very important job we have to do in person. We don't know when we'll be back, so enjoy the next few days without us. Water the pots next week if we're not back, please," Harry said to the porter before getting in, to which Pepe agreed and nodded with a smile.

"Don't worry, Harry, will do. Safe travels."

"Good morning, everyone. We'll get to our destination in an hour and a half. That's where we'll drop our luggage, eat, and draw up a plan." Martha started the car, and they went on their way.

Harry sat in shotgun, while Piotr and Angela were in the row behind them, leaving the back seats empty. Martha told them that they were heading to a farmhouse in the area that they had rented. Their cover was they were two couples staying there for a couple weeks on vacation to disconnect from their frantic city lives. The house was a little more than a mile from the nearest town, where there was just a supermarket with a bar restaurant and a few houses, a location that provided them with the necessary privacy to carry out their plan. They had paid an extra amount to have groceries and a stocked fridge upon arrival. Martha had given a list to the owners of the house:

-Beer (at least 30 liters)
-Whiskey (5 bottles)
-1 carton of tobacco
-7 pounds of spaghetti
-5 cans of fried tomato
-4 beef hamburgers
-4 bread rolls
-A pack of cheddar cheese slices
-8 cans of tuna
-4 packs of coffee
-4 cartons of milk
-3 bags of frozen potatoes
-1 bottle of oil
-10 frozen pizzas

While they were on their way, they discussed and shared the information they had. In the file on Abdul they had looked at, the information indicated that Abdul was in the villa with his wife Isabelle. Isabelle was French, Christian, and had converted to Islam after falling in love with Abdul while she was studying economics and finance at the same university as him in Switzerland. They were both forty-four years old, and even though Abdul advocated for radical Islam for everyone, paradoxically, he practiced the exact opposite with his family. Isabelle, beyond wearing a hijab that covered her hair, dressed in a Western European style and acted that way. She and Abdul practically formed a team. She wasn't a controlled or submissive wife at all; at least that was the information they had in the case file. The couple possessed a quasi-divine power over their followers, derived from the great charisma and conviction they had, such that all their claims went unchallenged. If Abdul said that women should cover their whole body with clothes and be submissive to the will of men, that's how it should be. But those obligations didn't apply to Isabelle. And it's not that no one argued it; it's that no one dared to even consider why they should or if there was some contradiction between his word and his supposed beliefs.

His rhetoric had spread throughout various regions of Pakistan and Afghanistan, and for several years, his followers had carried out attacks on Western interests in the area, as well as ruled several territories with an iron fist. That's why he was wanted by the authorities.

There were at least two other people in the villa: two supporters of Abdul, though possibly more. Apparently, from time to time, a vehicle would leave the property and come back after a bit. The most logical explanation was that one of his followers would get groceries, given that neither Abdul nor Isabelle left the property. What the van brought wasn't known, but apart from food, there would most likely be alcohol (Abdul didn't renounce that) or drugs (it was known that Abdul was addicted to opiates).

In the file on Abdul, there was a section with some of the most bizarre rumors, some more believable than others. There was one that said that Abdul liked to watch Isabelle while she had sex with other women. There was another that said he liked wild animals and that he had a real crocodile somewhere in the villa. Others mentioned gorillas. They were nothing more than rumors, so, for the time being, they couldn't take it as something they could use, unless they were proven to be true.

They were just about to arrive when Harry looked at his phone and saw that Sofia had responded to him. "Good," he thought. Now he could fully concentrate on the mission. It was evident that both sides would be ready and willing to fix things once he got back. For the moment, there were terrorists to kill.

They arrived at the ranch-style house with a porch with four chairs and a plastic table, like the ones from beachside bars[10].

---

10 Translator's note: The original Spanish text for "beachside bars" is *chiringuitos*, a word particular to Spain. They're small, informal beachside bars that offer snacks and drinks, with some also selling *tapas* and full meals.

Nothing glamorous, but very practical. The area was beautiful. There was hardly any noise, except for some birds, and, though the local weather was semi-desert-like, there were some trees around, indicating that the temperature was pleasant for that time of year. Harry figured that a couple of months later it wouldn't be as enjoyable to be there, but at that time it was pleasant. Martha put in the code 5420, provided by the owners, on a number pad next to the door, which then opened. Before them was a huge living room with a large table with six seats, along with a massive couch, a chaise longue, a couple of armchairs, and a gigantic TV hanging on the wall. In the back, there was an American-style kitchen openly connected to the living room and, on the other side, a door. Behind it was a hallway where there were two double bedrooms with their own bathrooms. The house was nice. Harry and Piotr left their bags in one bedroom, Martha and Angela in another, then they met in the living room.

"Okay, Harry, you're in charge from here. The fenced property with the villa is about four miles from here, past the mountain next to here. The weapons and all the necessary equipment for the mission are in the van, but if something is missing, let me know, and they'll bring it right to us. We have a direct link to the Conglomerate available to us for the mission," Martha said.

"Perfect. Thanks, Martha. Okay, the first thing we're going to do is open some beers and make some hamburgers and fries." Harry was a peculiar boss for what could be considered a standard one, especially for this type of work. He believed in some discipline, but in a mission that might take quite a while, you had to avoid being stressed the whole time. A hamburger and a beer would surely help everyone relax. At least that was his thinking, and, in the end, since he was the boss, the others had to obey. "I'll go ahead and make them. And meanwhile, I want a visual map of the fenced perimeter with the entrance points marked, cause in the file there weren't any, if I remember correctly. See if you can put it together based on the satellite photos and from what we know, and then project it on the

TV, even if it's haphazard. Alright, guys, let's go," Harry ordered, giving a couple of claps of encouragement.

Piotr opened a liter of beer and poured four cups, while Martha and Angela turned on their tablets. Piotr had perhaps the most expertise in that field. He was a telecommunications engineer with a degree in architecture from the University of Warsaw, graduating at the top of his class. So, putting a map together with some satellite photos and the information from the file shouldn't be too hard for him—at least that's what Harry thought. Piotr also had the military training that they gave him in the Conglomerate when they hired him. Angela, for her part, despite her youth, had trained in medicine and had a PhD in Psychology, specifically in behavioral sciences. Just like Piotr, she got the same military training when they hired her. In fact, that's where she met Piotr.

While Piotr, Angela, and Martha were at the table trying to put a map together, Harry put the four burgers in a pan, while in another he fried some frozen French fries. He opened four rolls and put a slice of cheese on each one. Quick, easy, delicious food—you couldn't ask for more. As he took a sip of his beer, he looked at his three colleagues and thought about how lucky he was to have that team. The bonus of also having Martha on the team, who was an excellent asset on the ground, was a true luxury. Moreover, the fact that she put herself to the side and let Harry be the boss of the operation, while being aware that perhaps she was a bit rusty to lead such an important mission, said a lot about the type of leader and person she was. There are things you either have or don't have, and class is one of those things. Martha had it, so it was impossible not to respect her.

The hamburgers smelled delicious. The meat seemed to be of good quality, and Harry had experience making them to perfection, like any respectable American citizen.

"Okay, guys, food is ready. Drop the beer and grab some water. That's an order," Harry said as he headed to the table with the burgers and the fries. They had a mission to fulfill. It wasn't a bachelor party weekend; they would drink later.

They already had the map of the perimeter of the property projected on the TV. Apparently, there was only one entrance point, with an unpaved dirt road that didn't seem to have too many potholes. The property had lots of trees, but the villa itself was visible in the back, nestled against a hill, also surrounded by a barb-wired fence at that end, like the whole property. From the property entrance to the villa there was between two-hundred twenty to two-hundred seventy-five yards. The pool was behind the house, not visible from the entrance. From one side, it was somewhat visible, though there were trees in the field of vision.

"Okay, for now, let's concentrate on observing the routines of the people in the villa for three or four days. The more we find out, the better. Information is everything in this job, as you all know," Harry said as he devoured his burger, which was cooked to perfection. "We'll get up close to the villa and set up shifts. So, without thinking too hard, how do we kill this bastard and make it look like a suicide or an accident?"

"I think the best thing is some kind of poison that can go undetected in toxicology analyses and that can simulate a natural death by a heart attack or something along those lines," Angela proposed.

It wasn't a bad idea, and Harry wasn't surprised at all by the response. There were statistics that said that women who murder someone plan it much more methodically than men, and poison was a common method for women. Men always tended to kill more by force and impulsively.

"That's a good idea. In the van we have a full kit of lethal substances that disappear from the blood within a few hours and that simulate a heart attack. We have pills, powders, and injectable substances," Martha pointed out as if she were talking about a washing machine catalogue.

"Another idea is to kill him with a sniper rifle at a distance," Piotr suggested. "It wouldn't look like an accident or a suicide, but no one would ever find out that it was us if we do it right. No fingerprints, no DNA, no pictures…. We could also use a rifle and ammunition that mujahideen militias typically use so that the obvious assumption would be that it was some rebel faction settling the score."

That wasn't a bad thought either, but that option didn't end up convincing Harry. It was obvious that a "natural" death of Abdul Akhbar would be investigated in depth as soon as he was identified, but the investigation would end much sooner without any culprits than it would for a death by gunshot. The job consisted of raising as little suspicion as possible.

"Well, in any case, grab some energy bars and water to spend the night outside. Let's get on the ground and set up a couple of full days of surveillance. I want patterns of behavior, who's going, who's coming, how many armed men there are…Any detail will be reported immediately on your phones to a central file for the mission so that whoever isn't on the ground can study it. Alright, go pee and we'll head out. And put a fire under it." Harry ordered.

They left the van hidden between some trees about nine hundred yards from the entrance of the villa and walked towards it, avoiding the main road. Once they arrived, Harry gave his orders:

"Okay, perfect. Piotr, you stay here until midnight. Hide and watch the entrance point. Martha, walk around the border of the property without being seen and you'll watch the back part of the house until midnight as well. Angela, you and I are going to go back around and go to the house. At midnight, we'll come back and switch. We'll park the van in the same spot and come to you guys. Don't move until we come back, got it? I don't want one minute to go by without the villa being watched. When we switch places, get in the van and go home. You guys will do two shifts; while one sleeps, the other will attend to the communications and analyze the information received. I hope that information is abundant and useful. Tomorrow at noon, you guys will switch with us, and so on until Monday at noon, and then we'll all go back to the house and figure out our next steps."

Everyone agreed. But they agreed with conviction; Harry saw it in their faces. They trusted him as a leader and would follow him wherever it was necessary. They would never question his decisions, but, at the same time, he wanted them to feel free to make suggestions at any point. He was smart enough to know that he wasn't infallible. There were times when his colleagues might have great suggestions, and a good leader had to know when to listen to them.

"Any suggestions, team? Please, don't hold back; anything to improve is welcome." They all shook their heads no.

"I'm going to grab a tracker that can attach to a vehicle in case someone leaves. It might be useful to know where they go when they leave the villa," Piotr noted.

"Excellent, good idea," Harry approved.

It was Friday at 3:50 p.m. and it was quite hot. Piotr took his assigned position, Martha set off towards where Harry had ordered her to go, and Harry and Angela went around the property from the other side.

The fence outside (which was barb-wired without anything complex—anyone with shears could enter) as well as the entrance didn't seem very secure. The entrance had a double padlock and opened manually. It had an intercom on the side without any cameras. In any case, the barb wire not seeming like a big deal might be misleading, given that it might have a silent alarm that would alert the people inside. Piotr took out his binoculars and saw that there were some birdhouses in the nearby trees. As he had foreseen, by looking carefully, he saw that there were cameras in them that pointed towards the entrance and around it. "Bingo," Piotr said to himself as he sent the pictures to the central file. As he had imagined, the soft security was only a front. Now he only had to wait a few hours and see if something interesting would happen.

Martha, meanwhile, reached the hill that faced the back part of the villa and hid between some bushes. From her position, she saw some security cameras placed on the roof of the villa that pointed near her. They weren't as hidden as the ones at the entrance. She also saw a couple of windows that, at that time, had the shutters closed. To one side, she saw a part of the pool, or as much as the vegetation allowed. With binoculars, she saw water moving, perhaps because there was someone in the pool in the part that she couldn't see. She took some pictures and continued to survey. Meanwhile, Harry and Angela walked around half-ducked down trying to camouflage themselves in the brush. They headed towards the main side of the pool, gradually moving away from it as they advanced to avoid being seen. Up to that point, there were plenty of trees visible inside the property, which camouflaged the villa quite well. Obviously, it was visible, and they knew that there was a house there, but the trees hid what was going on inside and along the perimeter of it.

Angela took out her binoculars and looked at the pool from afar. "Harry, there's a couple of guys in the pool, but neither of them looks like Abdul."

Harry took pictures and immediately grabbed the phone that the four FAI members had on walkie-talkie mode on a secure channel.

"Martha, do you see the pool from your position?"

"Negative, Harry. Just a small portion."

"OK, leave your position and keep going around the villa until you're right across from your current position, pretty much where we are now. I'll send you exact coordinates. That'll be your new position. Stay there until we change shifts. We're going back to the house to start studying what you guys are sending."

"Got it, Harry."

Harry thought it would be more useful to surveil that part of the property, since it was more likely that something would happen there. They went back to the van and headed back to the house. Once they were there, they began examining the information that they were receiving while the four of them communicated through the walkie-talkies.

For the time being, the entrance cameras, just like the ones in the back, made it unfeasible to jump over and try to advance towards the villa through that area. To the side of the pool, even if there were no cameras (there probably were, which Martha would find in her visual survey), there was plenty of open terrain to enter without being seen. They would be spotted instantly.

"In theory, we're screwed," Harry said. "But no one said that this was going to be easy. Piotr, do you see any option to deactivate or disable the cameras?"

"Harry, did you not see the pictures that I sent twenty minutes ago? There are solar panels on the house and a couple of wind generators. They most likely have gas motors, too, so I don't think we can cut their electricity from outside because they may not be connected to the network, and the breaker box might be inside," Martha interrupted.

"I know, I know. I was referring to if we could interfere with the transmission or something like that with some sort of chaff[11]," Harry specified.

"Shh, quiet for a second," Piotr abruptly said. "Over and out, be right back."

---

11 A type of grenade that releases aluminum clouds to confuse radar systems and similar devices.

# CHAPTER IX

A minute later, with everyone silent and anxiously looking at their phones, Piotr spoke again:

"A vehicle just left the property, Citroen C15 with tinted back windows, license plate 56520-R. I threw a transmitter on it."

"Received, good work. Angela, go follow them with the GPS to see where they go. *Echando leches*[12], as you guys say here," Harry ordered.

Angela got up from her seat, grabbed the keys to the van, and left the house. Harry would stay behind to coordinate everyone. It was 6:30 p.m., and things were getting interesting. He lit a cigarette and connected the transmitter from the tracker's GPS signal that Piotr sent to the TV. From what he saw, it went in the direction of the town, which wasn't strange at all if it was to get groceries. From what he saw on the GPS from Angela's van, she was going towards the town via a different route and would arrive about three minutes before him. That would be enough for her to leave the van discreetly parked and observe.

Angela arrived and parked the van between four other cars that were parked along a sidewalk to avoid drawing attention.

"Parked. Two minutes for the suspect's arrival," she informed.

The town was so small that she nearly saw all of it with her binoculars from her position. After two minutes, the C15 arrived

---

12 *Echando leches* or *echar leches,* literally translated as "pouring milk," is a slang phrase that means to hurry or rush.

and parked in front of the entrance to the supermarket. A tall, forty-something-year-old man, dressed in shorts and a Hawaiian shirt, got out of the car. He didn't give off the image of a terrorist, but rather a tourist on vacation. Angela sent several pictures to the central file, but no identity was found. He was probably an anonymous supporter of Abdul and his cause, unregistered and with no criminal record. It was within the realm of possibility. He entered the establishment and walked out ten minutes later with a couple of bags that, strangely, he didn't put in the back of the C15, but rather in the shotgun seat. He did a couple more rounds inside the supermarket to grab more bags and placed all of them in shotgun.

"There's someone or something in the back of the C15, it's obvious. He doesn't even want to open the back door to put the bags there," Angela said to her colleagues. "He seems cautious, calculating. I'm going to follow him to make sure he goes back to the villa."

The C15 drove off, and Angela left twenty seconds later. She didn't want him to see her, and with such little traffic, it would draw a lot of attention if a vehicle was right behind another one.

Plus, since it had the GPS tracker, there was no danger of losing him. To her surprise, she saw that he wasn't going the same way as he had gone before, which would have been the most logical thing since it was the shortest way back to the villa. Instead, he was going the exact opposite way. After five minutes, she saw the vehicle stop at a gas station. "Okay, maybe he changed course just to get some gas," Angela thought. However, according to the GPS information, that gas station had been abandoned for years. Angela arrived and parked at a safe distance to watch with her binoculars. The man, who had parked his vehicle in a parallel parking spot at the station which, indeed, was abandoned (there were three rusted pumps and a shop locked up tight with chains and covered in graffiti), opened the back door of the C15. Angela saw a girl get out of the car with her hands tied and a blindfold over her eyes. The man took off the blindfold, cut off the rope around her hands, gave her something that looked like cash, and pointed which way to go. The girl, who from Angela's position looked to be in her twenties, started walking in the direction that the man had indicated.

"Heads up, Harry, the man let a girl go who seemed to be in the back of the C15, and she's walking away. I'm asking for permission to follow her and question her. I think she can give us a lot of information," Angela requested on the phone.

"Yes, I think that's our best option. Do it. I know you can convince her to tell us what we need. Piotr, keep an eye out for when the man comes back in case you see something that might be useful for us. Angela, be careful. We don't know who this girl is. Keep communication open," Harry concluded.

He agreed with Angela. This mission was like a marathon, a race of endurance, and information was strength. What was certain was that, regarding the inside of the villa and the occupants there, they knew very little. Drawing up a plan to attack him without knowing almost anything was nearly suicide, and that was something that Harry wasn't willing to do. For the reward, it was worth it to spend a little time and dedicate a few days to studying the situation to ensure the success of the mission. When the time came to make a decision, Harry thought that there would be more options from Angela getting information from someone that had been inside the villa through her empathy and psychological observation skills, rather than watching the man in the C15 to see what he did in the abandoned gas station once he had left the girl.

"He may just take a piss or smoke a cigarette and go back to the villa," Harry's instinct told him. That would give them very little information, and they would have let the girl get away, a direct witness to what could be happening in the villa.

Angela stopped the van next to the girl as she was walking towards the town on the dirt path that served as a road. She put her window down.

"It's hot. Are you going into town? I can bring you, if you want. There's AC in here," Angela said, smiling.

The girl looked at her with a face that was a mix of fear, relief, and contemplation. Now that Angela saw her up close, she realized that she was indeed in her early twenties. She had Asian facial features and wore a black sleeveless top and a short jean skirt.

"Okay, thank you," the girl responded with a half-smile and an accent that confirmed her Asian origins. She opened the door and got into the van.

"What's your name? I'm Angela," Angela asked as she started the car to go into town.

"Melinda."

"Nice to meet you, Melinda. What part of town are you going to? I can drop you off wherever you want."

"At the entrance is fine, thank you."

"You sure? Really, it's no problem for me. Are you from around here? I don't know the area well. I could use someone who could help me with hiking routes and places to see."

"I'm sorry, I don't go out much. I can't help you. Really, you can just drop me off at the town entrance."

Angela realized that the girl was scared but at the same time needed help. She had gotten into a stranger's car, and she'd bet a hundred euros that she got in not only because of the suffocating heat, but to be close to another person at that moment. Angela also noticed that, even though Melinda's subconscious wanted to make her cautious, Angela gave her a feeling of trust. Melinda didn't show signs of nervousness. She wasn't biting her nails, her limbs weren't shaking, and she didn't stutter when speaking or refuse to look her in the eyes. Angela decided that she had enough information to trust her instinct and her training in behavioral analysis and psychological profiling.

"Melinda, you're safe. You can trust me. I saw where you got out, and I can assure you that you're safe. Okay?" Angela said with as comforting a tone of voice as she could. "Look, how about I take you to get something to eat at a restaurant in town and we chat for a bit? You can leave whenever you want, but let me try to help you."

Melinda nodded her head and started to cry. Angela stopped and parked the van on the side of the road because she knew what Melinda needed. She hugged her as she calmed her, telling her that she was safe. Minutes later, once she calmed down, they drove off into town, which was a few minutes away.

"Are you a cop?" Melinda wanted to know.

"No, I'm not, but I can help you. Look, we're here now. I heard they make sandwiches to die for...but not actually *die*." Angela tried to inject a touch of light humor to alleviate the heavy atmosphere.

They parked and went into a bar. It was a bar that could be described as old, with a supermarket section to supply the town. Nothing glamorous, but it did the job. There were some tables outside, and at one of them were four elderly men playing domino, hitting the table as hard as they could. Angela and Melinda sat at the table furthest away. It was about 7 p.m. Melinda ordered a Spanish omelette sandwich with mayonnaise, whereas Angela didn't want anything to eat. They also ordered a liter of beer for the two of them, which Angela knew always helped when it came time to talk and establish trust. Melinda almost literally swallowed the sandwich whole. It was obvious that she was hungry. She took out a pack of cigarettes from her pocket and lit one, blowing out a puff of smoke mixed with a sigh of relief and pleasure.

"That was good. You don't have to pay for me, really. I have money," Melinda said.

"I already saw that you got money, but this one is on me, don't worry. How old are you, Melinda?

"Twenty-one."

"Do you live here? Do you live with anyone?"

"For now, I live at the hostel at the end of the street. But enough about me, who are you, and what makes you think you can help me?"

Any other person would have been surprised at such a direct question from a young woman that they had just picked up and who, she intuited, hadn't had a great time in the villa. Not Angela, who, with the psychological profile that she had gathered while they were in the car, expected such a response.

"Okay, Melinda. I'm going to tell you everything so you can see that I trust you, but only if you promise to tell me whatever I ask you and to let me help you." Angela had decided to put all her cards on the table. All-or-nothing, as players of mus[13] would say. All-in, as poker players would say. She was going to do something that Harry wasn't going to like and that would undoubtedly lead to a strong reprimand, at best, but she believed that it was the right thing and knew that Harry would understand in the end.

"I work at an organization who has the goal of killing a dangerous terrorist that we believe lives in the villa where the vehicle came from which you got out of, who is this man." Angela turned her phone to her with a picture of Abdul Akhbar. "Does he look familiar?"

Melinda didn't respond. She poured herself another glass of beer and continued listening.

"Well, it turns out that you were in the villa, and we think that you can help us achieve our mission."

"And why should I help you guys?"

"That man's name is Abdul and he's a massive son of a bitch. If you want, I can show you what he's capable of."

"I don't doubt it, but why should I help you guys? I mean, I'm grateful that you've brought me here and all that, but..."

"Who from your family does Abdul have?" Angela had already seen this several times and, plus, Melinda was turning out to be an open book for her.

Melinda was petrified with a look of amazement. How was it possible that this stranger knew how to read her so well? It seemed like one of those American TV shows.

---

13  A popular card game in Spain and parts of Latin America.

"My father. He has him at our house in Manila." Melinda stopped for a moment and then kept talking. "He turned to dangerous men when his car repair business started to go downhill, and now, he owes a lot of money to people that he shouldn't. They threatened to kill him and sell his organs on the black market until his debt was settled, and I couldn't let that happen. I offered to do whatever. The next day, they told me to grab my passport if I didn't want to see my father carved up. I couldn't even say goodbye to him. A half an hour later, I was on a plane to Spain. Since they know that I speak Spanish, they brought me here and told me that I'd work here until my father's debt was settled and that, as you could imagine, if I escaped, my father would suffer the consequences. They paid for the hostel for me to stay for several months. When I get a text, whatever time it may be, I have to walk to that gas station where you saw me and that son of a bitch picks me up and takes me to the villa where another son of a bitch, who turns out to be the one from the picture, and the bitch of a woman that they have there do what they want with me. That's supposed to subtract from the debt, and they also give me money to keep me happy." There was a lot of anger in Melinda's face as she told everything.

"If you give me your father's address, I can have a team from our organization locate him and watch him to make sure that nothing happens to him. And as soon as we finish the mission, we'll bring him back to you. We can't before because, if not, Abdul would be suspicious, but your father would be safe."

"If you can make it so I can talk to him, I'll tell you anything you want. But I need to talk to him and know that you aren't bluffing," Melinda said, reaching her hand out to Angela. Angela gave her hers, and they sealed the deal. But Angela knew that she had to talk to Harry before, so she got up and called him.

"Angela, I heard everything. You told her who we are and the mission we have. You know very well that that goes against all the norms of the Conglomerate. It's not protocol, we don't know her, and she could put our entire mission in danger," Harry said with a strong tone.

"I know and I'm sorry, Harry, but screw the protocol. I was reading inside her completely and I knew that she could be useful for us. I had to gain her trust first. Melinda hates Abdul. She'll do whatever it takes to destroy him as long as we help her with her dad, which I knew perfectly well we could do with a couple of phone calls. Plus, let me say, I think we should recruit her. She's a survivor and she's really strong. With a few months of training, she'd be a valuable asset for the organization," Angela justified.

"Okay, Angela. I trust you and your judgement," Harry responded and then immediately added, "because now, I basically have no other option. If you make a decision like this again, I will unilaterally kick you out of the organization. Got it?" Harry hung up before getting a response, got up, and kicked the chair he was sitting in, sending it to the other end of the living room.

# CHAPTER X

Melinda told Angela where her father lived, gave her a description, and shared his address in Manila. Angela dropped her off at the hostel, telling her to continue her normal life, knowing that "normal" would only be for two or three more days, after which Abdul wouldn't call her again. She met with her the following day, Saturday, at 5 p.m. at the other end of town, far from anyone's sight so that she could talk to her father and see that they weren't bluffing.

It was nearly 9 p.m. when she went back to the house. Harry was there in front of his laptop analyzing information. He saw her walk in the house and raised his eyes with a not so friendly look.

"Tell me everything that girl told you about her father. I already have a team in Manila waiting for instructions," he told her. Angela talked about what they had discussed and told him that she had agreed to meet with her the following day at 5. Harry grabbed his phone and started talking to the team in Manila in English. After he hung up, he turned towards Angela.

"Melinda's father will get twenty-four-hour protection from the moment the team arrives at his house within a couple of hours. Tomorrow at 5, you'll get a call from that team, and they'll put that man on the phone so that he can talk to his daughter for a couple of minutes. As soon as Melinda hangs up the phone, you'll bring her here, and she'll tell us everything we want."

Angela nodded, showing her agreement with the plan. Then, Harry grabbed his phone and communicated to the team that there was a change of plans. They would pick them up at the spot where they had parked the van that afternoon, within an hour, and they would all come back home to relax. It didn't make sense to keep watching to get information about what happened inside the villa. They were going to have all of it the following day. Everyone agreed to Harry's order.

"Angela, I'm going to take a shower. Keep an eye on communication with your colleagues in case something happens. We'll go get them right away, okay?" Angela nodded and sat in the chair to look at the information and location of her colleagues. Harry went into his bathroom. He was furious, tense. But deep down, he understood what Angela had done. Why lie to himself? He probably would have done the same thing when he was younger. In a few years, she would understand that the rules and protocols were there for a reason, and that if they were followed, it was because they were proven to save you from problems in many situations. But for now, he trusted her instinct more than the protocol. She possessed that element of defiance against the norms that young people had. Harry knew that she was an excellent agent and that she had a great future within the organization. He only wanted her to understand the rules; he didn't mean to sabotage her in any way. He masturbated as he showered which alleviated the tension. When he got out, he texted Sofia: "I miss you. I think we'll be home sooner than planned, so we can talk right away if you want, sound good?"

He got a reply instantly with an animated image of a smiley face and "I can't talk now, I'm with my parents. When you're back, we'll talk."

A somewhat cold response for Harry, but the picture of the smiley face made it clear that the tone wasn't bad, so that was good enough for him for the time being. Now, he had to focus on the mission.

Harry walked out of the bathroom and saw that nothing had come up while he was gone, as expected. The C15 had returned to the villa a while ago, shortly after Angela stopped watching it. Piotr hadn't detected anything noteworthy when the vehicle got back to the villa. They picked everyone up right away, and around 10 p.m., the four members of FAI were at home making some pizzas in the oven.

"Okay, guys," Harry began, "as you all know, the plans have changed as necessitated by circumstances that you all know and that are no longer relevant to the case. With the help of the images that you guys have been sending, we're going to put everything we know up until now together if that sounds good to you guys. Piotr, please start."

Piotr had produced a sort of map with the semi-hidden cameras that were at the front of the property near the entrance. When projecting the angles of vision, thanks to the specialized software that they had, he verified that they were all placed in such a way that left no blind spots and covered the entire perimeter. He couldn't be sure of it, but they probably had night vision. The cameras didn't sound any alarm if they detected movement, since Piotr had seen several birds go in front of or fly by them without an alarm going off. That meant that that was either an internal alarm (unlikely because, with the animals from the mountain, it would be going off several times every hour) or there was someone watching the CCTV from the cameras and knew when something moving was an intruder or a bird. From the property entrance to the structure of the villa itself, it might take forty to forty-five seconds running.

The barb-wired fence didn't show any signs of being electric or of having any motion detector. Certainly, from the point of view of a hiker that passed through the area, the property was normal in appearance.

"If we find a way for the cameras to not see us, we could approach the villa by hiding in the trees on the property. That's the problem, the cameras not seeing us," Piotr pointed out to conclude his presentation.

"Okay. Martha, what do you have for us? What did you see from your position?" Harry asked right as the oven sounded to indicate that the pizzas were ready. Angela got up to take them out.

The pool was visible from Martha's position, or at least the part of it that the vegetation and the trees in the way allowed to be seen. Cameras camouflaged in birdhouses in the trees were also visible, like the ones that Piotr had described at the entrance, pointing towards the barb-wired fence that bordered the property. In the area of the pool, which was rectangular and about one-hundred ten or one-hundred twenty square feet, there were some deckchairs and a small cart with drinks that served as a bar. There was also a door that gave access to the inside of the villa. Everything seemed normal. Even though it wasn't easy to see that area of the pool, anyone looking at the landscape with binoculars that accidentally saw it wouldn't think that anything strange was going on there, except if someone was on vacation.

"It's the same thing here as what Piotr said with the entrance. It's all surveilled and covered with cameras. Plus, there's an added detail here: even if we did stay hidden, there aren't any trees on the way to the villa that can cover us. They're all right next to the pool. We'd have plenty of open field," Martha concluded.

"Interesting," Harry said as he took a bite of a slice of pizza. "Damn, it's good, isn't it?" he added as he swallowed.

"Ham and mushroom never fails, Harry. You already know," Martha responded, as Angela and Piotr laughed. "You really do love eating. You get excited about everything."

"Fuck off, you assholes," Harry responded, laughing as well.

It was necessary to have moments like that to remove the stress of the mission. That didn't mean that the mission was to be taken lightly in any way either, but Harry believed that being in a bad mood, serious, and focused the entire time during a several-day mission was counterproductive.

"Okay, do you guys realize what you both have said? There are cameras that cover every angle of the perimeter, all that. Got it. So, all the cameras point to the external perimeter, right? Then, based on what I've seen from your pictures, you haven't seen a camera that points towards the villa?"

Piotr and Martha shook their heads no. They had revised the whole property from their position with binoculars, inch by inch. And all the trees. There wasn't a single camera pointed anywhere other than the perimeter.

"Got it. Well, we already know that, if we somehow manage to avoid the cameras that point towards the fence, there won't be any other camera to worry about. There will probably be other things to worry about, but not cameras," Harry finished.

As far as the inhabitants of the villa, they had identified three men, plus the driver of the C15 and two women. They didn't carry rifles or machine guns, but they did detect small pistols on their waists. Martha couldn't tell if they were taser guns or pistols. They all wore Western European-style clothing. With Martha's pictures, they had managed to identify a couple of them and one of the women on the Conglomerate database, thanks to the modern system of facial recognition. They were followers of Abdul's cause, very well known by different intelligence agencies, and they all stood out for their loyalty to the cause and for being particularly ruthless. Regarding the rest, there was no trace in the database, but it was no surprise that Abdul had continued garnering new followers. Isabelle and Abdul had not let themselves be seen, and neither Martha nor Piotr had been able to capture a shot of them in the villa.

With the pizzas finished, Angela began to talk to them about the psychological profile of the subjects. "Abdul and Isabelle have proven to be powerful people. Their total and absolute lack of empathy towards other people might be one of their psychological features that stand out the most, but also their incredible self-assuredness. You can have someone locked away and derive a sense of power from that, but their power in this case goes beyond that. They have someone like Melinda at their disposal, and instead of having her locked up, they let her go because they know she won't escape. That indicates much more power over someone than a mere physical barrier. They don't do it from mercy or so that she has a little bit of freedom; they have no empathy. They do it to feel powerful. I think that we have to try to turn that against them. I think they're smart; if not, they wouldn't have been on the run for so long, but that degree of arrogance can be a weak point," she laid out.

After a brief, nearly imperceptible pause in which he had time to observe the attentive faces of his team, Harry began to speak:

"I think everything we know up until now is interesting, but what Melinda tells us tomorrow is going to be key to drawing up a definitive plan and accomplishing the mission. So, I suggest everyone gets some rest. Tomorrow morning we'll see about Manila and plan a set of questions for the afternoon. Do whatever you want now. At 8, we're on. Martha, can I talk to you, please?" Harry said. "Bring the whiskey and two glasses with ice. I'll wait for you outside," he added right after without waiting for a response.

Angela and Piotr went to their rooms to read, watch a movie, or whatever they pleased, as Harry opened the door and went out onto the porch to smoke a cigarette while he waited for Martha. He sat on one of the foldable chairs there. It was a beautiful night, with a little cool air, and the sounds of the birds singing could barely be heard (Harry didn't know which ones sang at night, much less about birds, nor did he try to). The near-full moon shone in the sky. As he let out a puff of smoke, Harry thought about Sofia, wondering what she was doing. Given the time, she probably would have already dropped her parents off at the hotel after dinner and would be at home or heading there. Or maybe she went out for a drink. Murcia was a city that welcomed that, given its atmosphere and its people. Either way, he had decided to give her a little space, so that's what he would do. He was more and more certain that he wanted to fix everything, no matter what it took, and he expected her to feel the same way. Martha came out onto the porch with a bottle of whiskey and two glasses with ice in hand right when Harry finished his cigarette.

"Thanks, Martha. Let's sit back and enjoy the night with this beauty."

"Your orders, boss," Martha responded as she set the bottle and the glasses on the table and sat down. Both reclined their seats as far as possible, at about a one hundred forty- or one-hundred fifty-degree angle. They sat there for a bit enjoying their drinks and the pleasant night.

"Do you think that bastard Abdul is capable of enjoying these small pleasures? Drinking a whiskey in silence, under the moonlight," Harry asked.

"That might be a question for Angela, but I don't think so. That type of person doesn't enjoy anything. The lack of empathy and sense of power and being above everything prevents them," Martha replied as she lit a cigarette and offered another to Harry, who grabbed it and thanked her with a nod of the head.

"Well, that son of a bitch can go fuck himself," Harry exclaimed with a loud laugh.

"Are you already drunk, Harry?"

"Are those beers I had at dinner showing?"

"Yep."

They both laughed.

He liked Martha. She was a tough boss, but sensible. She had her own way of doing things and had to be respected, as with the whole chain of command. But she was an honest, reasonable person, and, moreover, when she wasn't at work, she was quite pleasant. If he couldn't consider her a friend, she was certainly close.

"Martha, thank you for making this mission easy for me. I know that it may not be easy to accept that you're not the boss and that maybe the normal thing to do would have been to tell me to fuck off," Harry said, finishing his whiskey.

"Not at all, Harry. There has to be loyalty in an organization. It's no problem at all. It's the right decision for the mission," Martha replied, also finishing her drink.

"Have you ever thought about leaving?" Harry asked as he poured himself another whiskey and another for Martha.

"What I've thought about is asking to work in the field again, Harry. Coordinating sucks. So many meetings, traveling…but no action. Shit, just watching the fucking pool made me feel alive again," Martha responded with a glow of excitement in her eyes.

"*Well, if I left, you could go back to being the boss of FAI,*" Harry thought, but didn't say anything.

"Damn, Martha. Well, we'll see tomorrow, but I think you're going to have plenty of action in this mission. Let's fucking drink to that," Harry said, raising his voice a bit. Martha clinked her glass with his as she laughed.

"Harry, you're becoming quite the local." She then quickly added, "You have to leave that slut Isabelle to me, promise me."

Harry nodded his head and lit another cigarette. Martha finished her whiskey and decided that was enough and went to her room.

Harry stayed behind looking at the stars for a couple more minutes as he finished his cigarette and also decided that it was time to go to sleep. A rough day awaited them tomorrow, and it wasn't a matter of having too much of a hangover. However, this past Friday had certainly been quite intense, and it wasn't going to be easy to overcome it. But as Harry's mother used to tell him when he was little, "Never say never, son. Never say never."

# CHAPTER XI

Sofia had just read Loretta's text declaring her love for her and didn't know how to react then. She was in her car, shortly before going to work with her baggie of recently purchased weed (she wasn't an addict, but she liked to smoke a joint every now and then to relax) and an uncomfortable situation fell upon her. She knew for certain that she didn't love Loretta. Well, she did love her, but not in the way that Loretta wanted her to love her. Everything indicated that Loretta had wrongly interpreted what happened the night before. She didn't want to hurt her, so she would have to tell her in a gentle way, and even though she may be hurt initially, she hoped that they could still be friends. She decided that she would call her after work and meet with her in person as soon as possible. She had time before going to dinner with her parents. Yes, that's what she'll do. They would clear everything up, and life would go on. At least that's what she hoped.

The evening of classes went by incredibly slowly. If it wasn't already rough enough on a Friday afternoon (she didn't know why the language school had changed a couple of years prior and now offered Friday evening classes—it wasn't like that before), with the situation that arose and a hint of the hangover she still had, Sofia couldn't wait to finish. Since she was the highest-regarded teacher by her students for a reason, she let them go fifteen minutes early and called Loretta.

"Hey, are you home yet?"

"Yeah, I'm here."

"I'm heading there. Let's talk, okay?"

"Okay, I'll wait for you here."

She got in her car and started to think along the way about how to go about the conversation and how Loretta would take it. She ran through several scenarios in her head, some good, others awful. But before she could continue preparing herself mentally, she was already home. She opened the door and found Loretta on the couch watching TV. Sofia sat on the chair next to it and told her that she was very sorry if she had taken it differently, but that what happened the night before had been nothing more than a fun night. Then, she asked for her forgiveness if she had led her to believe something else, but that she really wanted to get serious with Harry and that what they had before hadn't turned out well, and nothing indicated that it would be different now. She took her hand and added, "But I want us to still be friends. I love you, but in a different way."

Loretta looked at her with a face of sorrow and told her that she needed time to process the situation and asked her to understand, to which Sofia agreed, as was only natural.

"I'm going to look for an apartment to move out, Sofia. I don't feel strong enough to keep living with you right now. You understand, right?" Loretta immediately added.

Of course she understood. She could have begged her and told her it wasn't necessary, that she didn't have to leave, but it would have been absurd. It was best for both of them.

"Whatever you want, Loretta, but don't rush. Take the time you need."

"My friend Barbara has plenty of space at her house. I'll call her tomorrow and talk to her to see if I can move in there soon. Don't worry."

"Ah, Barbara, the brunette you told me about one time. I don't know her. Doesn't she live with some guy?"

"No, she had a fling, and it seemed to be going well, but apparently not anymore. She said she'll tell me about it. Something crazy happened. I'll call her and see. Do you have plans with Harry this weekend?"

"No, he's away for work. I don't know what antique he had to leave to see if he could get it. It must be important because he said it could take several days. Listen, Loretta, I have to go soon. I'm going to dinner with my parents who came to see me. So, we're oaky, then, you and I?" Sofia wanted to know.

Loretta, with a tear rolling down her cheek, responded:

"Give me some time, but yes, we're okay." They hugged and gave each other a kiss, then Sofia went to her room to get changed.

When she walked back out ready to go meet her parents, Loretta had left. Poor girl. She felt bad. It must have been difficult for her. But she knew her well and that she was strong. She'd get over it. However, at that point, what she didn't know was that she would never see her again.

Either way, everything was said, so there was nothing to gain by ruminating over the matter. She called for a taxi to pick her up. She was going to the city center where it was difficult to park, and she didn't feel like driving around in circles to find a space. Plus, she wanted to bring her parents somewhere after dinner to have a cocktail and didn't want them to then see her get in the car, even if she were in a state to do so. They had a table at a restaurant near the hotel at 9:30, with typical Murcia cuisine. As usual on Friday nights, the city center was quite busy with people. Sofia let her parents know that she was on her way, and right when she got out of the taxi at the hotel entrance, they came out through the entrance and met her there.

She was happy to see them. It had been a while since the last time she was in Italy. She gave them a big, long hug, then they went to the restaurant. Her parents' names were Francesco and Arianna. For twenty years they owned a fairly large Italian footwear company that was doing quite well, so they had quite a bit of money. Sofia already knew the topic that would come up at dinner and, indeed, with *marineras*[14] as their appetizer, her parents told her that they were thinking about retiring soon. They asked her why not go back to Italy to take the reins of the family business. Meanwhile, she received a text from Harry that she responded to without giving it much attention, given that it wasn't a good time. Sofia had no intention of continuing the family business. She enjoyed being a teacher. She liked where her job was and loved Spain, especially living in Murcia, at least for the time being. Money wasn't something that worried her too much. With her job, she had more than what was necessary to maintain her current lifestyle. It wouldn't even be a problem for her to have kids in the future, if she decided to have them. Of course, everything that having more money would entail was great, and she didn't have anything against it, but she didn't want to give up her current life. Luckily, even though she could tell that it wasn't what her parents wanted to hear and that they were somewhat displeased, after finishing dinner, they told their daughter that they respected her decision. They would look for someone to be the manager and run the business, and Sofia would keep her stocks, meaning she would have the right to receive dividends without getting involved in the day-to-day management of the business. It would be in the hands of professionals. Moreover, those dividends, to be fair, would allow her to live quite comfortably without having to get involved in the running of the business.

*"Okay, another thing done, and it didn't even go that bad,"* Sofia thought, knowing that she had gotten through the situation reasonably well. The dinner had gone very well. Her parents loved the food, but they ate too much, so much so that they said they preferred to sleep instead of going out for a drink. They were tired.

Sofia said goodbye to them and agreed to pick them up the next day to take them to the Sanctuary of La Fuensanta, a must-see for

---

14 Typical tapa from Murcia consisting of a ring-shaped breadstick with Russian salad and an anchovy on top.

visitors of Murcia. It was early to go home, so she decided to drop by a couple of bars that were close by, in case she saw someone she knew who she could have a drink with before going back. She was just about to give up when someone tapped her on the shoulder. She turned around, and there was Alfonso, Harry's friend who she recognized even though she had only seen one picture of him that Harry had shown her.

"Hey, you're Sofia, aren't you?"

"Yeah, Alfonso?"

"Yeah, Harry showed me a picture of you. I wasn't sure if it was you.

"I know, same here. Nice to meet you."

"Well, I'm waiting for a couple of friends. Are you with someone or do you want to have a beer?"

"A beer would be great, yeah."

They went to a high table with a couple of beers. The bar, called El Lobo Marrón, was still half empty since it was early for what was usually the busiest time for people going out on a Friday night. At that point, there was a group playing pool, a couple of occupied tables, and some people at the bar, but not much else.

"Wow, so you're the one my friend is head over heels for, huh?" Alfonso asked, smiling.

"Well, I don't know. You tell me. Is he?" Sofia asked in turn.

"Hahaha. I mean, I've known him for barely a few months if I'm being honest, but yes: when he talks about you, his face actually changes and all that. By the way, where the hell is he?"

"I don't know. He's on a work trip for a few days and doesn't know when he'll be back, but he didn't tell me where." Sofia tried not to talk to Alfonso about the fight they had just had before he left. She didn't know him, and it wasn't his business. If Harry hadn't told him anything, she wasn't going to. What would she say to Harry's best friend? "Hey, Alfonso, since I just met you, and I'm not sure if you know, but the last time I saw Harry, we fought because he caught me making out with my ex-girlfriend. But it's all good."

"Wow, strange job that guy has, huh? He's like Indiana Jones, but boring," Alfonso said letting out a laugh that Sofia joined in on. "Looking for artifacts and old stuff. Have you seen the company website? Who the fuck would want to buy those things?"

"Well, I think it must be exciting to find the object, negotiate with the owner.... I don't know. According to him, every time he comes back from a trip, he comes back excited," Sofia pointed out, then immediately added, "But I also don't know who would buy most of those things."

FAI indeed had a website. If someone went on it, they found the following:

Image without changes from https://commons.wikimedia.org/wiki/File:Antig%C3%B-Cedades_%2857043898%29.jpeg

Then, from there, you could access a menu with a catalogue divided by categories and products, where there was everything from tools from different ancient cultures (from Aztecs to Celts and Romans) to

Spanish furniture from the early twentieth century, and even earlier, to Swiss clocks over one-hundred years old.

What Alfonso and Sofia didn't know was that those objects, in reality, obviously didn't exist. From time to time, some would show up with the "SOLD" seal and new ones were uploaded every now and again to give it the appearance of a real online store. Moreover, they would receive transfers from fake buyers created by the Conglomerate to simulate activity that the fiscal authorities would see. And if someone wanted an object listed on the website, they were either given the runaround or told it was already sold, or sometimes a perfect replica was made and that was what would be sent to them. The supposed merchandise warehouse was located in Rotterdam to have the port nearby for deliveries all over the world. That warehouse, of course, didn't exist either, but everything functioned with the perfect appearance of a legal business and an impeccable cover.

"So, are you meeting up with someone or are you hanging out alone?" Alfonso was interested.

"Well, I met with my parents for dinner who came from Italy, and since they went to the hotel and it was early, I decided to go out and see if I could find someone. And what do you know; I found someone after all," Sofia said, raising her beer for Alfonso to cheers with her.

"Great. Well, if you want to stay, you're welcome to. I'm meeting with a couple of coworkers; they're cool. You'll like them," Alfonso told her.

"Thank you, but I'm going to head out now. I'm tired and I have to be a tour guide tomorrow," Sofia said, taking one last sip of her beer and getting up from the stool. "Another time I'll hang out."

"Okay, as you wish." They gave each other two kisses[15] and said goodbye. Then, Sofia walked out of the bar heading towards the

---

15  Translator's note: It's common for Spaniards to greet and say goodbye to each other by giving a kiss on each cheek, even though, in reality, their lips don't touch their cheeks. The gesture has no romantic connotation.

closest taxi station. It didn't take long to get one. The taxi driver drove off, and when he was close to Sofia's house on a two-way street that had a roundabout, a boy on a bike suddenly came out from a house and crossed his path, making him slam on the brakes. Two seconds later, a car behind them hit the taxi, and Sofia was flung against the seat in front of her, the shotgun seat. The taxi driver got out of the car as if possessed. while the kid on the bike ran away.

"If I catch you, you're going to get it, you idiot. I'll break your ribs with your bike, you moron," the taxi driver screamed as he shook his fist and watched him run away.

Sofia, meanwhile, touched her forehead, where she hit her head against the headrest, but there was nothing there. She got out of the taxi, and the driver then turned his attention to her once his fit of rage was over.

"Are you okay? Do you need to go to the hospital?"

"I'm okay, I'm not hurt. I just want to go home."

"Don't worry. I'll call a colleague to pick you up while I take care of the accident with this woman. We're already close."

"Okay, thank you," Sofia answered.

The woman from the car that had hit the taxi went up to Sofia and apologized to her. Sofia accepted her apology, given that she had clearly seen that the fault fell on the cyclist. Meanwhile, another taxi that the driver from the accident called arrived and brought Sofia home. What a day. Just what she needed to cap it off. Luckily, nothing bad had happened to her, but if the car from behind had been going faster or closer, she may have gotten a serious injury and had to go to the hospital. Sofia went up to her apartment, and since the day called for it, she rolled herself a joint and sat on the small balcony to smoke it while she reflected on the day and waited to see if Loretta would come back, since she wasn't there. What a day: a hangover, a love affair, parents, the future, a beer with Harry's best friend, an accident.... It certainly hadn't been bad for a Friday. She finished the joint and decided to go to bed. She was going to wait for Loretta, but she didn't know where she was or how long it would take for her to get back and decided not to ask her. It didn't seem like a good time. She fell asleep right away, and at 8 a.m., when her alarm went off, she felt as though she had slept for four days straight. She showered, got dressed, and called her mom, who told her that they were ready.

She told them she wasn't ready; she would see them in twenty minutes since she still had to eat breakfast. She made herself a coffee with milk with the milk cold so she could drink it quickly, then grabbed a pastry from the kitchen cupboard. The rough day had begun, and she was already stressed. While she had breakfast, she realized that Loretta wasn't there and that there was no sign of her being home the whole night.

*"That's weird,"* she thought. It wasn't normal, but the situation with Loretta certainly wasn't either, so she may have decided to stay with her friend Barbara that night and would come get her things some other time. Nonetheless, she sent her a text: "Loretta, I just want to know you're okay. XO," she wrote. She would have wanted to open up more but decided that perhaps the situation didn't call for it. "Well, I'm sure she's fine," she said to herself as she grabbed her car keys and left the apartment.

She picked up her parents and brought them to the Sanctuary of La Fuensanta, a place in the mountains with some unbeatable views of Murcia. It was a must-see for all tourists, whether religious or not. Apart from the sanctuary, there were many hiking trails around the mountain that started in that area and was a place that Sofia, as a nature lover, liked a lot. It was a lovely day. She decided not to tell them anything about the near accident from the night before, since she didn't want them to worry or think poorly of the area where she lived. A lie could make you just as happy as the truth, maybe even more. And a lie wasn't even necessary; an omission of the truth would suffice.

As they walked along a trail, they asked her the question that they hadn't asked the night before, against all odds: if she was in a relationship. Sofia said she was, but that he wasn't around then, and that, moreover, they hadn't been together for long. She didn't want to say anything else for the time being. The conversation on that topic closed there. The rest of the day went by without anything remarkable happening. Francesco and Arianna loved the area around the Sanctuary of La Fuensanta, and since they were religious, even more so. They went back to Murcia and ate at another typical bar (this time a spectacular rice dish with rabbit that Sofia's parents loved, despite their initial reluctance). Then, later in the afternoon, they visited the old town, including the cathedral and its tower, as well as the Royal Casino of Murcia. Time for dinner. Francesco and Arianna decided to stay at their hotel. They had been tired the whole day. Sofia went back home and agreed to take them to the airport the next morning for their return flight.

She got home and found no trace of Loretta. She hadn't answered her text, either. Her things were still in her room: her clothes in the closet, her toothbrush and makeup in the bathroom.... This time, she called her, but her phone was off.

Now she was really starting to get worried. This wasn't normal. What if she did something stupid? What if something happened to her? She herself had had a small accident the previous night. Unexpected things can happen to anyone.

"Alright, Sofia, calm down for a second," she tried telling herself. "You spent a night with your ex-girlfriend, and the next day, you were rejected by her when you confessed to her how you really felt. Just assume she doesn't want to see you at all and leave it there." That's what it must have been. Just as it happens so many times in life, the most likely explanation is probably the right one. She had to respect her and not pester her. She had already sent her a text; that was enough. She was probably with her friend Barbara cursing her with a gin tonic in hand, and probably turned her phone off or blocked her, and the following week she would come for her things. She sat on the couch to rest for a bit and checked her social media.

Loretta didn't have any activity since Friday afternoon, so she was offline as well. "Okay, enough with Loretta already," Sofia said out loud. She turned on the TV, then her phone started to ring. It was a long number, so it must have been a call center. Were they really going to try and sell her something on a Saturday night? Normally, she didn't pick up calls from unknown numbers, but in this instance, without quite knowing why, she did.

"Hello?" she said, prepared to hang up as soon as they told her that they were from a phone company or something of the sort.

"Hi, Sofia?" a masculine voice asked on the other end.

"Yes, that's me. Who's this?"

"Hey, this is Pedro, Loretta's coworker. Sorry for calling you on a Saturday night, but it's just that she hasn't come to work and hasn't even called or anything. Is she okay?

Sofia didn't have a response to that question.

# CHAPTER XII

Harry woke up early, around 7:05. And he woke up euphoric, ready to go—ready to draw up a definitive plan that very day, to carry out the mission the following day, and to go home the next and see if he could sort things out with Sofia. But, above all, he was ready to kill Abdul and Isabelle. He especially liked missions whose objective implied that the world would be a better place, and this was one of them. And as it happens whenever you're eager to do something, you can't wait for the moment to come. He got up and was surprised to see that Angela and Martha were already having coffee. They didn't even bother to put on pants. They were wearing panties and a large T-shirt, as if they were at home or indeed at a vacation house with friends.

"Good morning, Harry. Coffee?" Martha asked.

"Gallons of it, please. Good morning, ladies," Harry replied.

"Did you sleep okay, boss?" Angela asked. "I was so nervous that I couldn't sleep. And we still don't even have a plan." Angela was glowing and even more eager than Harry, all the product of her youth.

"Yeah, I like getting up early, but not as much as you guys, evidently," Harry answered, trying not to raise the excitement he saw in Angela even more. Excitement and eagerness are like all things in life: it's not good to have too much because they can lead you to make mistakes.

He took a sip of his coffee which was just as he liked it: strong, with milk that's neither too hot nor too cold, and a couple of teaspoons of sugar.

"Thanks, Martha. The coffee's just how I like it," Harry said. "I know, Harry. I remember," Martha responded.

She indeed remembered. How could she remember? Harry and Martha had known each other for several years. They were together in El Paso for several months as well as in Harry's FAI training. They had a mission in Dallas once, when Harry was just an apprentice, though he had left his instructors in awe of his capability and know-how despite his youth. The mission consisted of surveilling a man, jumping him when he was alone, and beating him up without killing him. He was a rapist that had gotten out of prison, and the victim didn't think that being in jail would be enough for him. She wasn't confident that he would be rehabilitated at all and wanted to scare him in case he had thought about going back to his old ways, with her or any other girl. The instructions were to beat him up without anyone seeing, leave him alive, and give him a clear message out loud: don't do it again. The victim had plenty of money and was going to pay forty thousand dollars to the Conglomerate division of El Paso for doing the mission, a favorable amount for a quick and rather easy one.

They located the man in a café on the outskirts of Dallas and walked in acting as customers. A waitress was going around the tables taking coffee orders, and Harry said that he wanted a coffee with milk and put two teaspoons of sugar in it. Martha was surprised. In that part of the country, not many people put milk in coffee, which she told him.

"Damn, Martha, that's what you remember from that mission?" Harry asked, laughing. "We broke a few of that motherfucker's ribs, his nose, some teeth, and his ankle. And that's what you remember?

"That's how I am."

Indeed, she was. The mission was a success, and the subject got the message. He even peed himself when they gave him the message, so they were sure of it. Harry remembered the terror in his eyes, but apparently for Martha, the thing that stood out the most was Harry's coffee. Interesting.

Piotr then came out of the bedroom.

"What's with all this laughing? Is this the fucking comedy festival or something?" he asked as he yawned and stretched.

"Come on, man, don't be a grouch. Today's going to be a good day," Angela responded, hitting his shoulder as a sort of morning greeting. Piotr smiled at her and made his way to the coffee maker.

It was slightly cloudy that morning, but the forecast said it would clear up soon and would be hot and beautifully sunny the whole day. Harry's plan for the morning was for all of them to pose as hikers going out for a walk in the area. They would then watch the villa a little longer until about 1 p.m., once it was too hot and watching the place no longer provided them with anything important. Then, they would go back to the house, eat, and rest until 5 p.m. But beforehand, they had to make sure that their colleagues in Manila had everything under control.

Right before 8 a.m., Spanish time, Harry communicated with part of the Conglomerate's Asia team, the part that was in Manila. One of Martha's old colleagues was there that had been in Cambodia with her, Ronald. Ronald was a former artistic gymnastics champion of New Zealand. According to Martha, who had talked to Harry about him at one point, he could jump from branch to branch as if he were Tarzan himself. Since gymnastics wasn't something that would sustain his life, when he was recruited by the Conglomerate, he happily accepted. He quickly became the division boss and was the one leading the operation in Manila. Harry thought that Martha had had a romance with Ronald given how she talked about him, but he had never asked her about it, and Martha didn't talk about it to him either, so he couldn't be totally sure.

Ronald's team had Melinda's father located and was able to communicate with him and explain the situation. There was no hint of danger, but they would stay alert just in case until 5 p.m., Spanish time, which would be 11 p.m. in Manila. Then, they would pose as a delivery person and give him a phone to talk to his daughter for two minutes and complete what was outlined in the plan.

Harry communicated to the rest of the team that the Manila operation was going full steam ahead and to get dressed as hikers ready to enjoy the outdoors. After a bit, they got in the van and went to the exterior of the villa. They divided into two teams, and each one started walking on a different side, more or less parallel to the villa. Piotr and Harry went on one side, and Angela and Martha on the other, all of them with tracksuits and walking sticks to avoid standing out. They didn't observe anything relevant regarding what they already knew and had seen the day before, so even though it was likely a waste of time, they had to try. They went back to the house to eat something and get ready for the evening. Angela would go with Martha to meet with Melinda and gradually build her trust in the team. Harry could have gone, but perhaps another woman would make Melinda feel more relaxed at that point. That's why Harry had thought it would be better if Martha went. It was fundamental, assuming that the Manila team was going to fulfill their end, that Melinda felt the trust necessary for her to reveal as much information as possible to them about Abdul's life inside the villa and the villa itself. If not, they would turn to plan B, which was basically to do whatever it took to force her to talk, but Harry didn't want to even get close to that point. Firstly, he would hate to force or even torture a victim to get information from her. He didn't want to become like the people they were trying to get rid of who carelessly exercise their power, though in some instances, he had to do it. Secondly, because it's always much more effective when someone tells you something on their own volition than by coercion. It was shown (at least that's what Harry thought) that even if the information were the same regardless of how it was obtained, it wasn't truly "the same" because highly important details would fall through. But Harry was also certain that if he had to force her to say something, he would do it and not let anyone have any doubt about it.

At 4:30 p.m., Angela and Martha got in the van and went to the meeting point to meet Melinda, with plenty of time to resolve any contingency along the way, given that a flat tire could always happen. Harry was obsessive about time, and from the time he lived in Spain, he had become so even more. From what he observed there at large, people didn't take punctuality seriously at all. He didn't know if it was a coincidence or if people in Murcia or Spain were like that as part of the general culture. From what he had been told, it may have been the latter, but he had set out to not fall into that habit and arrived everywhere before the scheduled time. On a mission of this caliber and importance, he wasn't about to let something go wrong due to not leaving early enough. So, he made Martha and Angela leave thirty minutes early. That's what he was the boss of the mission for.

When they got to the "rendezvous," as Martha said, they had to wait. It was the town entrance, and there was an open field to the side of the road with some trees. There was no other car parked, so they parked there half camouflaged between the trees and waited. At 4:55, they saw a feminine figure appear walking towards them. It was Melinda. She was walking quickly with a miniskirt and a dark-colored top. Right when she got to them, she said, "Is my dad okay?"

"Don't worry, Melinda, your dad is okay. My colleagues will call me soon and you can see for yourself. This is Martha. She works with me. You can trust her," Angela responded. Martha smiled and waved at her, to which Melinda responded with a smile. Right then, Angela's phone rang. She looked at Melinda and told her before picking it up:

"Once I give you the phone, you'll have two minutes, not a second more, for security reasons." Melinda nodded her head as a few tears started to well up in her eyes.

"Angela speaking," Angela said after picking up the phone. "Yes, one second," she answered in English, then handed the phone to Melinda.

Melinda grabbed it and started talking excitedly in Filipino. Neither Angela nor Martha understood a single word of what she was saying, but they did understand the non-verbal part; Melinda looked excited, as well as relieved and happy. After a minute, Angela lifted her index finger to let her know that she had exactly one minute left, to which Melinda smiled in response. When there were ten seconds left, she opened the palms of her hands so that Melinda could say goodbye and put her hand out so she would give her the phone. When the time was up, Melinda gave her the phone without any fuss.

"How was it? Is he okay?" Martha asked, trying to start gaining Melinda's trust.

"Yeah, the poor guy is confused because he doesn't quite understand the situation, but he's fine. He says that your agents, or whatever you call them, are watching him and that he's safe, and that it seems like he can trust them. But he doesn't understand them that much; the poor guy doesn't speak English well," Melinda responded, drying her tears as she added, "Thank you so much, really. Now I'll fulfill my end of the deal. What do you guys want to know?"

"I'm very happy, really. Soon, you'll be with him again and you'll leave this whole nightmare behind. Now, if it sounds good to you, you can come with us to our operations base, if you can call it that, and we'll ask you some questions there. Sound good?" Angela said, opening the van door. "It's not far. You can trust me and my team. You already saw that we fulfilled our promise. We're here to help you."

As they got in the van, Martha told Harry that everything had gone well and that they were heading to the house. Meanwhile, Harry and Piotr prepared as comfortable a space as possible for Melinda's interrogation. They would give her a comfortable armchair with a table next to it to put her drink if she wanted, and an ashtray. Angela would sit on the couch next to the armchair in the spot closest to her to give her a sense of trust, and to be able to hold her hand as a sign of closeness if it were necessary to console her. Martha, for her part, would sit on the same couch. There would be nobody on the other side of the couch so that Melinda at no point felt that she was being trapped or surrounded. Harry would sit in a chair across from her to conduct the interrogation, about six feet away to give her enough space so it wouldn't feel like a police interrogation. Piotr, meanwhile, would be at the table listening to everything and taking notes in an innocent looking way. In reality, apart from the notes he would take, he would be monitoring Melinda's voice with his computer, looking for possible fluctuations or abnormal patterns in her responses. In short, anything that could indicate whether Melinda was comfortable or not, if she was lying, if she was getting more nervous at certain points…. They suddenly heard the engine of the van, which cut off after a few seconds. The door opened, and Martha walked in first, followed by Melinda, and lastly Angela, who closed the door and introduced Melinda to the rest of the team. Then, Harry tried to explain what was going to happen.

"Hi, Melinda. We're glad your dad is safe, and we're confident that you'll be with him again very soon. I'm Harry, and if it sounds good to you, I'm going to conduct the conversation we'll have. Piotr will be at the table behind us listening and taking notes. Don't get overwhelmed if you see him take a lot of notes; it doesn't mean you're doing something wrong or anything like that."

"I take notes about details that may seem insignificant, but which may help a lot later. That's all," Piotr added, raising his right thumb.

"Exactly." Harry continued, "As long as you're okay with it, we thought you could sit in this armchair. Angela will be next to you on the couch the whole time. We can speak in English if you prefer. If you want to smoke, no problem. There's an ashtray there, and if you don't have cigarettes, we can give you some. Would you like something to drink?"

"Do you have a beer? I have cigarettes, thank you. It all sounds fine to me. Spanish is fine," Martha replied.

"Yes, of course. Martha, grab a beer, please. Before starting, I want to let you know that if you need to stop at any point, simply say so and we'll stop. I also want you to know that it's not our intention to make you remember anything to hurt you, but it's of vital importance that you respond to everything we ask you to the extent that it's possible if we want our mission to be successful, and we can all go home happy. You understand, right?" Harry concluded.

"Don't worry, I'll do the best I can. Shall we start?" Melinda answered, grabbing the beer that Martha was handing to her and sitting in the armchair.

Harry smiled and nodded his head. He started by asking her about what she could tell him about the inside of the villa, and Melinda began her story.

"The inside of the villa is two floors. If you walk through the front door, there's a room to the left that's aways closed. I don't know what's inside, but one time I saw a guy come out and another one go in, and out of the corner of my eye I was able to see screens and, like, consoles with keyboards, I'm not sure."

"Could it be a surveillance center that controls the cameras on the property?" Harry asked.

"I don't know. I guess it could be, yeah. I have no idea. It's not locked; when I said closed, I was referring to just the door. When they go in and out, they don't use any key. There's no sensor or key-cards, nothing like that," Melinda responded.

Harry, without taking his eye off her, made a gesture to Piotr with his hand. Anyone that would have seen it would have confused the gesture with the one used to ask for the check at a restaurant[16].

"Okay. Continue, please. What else is on the first floor?"

Harry lit a cigarette and offered one to Melinda, who took it and thanked him. As she lit it and let out the first puff of smoke, she went on.

---

16  Translator's note: In Spain, to ask for the check at a restaurant or bar, you make a motion with your hand in the air to the waiter as though you're signing a check. As opposed to restaurants in the US where the waiter frequently visits the table, in Spain, you often have to call the waiter over by signaling to them.

"As I said, that room is to the left entering through the front door; if, from that room, you start looking to the right, the next thing you see are some stairs that lead to the second floor.

"Would you mind describing the stairs, please, Melinda?"

"Well, there might be like fifteen or sixteen steps, I'm not sure. They're wooden. They seem new. And the railing is a really ugly dark brown. It's straight. From below, if you look up, you can see the door that opens to the second floor."

"Okay, great. Continue, please."

Melinda took a sip of her beer and continued.

"To the right of the stairs, there's a big, long room that's a bowling alley. That motherfucker and his whore of a woman like to bowl a lot. There's only one lane and a small bar when you walk in with a bench to sit on, plus a closet with bowling shoes."

"Does it have windows? How many doors does the bowling alley have?"

"No, it doesn't have windows. And it only has one entrance door."

"Are you sure?"

"I spent a lot of hours dancing naked in that room and serving drinks to those two while they bowled. So, yes, I'm sure."

"Got it. Sorry, I didn't mean to make it seem like I was doubting you." Harry genuinely apologized. He knew that Melinda was a fragile witness at that moment, despite the composure she showed, and he didn't want to distress her emotionally, among other things. It wouldn't help them at all in the mission. He noticed that Angela grabbed Melinda's hand, who in turn squeezed hers.

"Take the time you need before continuing. Martha, bring some peanuts from the kitchen for everyone. That would be nice," Angela said.

Martha complied and brought peanuts for everyone. Nuts provide energy and clear the mind. It was what they needed at that moment. Everyone grabbed a handful, and Melinda decided to continue, without letting go of Angela's hand.

"Next to the bowling alley, directly in line with the front door, there's a room. That room belongs to what we could call the bodyguards. That's where they all sleep. I didn't tell you guys this, but there are six guys and two women in the villa apart from the couple. There are six beds and a bathroom in that room. As always, there's someone on guard. They always have beds for everyone. Sometimes, when Abdul and Isabelle were done with me or got tired of me, they would leave me in that room with those animals for a bit before ordering them to take me back home. The two women, even they enjoyed watching…. I need to take a break, please." Melinda got up, drenched in tears, and went to the bathroom. Everyone looked at each other with an expression of contained anger. How could such people exist in the world? Certainly, if they took one of them out during the mission, no one from the FAI team would be all that sorry about it.

Ten minutes passed. Harry made a gesture to Angela for her to knock on the bathroom door. "I'll be right out," was heard from inside, and a couple of minutes later, Melinda came out. She sat back in her seat, ready to continue.

"Alright, Melinda, please describe that room as best you can," Harry asked.

"Well, it's big, rectangular. It has a bathroom in the back. Like I said, there are six beds and a couple of big closets. Apart from that, there's no other furniture, except for a nightstand for each bed. Ah, and there are two windows that look outside. There's not much else to point out."

"Okay, great. Continue, please."

"Hm…. Attached to the room on the outside, there's another bathroom. Actually, I didn't mention that there are small windows in the bathrooms, in that one and the one inside the room. No one could fit through, not even a child, maybe. Then, over to the right, there's a big glass door that gives access to the pool and the backyard. That door, as far as I know, has no key, just a handle to go in and out, which doesn't open from the outside if it's locked on the inside. Right next to that door is the kitchen. The kitchen has a couple of windows, one that looks out onto the pool and another onto the wall perpendicular to it. It doesn't have direct access outside, only an access door, which is perpendicular to the door that goes to the pool. There's a big countertop and a washing machine, a dishwasher, refrigerator, oven, and a huge sink. Next to the kitchen, there's a room that's used as a pantry. Ah, I forgot. Right in between them there's a door which I don't know where it goes to."

"Could it be another door that goes outside?"

"I guess it could be, but it's not as tall as the wall. If it's another exit, there'd be a small hallway before getting outside, which doesn't make much sense."

"Harry, from our pictures of the outside there's no door there. I didn't see anything there. It must be a small room, a closet…I don't know, but it's not an exit," Martha interrupted.

"That door, did you ever see it open?" Harry asked.

"No, I never did, actually. I don't know what's there," Melinda answered. "The thing is, as I said, it's between the kitchen and the pantry. They use the pantry to store food and drinks, and to lock me in for hours when they say that I've misbehaved. It can be locked with a key from the outside."

Truly, Melinda's testimony was unbelievably heartbreaking. Harry couldn't even imagine in the slightest how difficult all this had to be for that poor girl. Certainly, she was becoming yet another incentive to carry out the mission, besides the money. And she still hadn't even talked about the second floor where the main bedroom would be and where he imagined the worst was done to Melinda.

"And next to the pantry is the living room. It's massive and stretches all the way next to the front door. It has a fireplace on one side, three massive couches, and an enormous TV. The bodyguards are usually there if they aren't sleeping or on duty. There's also a big table that could fit about twelve to fourteen people. And that's the first floor. There's not much else to say, except that it has a big window that faces the side of the façade, about half the height of the living room.

"Excellent, Melinda. You're doing great. How big is the fireplace?"

"I'm not sure. It's big."

"Would you say that a person could fit through the hole in it?"

"I didn't look through the hole, but at first glance, I'd say so."

"Great, Melinda. If we go upstairs to the second floor, what do we find?"

"As you go up, there's a dressing room for Isabelle. It has a ton of clothes and shoes, a bench to sit on, and a mirror. There aren't any windows. Then, to the left of the stairs, there's one single main bedroom that takes up the whole length and the width of the second floor. It's the biggest room I've ever seen. It has a bed that can easily fit four or five people. When you enter the room, there's a huge bathroom with a jacuzzi and a sauna to the right. Then, to the left, on the other side, at the corner of the villa, there's a terrace with a table and four chairs. There's a couple more windows in the room, small, one next to the bathroom and another perpendicular to it. That and the light from the terrace are enough." Melinda sipped her beer again and took a brief pause, looking at the ceiling. "I want to help you take these motherfuckers out. I want to kill them myself."

# CHAPTER XIII

Harry understood Melinda very well, which is precisely why he responded the way he did.

"That option is completely off the table, Melinda."

Melinda started to protest energetically. She sat up and exclaimed:

"You guys have no idea what they did to me."

"No, Melinda, we have no idea, which is exactly why I can't fulfill your wish," Harry replied without faltering in the least. "Firstly, we've broken every protocol there is and more by telling you who we are and the operation we're doing. But there's still one that we haven't broken and that I'm not willing to break, which is letting a civilian actively participate in a mission, because it can be dangerous for you, and also because it can put us and the mission itself in danger since you're not trained or prepared. There's nothing more to talk about. You're already helping us plenty. You're serving as a key part here; in fact, without any of this valuable information that you're giving us, it would be much harder to carry out the mission. You'll have to settle for that."

"Melinda, it's best for everyone," Angela reinforced in the most comforting tone she could.

"What can you tell us about the other eight people in the villa with Abdul and Isabelle? Any detail could be useful for us," Harry asked in order to close the discussion about Melinda's active participation in the mission.

Melinda's face was a combination of resignation and understanding. It gave the sense that, though her thirst for vengeance was strong and still present, she understood that they were the professionals who knew how to best accomplish the objective, which, in the end, was mutual and most important. Thus, she would continue trying to help them.

"Well, there are two of those motherfuckers who are Arabs. The rest are western, including the women. I couldn't say where they're from. The women seem Spanish by the way they speak, and another two as well, including the one that picks me up and drops me off. The rest speak Spanish, but with a foreign accent, each one different from the other. They all speak Spanish with each other, including the women. They always have a pistol, the women as well. They're all pretty strong. With Abdul and Isabelle, there's always at least two of them at the door of whatever room they're in. The rest are in that room that you mentioned might be for surveillance. Some are outside, always making their rounds.... I'm not sure."

Harry prompted her: "We need to know routines, Melinda. I'm going to summarize, and you tell me given what you know if I'm right. Please, focus. Given what you say, two of the eight are always with, let's call them, the targets. I understand that there are some on guard, one always in what we've called the surveillance room (Melinda nodded her head), leaving five. Am I right?"

"Yes, Harry."

"Of those five, at least two of them are, let's say, patrolling the property or the house. Is that correct, Melinda?"

Melinda sat there pensively as she took another sip of her beer, then said:

"Yes. From what I remember, they're always together."

"Great. Thanks, Melinda. I think we have everything we need. Would you like to add something else, anything? Any tiny detail might help," Harry asked in order to conclude the interrogation.

"Hm. No, I don't think so."

"Excellent. Either way, if you think of anything, call us. Angela will bring you home now and will give you our contact info. Just act normally, with your normal routine. If they call you from the villa, let us know immediately, whatever time it is. We hope, either way, to accomplish the mission soon. If we're lucky, they won't have the chance to call you anymore. Once everything is complete, we'll let you know somehow," Harry concluded as he stood up. Angela and Martha also got up, followed by Melinda. Piotr was still immersed in his equipment, typing away.

"You've got guts, Melinda. You did great. When all this is over, would you like to join us or others like us? We think you could be a great help. And it's a well-compensated job. No need to give me an answer now. In fact, don't. When everything is over, we'll talk," Harry said, stretching his hand out to her. Melinda smiled without saying anything. Then, she left with Angela.

"We'll wait for Angela before talking, right?" Martha asked.

"Right," Harry answered. "You got everything?" he added, looking at Piotr.

"Yes, boss. I made some plans based on what she said. I'll show them to you guys, and we'll take a look," Piotr replied.

Harry gave a couple of claps of approval to his colleague and went to the kitchen to open a bag of potato chips. He was happy. As long as his plans were somewhat acceptable (something he didn't doubt for even a second), with everything that Melinda provided, he was sure that they could draw up a plan with some certainties, if you could talk about certainty on a mission like this. He had completed missions with much less information than this one. Once, for example, he rescued a little boy from a kidnapping without even knowing how many kidnappers there were. He was told that he had to go into an abandoned ship and rescue him. It was the son of a Japanese diplomat kidnapped in Connecticut. He had to rescue him before a conflict between countries broke out, so he didn't have time to collect any more information than the bare minimum. He went into the ship in the dark and managed to rescue the boy and avoid the diplomatic crisis, confronting four kidnappers when it seemed that there would only be two. Luckily, he was okay, but he was quite fortunate. This time, he had all the information. Plus, he had a wonderful team.

Angela came back right away, and they all sat around the table, where Piotr showed them the plans of the property (he had done it with the visual information obtained on the ground and the preliminary information about the mission, since Melinda always entered and exited the property with a blindfold on) as well as the first and second floor:

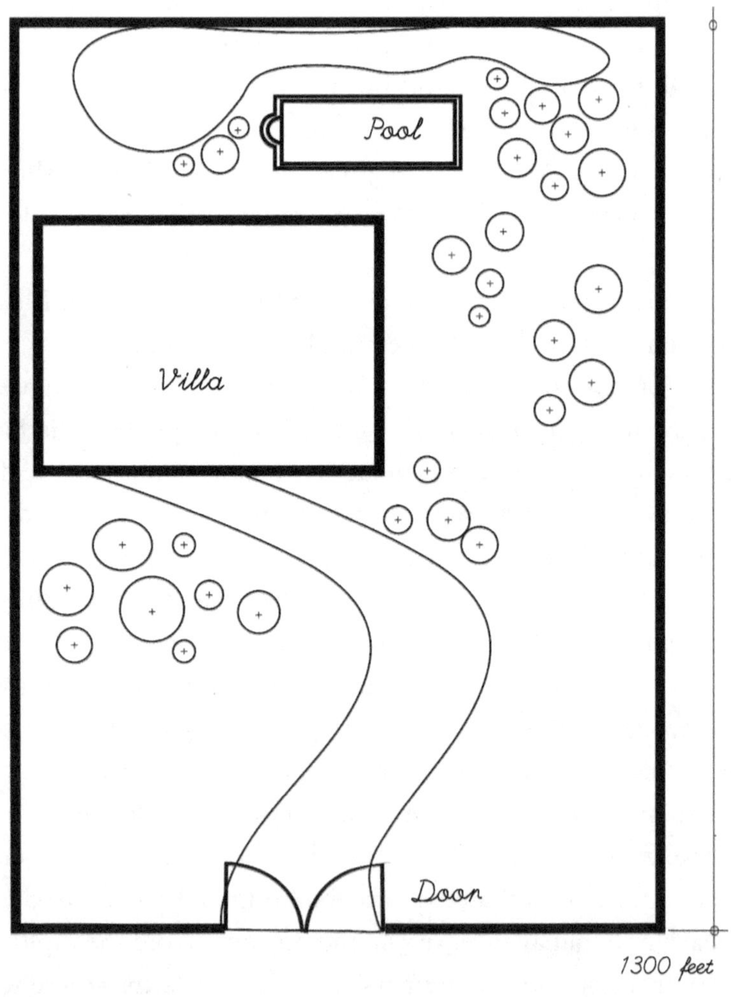

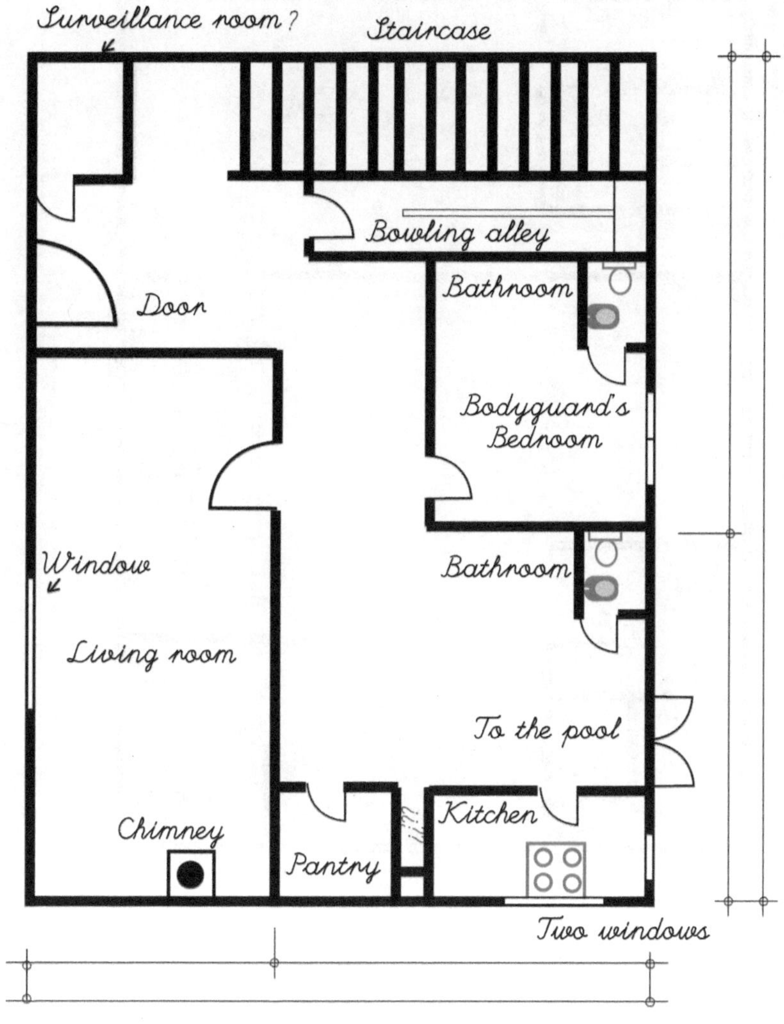

Surveillance room?
Staircase
Bowling alley
Bathroom
Door
Bodyguard's
Bedroom
Window
Bathroom
Living room
To the pool
Chimney
Kitchen
Pantry
Two windows
- 25-acre plot of land
- Two floors

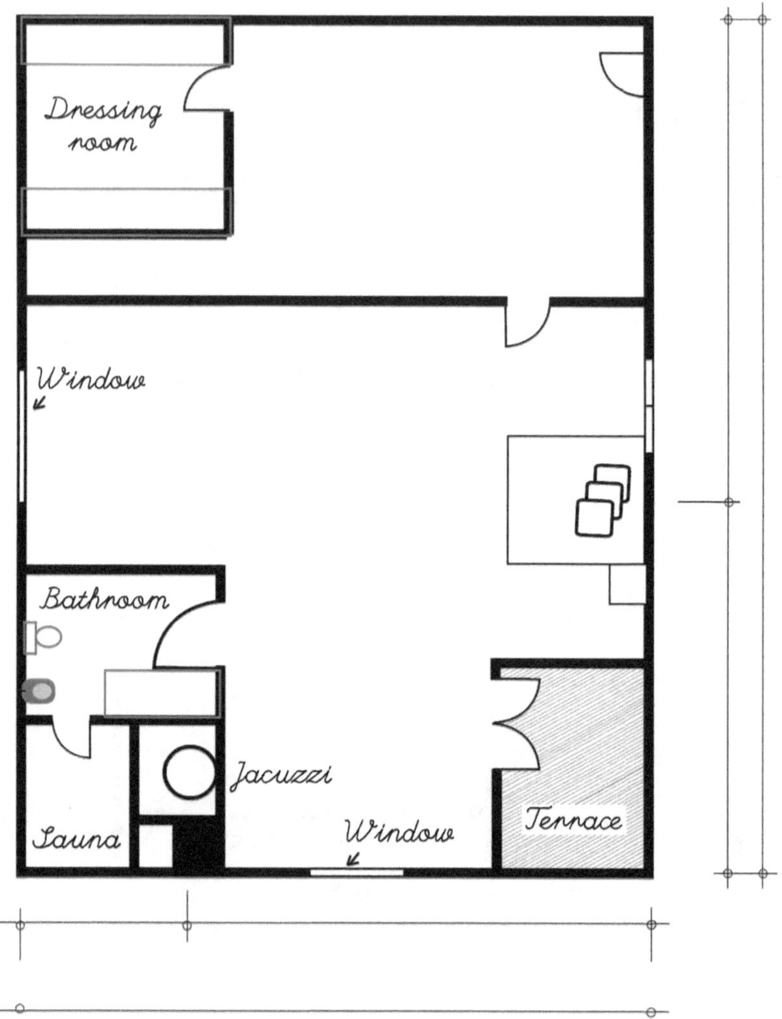


"In my opinion," Piotr began, "and from seeing the villa, there are various entrance points that could be feasible if we trick the security cameras and the patrol, which we'll go with now. On the first floor, apart from the front door, we would have the glass door at the pool, as well as one of the windows. The door to the pool shouldn't be very hard to force open with a crowbar. The problem is getting there. There are trees if we jump from as far back as possible, but there are cameras in them and on the roof. We'd also have the same problem if we wanted to get in through the windows. Another possibility I see, even though it's probably something you only see in movies, is the chimney. If we could land on the roof, we would avoid the cameras. Melinda said that she thinks a person can fit through the chimney. With the satellite image, we can measure the length of its side and estimate the average width of a chimney with those characteristics on the market to see if it's feasible, at least for Angela since she's the smallest of the group.

"It's a possibility, Piotr, though a risky one. Angela would land in the living room where there might be a bodyguard hanging out. We couldn't know," Harry pointed out.

Angela said that she was willing to do it, to which Harry replied that he didn't doubt it for a second, but they needed another idea. Harry wasn't convinced about pulling a Mary Poppins. They needed to have more control over the enemy. Simply showing up inside left too much to chance. They needed the enemy to do whatever they wanted him to do, and for that, they had to locate the weak link.

Melinda had said that the patrol was always a pair, another two with the target, and one more in the surveillance room. The other three were on break. The ones watching over the target and the one in the surveillance room were probably ordered to not leave their positions. Therefore, they would be monitored. Their position in the villa could be monitored with infrared binoculars, which they wouldn't move from. But the others would go check on anything unexpected, even if they were on patrol or on break.

"Okay, guys, this is what I'm thinking. We do something that makes the patrol and the three on break come out of the villa where we can neutralize them. Something that causes Abdul and Isabelle to have to remain hidden, probably in their room. I'm thinking a fire on the property or something like that. That way, Angela can go in through the chimney, if we confirm that the measurements allow for that, and neutralize the one in the surveillance room while the rest of us neutralize the five others outside. From there, we'd have the villa and the target to ourselves and all forces equalized. What do you guys think?" Harry laid out his plan without thinking it over much, but his actual goal wasn't to have the definitive plan then, but to encourage his team to start brainstorming.

"I think that would draw too much attention, Harry. It's putting them on alert unnecessarily and too soon," Martha responded.

"And what do you suggest, Martha? We can't wait for them to open the door and happily let us in."

Martha smiled and gave Harry a pat on the shoulder.

"That's exactly what I'm thinking, Harry," she said. "Let me explain my plan."

"I'm all ears."

# CHAPTER XIV

Loretta was a responsible person at her job. She wouldn't have missed work, save some act of God, and if she had had to, she certainly would have called her coworker/manager and repeatedly apologized. At least that's what Sofia thought. Something was wrong.

After the call with Pedro, and though it was already quite late, Sofia decided to get in the car and stop by the police station to file a report. She was sincerely worried. She couldn't help but think that something may have happened to her, or that it may also be her fault. When she went downstairs, she noticed that Loretta's car was still parked at the entrance. She arrived at the police station very late, past midnight, where an officer received her who, after Sofia told her that she came to report a missing person, kindly told her to wait a minute in the waiting room. After a minute, she had her go to a small room where there was a writing desk and a computer and told her to sit down and tell her what happened. She had never been to that police station, but it certainly didn't look anything like the ones from a movie or a TV show. In fact, it seemed rather old and dilapidated to her, undoubtedly in need of renovation.

Sofia explained the situation to the officer with painstaking detail. She felt a bit embarrassed about the part where she rejected her after spending the night with her, but it didn't matter. The most important thing was finding Loretta safe and sound; the rest was secondary. In any case, Sofia didn't sense anything in the officer that would indicate that she was judging her in any way, which helped her gain a sense of trust.

"So, you suspect that something may have happened to her?"

"Yes, it isn't normal that she just vanished, didn't go to work, didn't post anything online, and that her phone is off."

"Do you fear for her life?"

"What do you mean?"

"Do you think she could have attempted to take her own life?"

"God, no."

"Have you called her family to see if they know anything?"

"Her family is in Italy, her father, her older sister. And her sister's kids (her nephews). Her mom died when she was little. I didn't call them. I didn't want to worry them."

The police officer typed away on her computer at a rapid pace. She finished a few seconds after Sofia had told her everything and responded to the questions she asked. Then, she added:

"Okay, look, ma'am, I'm going to be completely honest. This seems to be an outburst from what happened between you two. Sometimes, something makes us so angry that we blow up, and each person goes off in who knows what direction. In this case, she may have decided to go away for the weekend to let loose a bit, and given the circumstances, you were the last person she wanted to tell. Missing work without saying anything is certainly perhaps abnormal, but as I said, everything blew up, so she doesn't care about anything right now. I've seen cases like this. So, I'll tell you what we're going to do. It's Sunday, so go home and relax. Your friend will most likely show up within a few hours after a weekend of retaliation. If not, try calling or sending a message online to her family or the friend that she mentioned had a place at her house for her to see if they know anything. And if on Monday you still haven't heard anything, call me on this number." The officer gave her a card with a phone number and her name: Officer Suárez.

Sofia took the card and smiled. She found her to be convincing and empathetic toward everything she had told her. Sofia was probably blowing things out of proportion. Loretta was an adult, and Officer Suárez was probably right. The spite and anger of the moment probably made her get a taxi to anywhere with nothing but the clothes on her back. Perhaps to the airport to go to Mallorca for the weekend, or maybe to Italy to see her family. Perhaps, if she had called her sister, she would know that she was with them and that she was okay. But she didn't want to worry them since they were far away. Missing work certainly wasn't normal, but it wasn't like it was the job of her life. If they fired her, she could work in any other store or restaurant or some other place. Moreover, her father had plenty of money, tons of it. Loretta could never work again if she wanted. She wouldn't need anything, though she had never wanted to depend on her family financially.

Sofia left the police station around 3 a.m. She was still worried, but for now, she couldn't do anything. As she left the station, a patrol car parked at the entrance and two police officers got out. They opened the back door of the car and took out a man in handcuffs that Sofia immediately recognized. It was the taxi driver who was taking her home the night before and got in the accident. What in the world was he doing to get arrested? Did it have to do with the accident from the previous night?

"Excuse me, I know this man. Did he do something?"

"You know him? Where do you know him from, ma'am?" one of the officers asked.

"He's the taxi driver that was taking me home last night."

The taxi driver was handcuffed and dejected. He didn't even deign to look at Sofia when she spoke. He seemed in shock at that moment.

Both officers looked at each other, and one made a gesture to the other to get the taxi driver inside. When they walked into the building, the other officer asked Sofia if she would mind coming inside and telling him what happened the previous night. Intrigued, Sofia accepted.

She sat in the same reporting room where she had been a moment ago, but at another table in a corner, with some separation from the rest. Sofia figured that the police in that spot had a superior rank to that of Officer Suárez, since the desk was bigger and had more empty space around the seat. It seemed somewhat more comfortable, though certainly nothing otherworldly. The officer that had invited her in arrived immediately and introduced himself as Seargent Sánchez. He explained to her that they had arrested the taxi driver from the previous night because a woman had reported him for attempting to physically abuse her the night before. It turns out that the woman in question was the one from the car that had hit the taxi driver from behind in the accident when Sofia was in the taxi. Sofia confirmed those events, but the only thing she could add was that another taxi driver had taken her home, and the suspect in question had stayed behind to sort out the paperwork for the accident with the woman. She didn't see anything else. The Seargent thanked her and asked for her information to contact her if necessary.

"Seargent, tell me the truth. Is he guilty?" Sofia asked as she got up.

"It's not my job to determine that, ma'am."

"Sure, but do you think he is?"

"I can't tell you anything, ma'am. Understand that we haven't even heard his testimony. The woman reported him and definitely seemed upset, but we have to prove the facts. Sometimes, things aren't as they seem." Sofia understood and left the station, hopefully for the last time that day.

As she walked to her car, which was just a couple of minutes away, she thought about how she may have been in the taxi of a rapist last night. Perhaps this wasn't the case, but for the moment, it just as well could be. And if so, even though he hadn't touched her, he did touch the next woman that he had contact with. It was possible that she had narrowly escaped. What if the taxi driver had ended up taking her home and forced her to let him go with her up to her apartment? Even though she knew how to defend herself alone, it wouldn't have been fun and could have been dangerous.

She got in her car and immediately locked it. She sat there behind the steering wheel for a minute, thinking about the dangers that may be out there in mere everyday situations, even if it were in a city like Murcia, which wasn't dangerous or unsafe at all. Sometimes, ignorance is bliss. If she hadn't found out about the taxi driver's arrest, she wouldn't be terrified then. She drove off and got home at 5:05 a.m., locking the door behind her. Then, she texted Harry asking if he knew when he'd be coming back, saying she wanted to see him. To her surprise, Harry immediately called her. Sofia picked up:

"Sofia, is something wrong? It's five in the morning."

"No, nothing. I couldn't sleep and was thinking about how it would be nice if you came back soon." Sofia lied because she didn't want Harry to get worried. He couldn't do anything now anyway. "Do you know when you're coming back?"

"Soon. We might close negotiations with the client tomorrow and finish up the deal, and then we'd be back Monday if all goes well."

"Tomorrow meaning today, Sunday?"

"Yes, right—today. How's it going with your parents? Do they like Murcia?"

"Really well. Yeah, they like it a lot. They leave tomorrow. Well, today, I mean. Anyways, I'll let you get some sleep. Sorry for waking you up. Keep me updated about when you'll be coming back. Hope the deal goes well."

"Are you sure you're okay? You seem off, like worried."

"Yeah, I am. I woke up to go to the bathroom and couldn't go back to sleep, so I texted you. But I'm okay, really."

"Okay, well, get some sleep. It's early still."

"You, too. Sending you a kiss."

"Sending one to you, too. Bye."

Good news. Apparently, Harry would be back soon. The sooner he got back, the sooner they'd talk. She was more and more convinced that he would forgive her, and everything would go back to how it was before. Good, but for now, she had to focus on Loretta. Either way, she still couldn't sleep, so she turned on her computer and searched for Barbara, Loretta's friend, on all social media she had. She found her (or so she thought; there was only one Barbara in Loretta's contacts) and messaged her telling her who she was, what happened without going into detail, and left her phone number so she would let her know as soon as she heard from Loretta. Later, around 6 a.m., she smoked a joint next to the window in her room to end the long day. With the high it gave her, she fell asleep right away.

When her alarm went off at 9 a.m. on a Sunday, she cursed all the saints she knew and threw her old alarm (Sofia didn't use her phone alarm) against the wall. Why had she set the alarm for 9 a.m. on a Sunday? She then remembered that she had to take her parents to the airport. "*Porca miseria*[17], fucking hell. I forgot," she thought. She struggled to get up, dragging the heavy load of exhaustion through-out her whole body, and got in the shower. She put on some music to wake herself up as she showered. When "Sweet Child O' Mine" by Guns N' Roses came on, she started to get some energy. Her burst of energy continued when she got out of the shower and made herself a huge cup of coffee with milk. That would have to be enough for her to function.

Luckily, it was. Sofia was someone who quickly gathered strength to get going; she got energized easily. She got dressed and went down to her car. Fifteen minutes later, she arrived at her parents' hotel and saw them at the entrance with their luggage. She decided not to tell them anything about last night. She wasn't going to worry them when they were about to leave the country. And it would most likely be worry for nothing, because everything would soon go back to normal. She was convinced of that, or at least tried to convince herself.

When they got in the car, they told her that she seemed off. She told them that she hadn't slept much because she had gone out for

---

17 Translator's note: *Porca miseria* is a common exclamation in Italian, roughly equivalent to "Damn it" or "For God's sake."

some drinks with a couple of friends, but that was all. The Murcia airport is close to the city, about twenty minutes away, so they arrived quickly. Her parents invited her for a coffee (which she definitely needed) at one of the coffee shops in the airport before going through security. They had plenty of time, since there was more than an hour and a half before takeoff and didn't have to check any bags. Plus, judging by how few people there were, they would take three or four minutes at most to get through security. As they had their coffee, Francesco and Arianna invited their daughter for a family weekend in July at their Tuscany villa for Arianna's birthday, the final weekend of that month.

"So, Sofia, are you doing anything the last weekend of July?" Arianna asked as she stirred her coffee with a spoon.

"And if you are doing something, you should cancel and come for your mom's birthday," Francesco intervened before Sofia could say something abruptly, but with a pleasant smile.

Arianna was turning sixty-five years old, and it was a special occasion, so they had planned to throw a party in grand fashion and invite the whole family and friends. "Bring a guest if you want. They're invited," her father added to conclude the invitation. They knew that she didn't have any more classes at the language school at the end of July and told her they would pay for the plane tickets, so Sofia had no excuse not to go. Plus, it was her mother's birthday, so she already figured she would be there.

The family villa in Tuscany was one of Sofia's favorite places in the entire world. Her parents had had it for forty-five years, before she was born. It was close to Florence, surrounded by small hills with lush green trees. Sofia remembered playing there as a kid, running up and down the hills, and how her dad would take her to see the deer that wandered nearby to take pictures of them, and how, as soon as it started to get hot, she would splash around in the pool at the villa while Mario, the chef, prepared barbecue. Then, when she was older, she would spend weekends there throwing amazing parties with friends. Her parents left her the keys whenever she wanted, since they would always arrive after to find the house spotless. Plus, she had lost her virginity there with her first boyfriend, Marco, in a hammock by the pool with a vast landscape in the background. Even though, as it normally occurs, the first time that someone has sex isn't objectively great, you don't forget it. She had unforgettable memories at that place.

The villa had plenty of open land, and the pool was quite big, about thirty-five feet long. Moreover, the inside of the villa was about thirty-two hundred square feet. It was no Beverly Hills mansion, but it was beautiful and very well maintained. It had been a couple of years since the last time she went, so when they told her to come, she very much wanted to go back. Whether she would go with a guest or not, she still didn't know, but either way, she would go.

Sofia gave her parents an affectionate goodbye and then went back to the city. Francesco and Arianna's visit had turned out to be pleasant, if she thought about it rationally. But, of course, it couldn't have come at a worse time for her, given all the circumstances she found herself in. Even so, both Sofia and her parents had spent nice moments visiting the city that weekend. She could say that her goal had been accomplished, despite the visit having been at the worst possible time. Sofia herself would say that it provided a distraction for her.

It was Sunday, but one of the Sundays when shops were open, so she decided to go shopping for a bit. She could use a wardrobe renovation. She checked her phone, but there were no notifications from Loretta or Barbara or anyone. In any case, since she couldn't really do much except wait, stopping by the beautiful shops in the city center would serve as a distraction for her. She parked as close as she could to the pedestrian-only area and walked towards where various pedestrian streets and shops were concentrated. She sat on a patio in that area for a coffee before starting her tour. They were streets with plenty of history. It was intriguing to her that they all had names from medieval times according to the professions that each one was home to. The two most famous, Trapería and Platería[18], were often confused even by people from Murcia. Sometimes, on the street, you could hear people say things like, "The shop is on that street where the Casino is. I'm not sure if it's Trapería or Platería." It was common.

It was a beautiful morning. She enjoyed a nice cappuccino, like the proper Italian she was, as she watched the people pass by. Some had shopping bags, while others were simply taking a stroll, while some were tourists.... When she asked for the check, a familiar face approached her. It was her coworker Martin, a German professor at the language school.

"*Guten morgen*[19], Sofia. How are you? What are you up to?"

She liked Martin. He was a fun person. At the Christmas dinners, he was always one of the last to leave, and since Sofia was as well, they hit it off. Moreover, his wife, Gema, was genuinely charming.

"Not much, having a coffee before I go shopping. What about you?"

"Good. I'm meeting up with my brother-in-law for a beer while I wait for Gema. She went to see her mom. And before that, I'll stop by the cell phone store to see if I can find a case for my phone since it broke."

"That's great. I'm happy to see you."

"Same here, Sofia. If you'd like, we'll be around the Plaza de las Flores somewhere later on; come by for a drink.

"Okay, thank you, Martin. I'll see you later. If not, I'll see you tomorrow. *Ciao*."

Sofia paid for her coffee and started her shopping tour. Approximately an hour and a half later, with two bras, three dresses, and a

---

18  Translator's note: In medieval times, *trapería* referred to where clothing, textiles, and fabrics were traded, while *platería* referred to silversmithing, i.e., where artisans crafted and sold silver goods.

19  "Good morning" in German.

couple of pairs of shoes, Sofia had finished her morning shopping. She didn't feel like stopping by Plaza de las Flores to see if she would catch Martin. She was still worried and didn't have the energy to put on a brave face for other people. She liked Plaza de las Flores, a plaza full of outdoor restaurant patios with a fountain in the middle and a lively atmosphere, but now wasn't the time. So, she headed towards her car as she thought about ordering some food for delivery and continuing her online search for Loretta. When she got to the car, she texted Martin to tell him that she was going home since she was tired. When she finished the text, her phone started to ring and vibrate. It was an unknown number, and she normally didn't take those calls, but given the circumstances, she decided to do it.

"Hello?"

"Sofia Lombardi?"

"Yes, that's me. Who's this?"

"This is the Murcia police. Can you talk for a moment?"

Sofia said yes and listened carefully to what the police officer told her without saying a single word. She couldn't believe what she was hearing.

# CHAPTER XV

"Go ahead, Martha. Tell us your plan," Harry said. "We're all ears."

"Thank you, Harry. Alright, team, from what Melinda told us, there's one person that leaves the villa somewhat regularly to pick her up and buy groceries. So, Angela and I will go back to the villa with that bastard posing as a couple of poor girls willing to do anything to get some money. Once we're inside, we'll give you guys the green light to go in. It's simple."

It was truly a great idea. They would get the enemy inside the villa voluntarily, and once inside, everything would be much easier. And it wouldn't be with Melinda's active participation per se; she would only accompany them until they went inside, and then they would get her out of there. "Shit, of course," Harry thought.

Truth be told, it was a good initial idea. They were lucky to have Martha on the mission.

"I like it," Angela said.

"It might work," Piotr added.

"Martha, have I told you that I love you?" Harry asked.

"Harry, I don't like liars. I already told you that." Everyone laughed.

"Okay, team, let's eat something for dinner and get some rest. We'll sleep on it so we can figure out the specifics with this idea as a starting point. Tomorrow morning, we'll sit down and won't get up until we have a clear plan." Harry ordered.

Dinner went smoothly; the atmosphere was palpably upbeat, but not euphoric. They were all aware of the importance and the danger of the mission. At the same time, they wanted to get it over with successfully, and after that day, they could see the end getting closer and closer.  Everyone went to their rooms shortly after, and Harry fell asleep immediately. Around 4 a.m., he woke up and started ruminating on everything. They already had the initial plan, which was great. It would allow them to avoid all the security measures to enter and not put the enemy on high alert, which was a great advantage. But how would they get to that point? Neither he nor Piotr could knock on the door and offer prostitutes to the house. It was too suspicious, keeping in mind that nobody knew who was in the villa. It would put them on alert. Waiting for them to call Melinda again and for her to be the one to introduce Martha and Angela as friends looking for some money was the best option. Abdul wouldn't be suspicious about Melinda, since they had her father hostage in the Philippines, or about a couple or whores, which would be the only thing he would see in Angela and Martha. That may be a good plan to get in.

However, there were a couple of problems with that. The first was that they had to be ready for when Melinda got a call from the villa, and they didn't know when that would be. They imagined that it would be soon, but they didn't have a calendar with the event marked off. They may be waiting for a week, but it may also be in the next ten minutes without them being prepared for the mission. The other problem was Melinda herself. She was still a civilian, and having a plan depend on an untrained civilian was always risky. In fact, the Conglomerate protocol expressly prohibited it, except for extremely rare cases. Whether it fits within the protocol wasn't something that worried Harry, given that, as he always said, anything in life can be defended and justified with a bit of imagination. However, the risk of Melinda ruining everything was real. Some stuttering, one too many words, behavior that the enemy considered suspicious, and everything could fall apart. On the other hand, Melinda had demonstrated great composure and a desire to help, and the risk would essentially be limited to the van route; once inside, everything would then depend on the FAI team.

Harry had doubts. He started sweating and got up to drink a glass of water. Upon getting up, he realized that Piotr wasn't in his bed. "*That's weird*," he thought. Harry had already been awake for a bit with his thoughts, and no one had either gone in or out of the room. He got up and, as he approached the door, started hearing a noise from the living room. It was a more or less rhythmic noise. He opened the bedroom door very slowly and saw that the hallway door, which went to the kitchen and the living room, was ajar. As he approached it, the noise became more intense. Harry already had an idea of what was happening, as a subtle smile appeared on his face. When he got to the slightly opened door, he carefully stuck his head through, and, indeed, it was what he thought. He saw Angela on her knees on top of Piotr on the couch having sex. Harry decided he would grab the glass of water from the bathroom in his room. He didn't want to bother his colleagues while they were exchanging thoughts about the mission in such an intense way. If this was part of a new pre-mission ritual that they had agreed upon, Harry thought it was great.

Piotr was several years older than Angela, though he did look younger. He was divorced and had a daughter in Warsaw who he barely saw due to work. Angela, for her part, was single and had no commitments, so it seemed normal to Harry that they both felt like having fun at some point, even more so in a tense atmosphere prior to an important mission. Who knew if it would be their last night on Earth. Of course, it wasn't Harry's plan to do anything to prevent it; it was none of his business. He wasn't like those football coaches who want to have every single detail figured out before games. He didn't want to control their diets, whether they went out and partied, whether they had sex.... No, Harry wasn't like that. Of course, if he saw that they performed poorly during the mission, he would be the first to find out why. But if his colleagues wanted to have sex before a mission, great.

So, he went back to his room, went into the bathroom, and drank water from the sink like a cat given that there were no glasses in the bathroom. He went back to bed, and- before he could start ruminating on the plan for the mission, his phone vibrated on the nightstand. It was a text from Sofia:

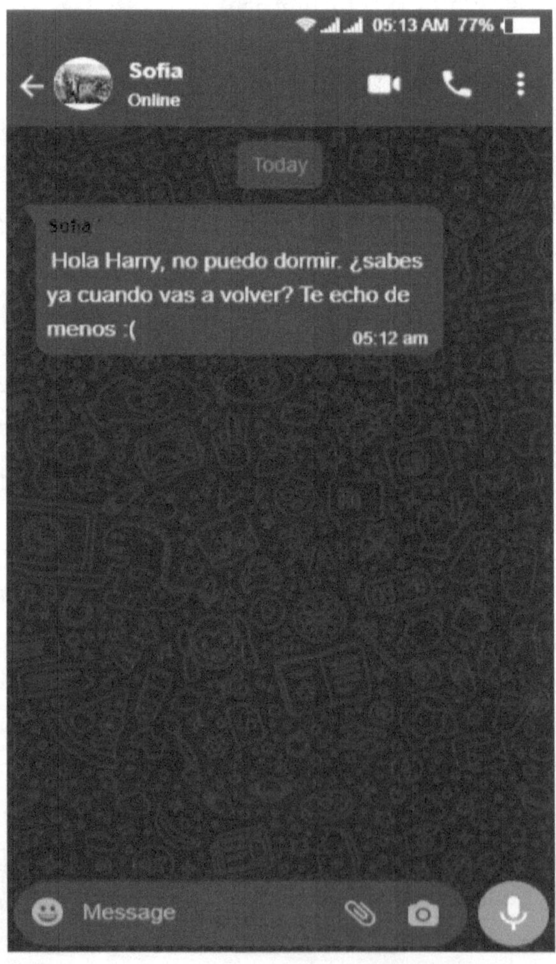


*"Hey Harry, I can't sleep. Do you know when you'll be back yet? I miss you."*

Harry decided to call her. It wasn't as though his roommate would get upset if he talked on the phone at that point. It wasn't a very long conversation. Harry could tell that she was worried about something but probably didn't want to tell him because it was something she would rather talk about in person; still, something was wrong. And he wasn't sure if it was just Sofia wanting to resolve things with Harry. It seemed like something else was going on. However, since he couldn't do much more at that point if she didn't tell him anything, he decided to try to avoid thinking about it. So, he hung up and started thinking about the plan again.

Once the girls were inside, they would have to facilitate access to the guys. For that, they would have to deal with various problems: the surveillance room, the patrol, and taking care of the people that were on their break. How could they do all that at the same time? Before he could answer that question, Harry was overcome by sleep.

He woke up around 8:15 to Piotr shaking him.

"Wake up, boss. We have to draw up the plan."

Harry opened his eyes, taken aback. Damn, he fell asleep? What a terrible leader of mercenaries he was. He jumped out of bed, still dazed, and nearly fell to the floor.

"Don't worry, boss. We'll wait for you outside. Five more minutes won't make or break the mission," Piotr said to him, laughing.

Harry got himself to the bathroom sink to wash his face as he thought about how much he had slept and if everything had been a dream. He looked at his phone and saw Sofia's text, so that much was real. Did he really see his colleagues in the middle of having sex, or did he dream it? It seemed very real to him the way he remembered it. He wasn't going to ask them, either: "Hey, you two were fucking last night, weren't you?" Harry laughed at the thought as he got dressed. Five minutes later, he went to the living room and saw everyone sitting at the table, each with their cup of coffee.

"Good morning, everyone. Sorry for the delay," Harry announced.

"Good morning, Sleeping Beauty. Did the prince give you a kiss to wake you up?" Martha asked, which made Angela laugh and Piotr smile.

Harry also laughed and went along with the joke that Martha had started:

"No, he did other things to me that I like better. Do you have coffee?"

Angela handed Harry a cup, then he poured himself coffee from the pot as he grabbed a chocolate muffin. He wanted something sweet for breakfast this time. He always ate an American breakfast of eggs and bacon, but there were no eggs, so he had to adapt.

"Okay, team. I think that, going off the idea that Martha had yesterday, we have several things to figure out:

1) How to get them to let Martha and Angela in the villa.

2) How to take over the surveillance room.

3) Taking care of the patrol.

4) Taking care of the ones that are on their breaks. From there, Piotr and I, or one of us, will be able to enter and go up to the first floor where we'll have to see:

5) How we get rid of the bodyguards, and…

6) How we kill Abdul and Isabelle and make it look like a suicide or an accident.

Suggestions?"

It was about 8:30 in the morning. They were mulling over the solutions to all those problems and to everything laid out before them. At around 5 p.m., after a multitude of ideas put together, some moments of frustration and others of euphoria, they had it all set and got out a bottle of whiskey to celebrate. Each of them drank it in their favorite way: Harry and Martha on the rocks, Piotr with an orange slice and orange soda, and Angela with only one ice cube and a bit of water. The plan was clear and solid, in Harry's opinion. The only downside was that it all depended on Melinda getting a call from the villa. If that didn't happen, there would come a point where they would have to change their strategy, given that the risk of Abdul and Isabelle leaving the country increased. But what the hell! They had gone to play, and if they had to go all in, then so be it.

Melinda would go with Martha and Angela when she got the call. Then, she would ask Abdul's bodyguard in charge of picking her up if they would be interested in a couple of friends who were looking for work. There was no chance that he would say no. It was six guys apart from Abdul and Isabelle. And the other two female bodyguards didn't seem bothered by Melinda's presence, so two more whores would be too sweet a deal to pass up.

They hadn't finished drinking their whiskey when Angela got a call from Melinda. She picked up, listened, and lifted her thumb to end the call, saying, "In forty-five minutes, I'll pick you up and explain everything. Be on time. We have some sons a bitches to kill today."

Coincidence, fate, an aligning of the planets, who knows what, had made it so that Melinda got a call from the villa at that very moment for her to be ready in an hour and a half, right when they had just established the plan. There was no time to waste. Martha and Angela went to get changed. Twenty minutes later, they all left to get Melinda. They described the part of the plan to Melinda that they needed her to know and made sure she understood it. They couldn't tell her all the details, only the ones that concerned her. Sharing the entire plan with a civilian may only lead to her getting overwhelmed with unnecessary details, which might make her act suspiciously toward the enemy and accidentally ruin the plan.

Melinda understood everything perfectly, or at least that's the sense she gave. They headed to the pickup point. Harry and Piotr dropped them off about five hundred yards away and drove away to get themselves in position near the villa. Martha, Angela, and Melinda arrived at the abandoned gas station which served as the pickup point. Then, like clockwork, after a few minutes, the C15 they were waiting for showed up. It was 8 p.m. The vehicle stopped about fifty yards away from them. The driver then took out a gun and pointed it at them.

"Listen, you whore, you have fifteen seconds to explain to me who your friends are and what they're doing here," he said, addressing Melinda.

She lifted her arms and started stuttering, "They're lo…lo…locals. They need money—they can be trusted. I…I…I told them you guys might be interested in a couple more girls. I…I…I'm sorry. Please, don't kill me." Then, she broke down crying, as Angela and Martha stayed silent with their arms in the air.

The driver lowered his gun and put his hand on Melinda's head. "Shhh, don't worry. Don't cry, it's okay. I believe you. We can always use more girls. So, she told you two about the job?" he asked Angela and Martha.

"Yeah. As long as it pays well, there's no problem," Martha responded.

"But there has to be a confidentiality agreement. You understand, right?" The driver got closer and closer to them and started lifting the gun.

"Don't worry, we won't say anything," Angela said.

"Right, but, you see, it's not going to be that simple." He started poking Angela's chest with the gun. "Give me your IDs now," the driver ordered.

Martha and Angela took out their fake IDs and handed them to the driver. He looked at them and took a picture of both sides.

"So, you're Alba, and you're Jasmine. Okay, Alba and Jasmine, now you know that we know who you guys are and where you live, and we can find out who your loved ones are. Everything will go well, and you'll be well paid, as long as you keep your mouths shut. If not, everything could go wrong. And I guarantee that you won't be able to hide. Sound good?" the driver asked as he handed them their IDs.

They both agreed. Then, Melinda asked, "Are we leaving now? It's hot out here." She seemed calmer already, or perhaps it was an act; Angela wasn't sure. If it had been an act, it was certainly Oscar-worthy.

The driver looked at her and shook his head no. She opened the back door of the C15 and sat down.

"Before giving you guys the job, I'll have to see if you guys are fit for it. You seem like you are. I'm going to trust my instinct and say you pass (looking at Angela). But you, I'm not sure. Come here," he said, making gestures to Martha with his gun in hand to come towards him. Martha approached, and the driver showed her his private parts.

"Let's see how you manage down there, Jasmine. And careful with trying anything, or else I'll blow your brains out." Martha looked at him and knew she had no choice. Of course, she would have preferred not to get to that point; it wasn't the initial idea of the plan. However, she had done hundreds of missions and knew that sometimes you had to do things you didn't want to do, which she understood. She got very close to the driver and looked him in the eyes as she took off his pants. She wanted him to see in her eyes that she wasn't afraid of him and that she was there by necessity. The driver thought that the necessity was because she was another whore in need of money, and she knew that the necessity was to complete the mission. However, the sense that it was necessity and not fear motivating her to do this was evident in her gaze. She pulled down the driver's pants and underwear and slowly bent down, got on her knees, put the penis in her mouth, and did what the driver expected, while Melinda and Angela made sure not to look.

A moment later, the driver, now convinced, blindfolded the three of them, put them in the C15, and headed to the villa. What the poor bastard didn't know was that Martha had him on the list in her head. And whoever Martha had on her list only got off it one way.

# CHAPTER XVI

En route to the villa, with her eyes blindfolded, Angela thought about what had just happened. She was thinking about how great it would have been if Martha had bitten off that bastard's dick. It would have looked like a scene from a Quentin Tarantino movie, with blood everywhere. Damn, that would have been great. Guys like him made her sick. But Martha had put the mission first, as everyone imagined she would, though she would probably have her opportunity for revenge. And, if Martha didn't have it, Angela would do it in her name. From what she had seen, the driver was the typical high school or neighborhood bully who held certain power, but who had someone in the background above them that terrified them (in this case, Abdul). That's why, when he could, he had to assert his share of power over those weaker than him to feel fulfilled in his bully mentality. However, in this instance, they were only weaker due to the circumstances of the mission, which the driver wasn't aware of. What had just happened was a clear example. He had done it simply because he felt he could, and his conviction that he truly was someone important with power was reinforced. He hadn't done it because it was necessary or because his superior had ordered him to do it.

In the concentration camps of World War II, the figure of the *kapos* was common. They were nothing more than prisoners who were given supervision roles over other prisoners in exchange for better conditions, like better food or less demanding jobs, among other ones. In the end, a *kapo* was still just another prisoner who the SS could decide to kill at any moment, but having certain power over weaker individuals still strengthened their self-esteem and produced a false sense of control that provided them comfort. The driver had the typical behavior of a *kapo*.

It was quite possible that the rest of Abdul's personnel had a very similar behavioral profile, though she couldn't be totally sure. In any case, she didn't have much more time to contemplate, as the vehicle quickly stopped, the door opened, they drove a few more seconds, and then made them get out. With the blindfold still on, they entered the villa where they were given permission to take it off. Angela took a look around and saw that it was all as Melinda had described, and Piotr had reflected it in his plans. Two bodyguards showed up, a man and a woman, alongside the driver.

"Hold on a second," the driver said as he grabbed what looked like a metal detector from a drawer. This was as they had expected. They weren't going to let strangers in without being searched, not even Melinda, even though they already trusted her. They had nothing suspicious, so the detector didn't go off.

"Good. Good girls. Do you think the boss will like them?" the driver asked his two colleagues that were there.

"Isabelle's going to love this one," the female bodyguard said, looking at Martha, as the driver and the other bully nodded their heads. "Oh, yes, she will." Everyone laughed out loud.

Suddenly, they heard what sounded like firecrackers right near the villa. Everyone got startled. The driver grabbed his walkie talkie and said:

"Patrol, take a look. We expect a report in two minutes." Then, he told his colleagues, "Stay with these three whores in the living room until I say so." He then went upstairs.

Just as they had imagined, being a fugitive like Abdul made it so the security measures were maximized. Continually changing refuge was an unequivocal sign that they took their security very seriously. With this attitude, it was obvious that anything unexpected would be handled with the utmost caution. A strange noise near the villa could be one of the things that would activate their security protocol until it was confirmed that it was all a false alarm. The protocol wouldn't include taking strangers to Abdul, but it would mean going to check out what was happening. Therefore, they would get the patrol right where they wanted them.

Melinda, Martha, and Angela went to the living room with the two bodyguards and closed the door behind them. Then, Angela and Martha began their plan.

"We shouldn't have come. These guys are crazy. I'm scared, Jasmine. I shouldn't have listened to you."

"You need money, don't you? Well, here it is. Stop whining."

"I want to go home."

"Stop fucking whining."

The supposed argument was becoming increasingly heated, as the two bodyguards looked at each other incredulously. The woman, a bit annoyed, approached them, took out a gun, and pointed it at them. As soon as she approached, Martha grabbed her arm and twisted it, which made her let go of the gun. Then, Angela grabbed it and pointed it at the man.

"Hands up or you're dead," Angela said as she gestured to Melinda to take the man's gun. She complied and handed the gun to Martha, who let go of the woman's arm and violently pushed her back.

Martha, seeing the gun, looked at her for a couple of seconds, then shot the woman three times and the man another three. Angela realized that what Martha had seen was a silencer on the gun. Therefore, a few gunshots wouldn't draw any attention. Two down. About a minute and a half had passed since the driver had gone upstairs, which meant they didn't have much time for the next phase of the plan. Angela left the living room and headed to the surveillance room. There should have been only one person alive, apart from the three girls, on the first floor at that point. Just as Melinda had told them, the room wasn't locked. She opened the door and shot the watchman, who, in this case, was the other female bodyguard from the crew. She closed the door and blocked it with a chair. Then, she looked at the screens in front of her. On one of them, she saw that the patrol had gone to check what was going on; they found the remains of firecrackers by the side of the pool. Then, she heard the walkie talkie from the dead woman in the room.

"False alarm. It must have been some kids throwing firecrackers through the fence to be funny. Let's go back to the villa to go to the bathroom before going back on patrol. Over and out."

"*Shit*," Angela thought, "*we have to hurry.*" She grabbed the walkie talkie and said with as neutral a voice as possible, "Pick up the firecrackers before coming back. Over and out." She saw on the screen that the patrol started picking up the firecrackers, which would give her an extra minute for what she had to do.

The CCTV system was quite simple to operate. The villa property was divided into quadrants, each quadrant with several cameras. With the keyboard, she went from quadrant to quadrant, and when she wanted to choose one, she clicked Enter and could then move from camera to camera. She moved to the northeast quadrant and turned off all the cameras. She waited thirty seconds, then turned them back on. She saw on the screen the two patrol members down on the ground. Everything was going as planned. Now she had to wait.

Piotr, for his part, was positioned on a hill near the property fence on the east side. He was looking through the scope of his sniper rifle and had the two patrol guards located, but he had to wait for the signal. As soon as he saw the small red lights on the cameras turn off, he killed the two patrol members with a shot to the head. He folded his rifle, put it away, and went towards the car with the satisfaction of a job well done.

Harry, as soon as he saw the two patrol members fall down, opened a hole in the fence and slipped into the property. He quickly but discreetly headed towards the area around the pool to the door that provided access inside. Martha was waiting for him with the door open. Melinda walked out, and Harry told her:

"Run to that side and you'll see a hole in the fence. Go through there. Piotr will be waiting for you. We'll handle the rest." Melinda hugged Harry and left. Harry went inside with Martha, and they closed the pool door behind them. Then, the driver's voice came through the walkie talkie:

"Security protocol complete. Get those three whores up here."

Everything was seemingly going according to plan, and the people upstairs thought that everything had been a false alarm. As far as they were concerned, a few troublemakers had thrown some firecrackers, as the patrol had confirmed, and no one else had reported anything strange. What they didn't know was that they hadn't reported anything strange because they hadn't had time, not because there was nothing to report.

They knocked on the door of the surveillance room where Angela was, using their knuckles to tap out the chorus of "Oh, Susana" so she knew it was them, and Angela came out. Harry was armed with an assault rifle, and Martha and Angela with the pistols with silencers. They started slowly walking upstairs. The door up there was closed. They reached it, and Harry grabbed the knob and started turning it very slowly. It didn't open; they had locked it. They knocked on the door and heard a voice from the other side: "Coming." Then, a few seconds later, there was a key turning from the other side opening the door.

Someone who must have been one of Abdul's other bodyguards opened the door, who barely had time to see Angela fire two rounds of the pistol through his stomach. His inert body rolled down the stairs. They saw the door to the dressing room, which was right across, slam shut. Harry signaled to Angela to go there and then to Martha to go with her to the main bedroom to the left, whose door was wide open. Whoever was inside must have realized by then that something was wrong.

Harry and Martha leaned against the wall, each to one side of the door. Harry signaled to Angela for her to stay in her position beside the dressing room door. Then, he looked at Martha and took out a small mirror from his pocket to look inside the bedroom. He identified a gun pointing from the edge of the bed. If his calculations and suspicions were correct, it would be Isabelle in the dressing room, and Abdul and the two bodyguards remaining (the driver and another one) in the bedroom. All he needed were two more guns pointing at the door. He continued to turn the mirror as much as he could but didn't see anything else. They may have been in the bathroom or on the bedroom terrace. He had no way of knowing. But after seeing the room, a plan occurred to him.

Angela, meanwhile, watched the closed dressing room door. She had to keep Isabelle in there until the others killed off Abdul. There was no other exit from the dressing room other than that door; thus, as long as it was closed, there was no danger.

Harry grabbed the mirror and started counting down with a normal tone of voice that could be heard from inside the bedroom. Three, two, one. When he got to one, he threw the mirror inside the room. Nearly instantly, they heard "Take cover!" and Harry took advantage and snuck in rolling on the bedroom floor all the way behind an armchair near the door, where he had a full view. He had used the old trick of the false grenade, making the enemy believe that he threw a grenade to distract him, having just that half second that he needed to enter the room that the enemy was using as a trench and from which he had an advantage to defend himself. From his new position, he could now see everything. The mirror-grenade (which had broken into pieces upon hitting the ground) had made Abdul and the driver seek refuge on the terrace, where Harry could easily see them through the glass. The other bodyguard was in the bathroom, where he was sticking his gun out the door. Harry shot a couple of times towards there, and the bodyguard returned the shots. Harry signaled to Martha to come in and started advancing on the floor of the room until he was under the bed, while Martha took the armchair spot.

"Are you finished in the bathroom yet? I have to use it—it's urgent," Harry shouted at the man entrenched in the bathroom. "You don't want me to take a shit here in the room, do you?"

Then, a muffled shot and a scream of pain from the bodyguard in the bathroom were heard. Martha had hit him right in the hand that was sticking out to return the shot. Great aim. Harry then leapt on the bodyguard who was writhing in pain and clutching the hand where Martha had shot him with his other hand. He punched him so hard that he fell to the floor. He grabbed the gun and killed him with a shot to the head.

He left the bathroom, looked toward the terrace where Abdul and the driver were with a table knocked over, serving as an improvised barrier.

"Hey, you, the guy who got his dick sucked before. Hand us that piece of garbage next to you and we'll let you walk," Martha screamed.

Harry understood Martha's strategy. In such a situation, where it could go on eternally like a chess match in which only the two kings remained, attempting to confuse the enemy and even make them betray each other might be a good option. Especially keeping in mind that a *kapo* would always try to save himself over any type of loyalty.

"That's right," Harry reinforced Martha. "Give us Abdul, dead or alive, and we'll let you go. He's who we want."

The terrace door was half-open, so they could hear them.

"You don't believe us, do you? I get it, but you're running out of options. You guys can't stay on the terrace forever. We can just as easily wait for you guys to jump down thirty feet and kill yourselves that way, or die of thirst, or come in the room and surrender, and we kill you both, because that's what we would do. We can do that, or you can give us Abdul, which is who we came for, and then we'll let you walk. Choice is yours," Harry concluded.

"Come on, hon. If you're worried about what happened before, it's forgotten. I've eaten worse things, trust me," Martha added with a laugh.

Then, shots came from the terrace towards Harry and Martha. Apparently, the job of negotiator they were doing wouldn't be so easy. But they had everything in their favor, given that time was on their side.

Meanwhile, Angela was still posted at the dressing room door waiting. Suddenly, she heard a voice speaking in Spanish with a French accent:

"Who are you and what do you want?"

"We're from the electricity company. We came to check your meters. Have you thought about switching to natural gas?" Angela replied.

Isabelle didn't respond, and Angela didn't make any attempt to continue the conversation either. She had no interest. Time was also in her favor. She only had to wait for Harry and Martha, and between the three of them, they would make her come out, especially since, if Isabelle spent time trapped in there, she would get desperate.

About forty minutes passed. Harry and Martha kept trying to make the driver-*kapo* turn in Abdul.

"Come on, guys. Are we really going to have to be here much longer? It doesn't matter to us, but, fuck, we'd rather be at home sleeping. When something is inevitable, it's not worth it to delay it. But whatever: your house, your rules," Harry said.

"I'll die before turning myself in to you guys. We're not afraid of death," Abdul suddenly shouted.

What happened next was as anticipated. The driver shot Abdul in the head, threw the gun on the ground, and went into the bedroom with his hands on his head.

"Stay still—don't move. Don't put your hands down," Harry said. As Martha pointed her gun at him, Harry searched him to make sure he had no other weapons, which was the case.

"You did the right thing," he added as he grabbed his hands and restrained him in handcuffs he had brought, fastening him to a railing on the terrace door. "You've proven to be a disgusting rat that would let his own mother die to save himself, but you've done the right thing."

Then, he approached the then lifeless body of Abdul and confirmed exactly that: that he wasn't playing some perfectly executed trick. He wasn't. Abdul Akhbar was dead.

# CHAPTER XVII

"Alright, Martha, I'm going with Angela to take care of Isabelle. You coming?" Harry asked, intuiting her response. Martha smiled and replied:

"Of course I'm coming, Harry. Just give me five minutes and I'll join you guys. Sound good?" She said all this while looking at the handcuffed driver.

"Hey, man, you promised me you wouldn't do anything to me if I gave you the boss," the driver said with an uneasy tone. Harry completely ignored him, gave a thumbs up to Martha, and kissed her on the cheek. Then, he left the room and closed the door behind him. Angela, meanwhile, was still leaning against the dressing room door with Isabelle inside. Harry looked at his watch. It was 5:03 a.m. at that point.

"Anything noteworthy?" he asked Angela. Angela said no; she hadn't heard anything from inside the dressing room.

Harry signaled to Angela to grab her gun and to position herself next to the dressing room door. Meanwhile, they heard a harrowing scream coming from the bedroom. Apparently, Martha was having her way with the driver. Harry counted to three with his hand, and when he got to three, Angela turned the knob and opened the dressing room door as Harry pointed his gun inside.

Isabelle was sitting on the floor, leaning against the opposite end of the dressing room door, in underwear and with her hijab tossed on the ground next to her. Her long brown hair was visible, and Harry realized that she was quite an attractive woman. Isabelle didn't bat an eye upon seeing the door open and Harry pointing a gun at her. He stopped pointing when he saw that Isabelle didn't have a weapon on or near her.

"You guys came to kill us, right?" she asked with a firm voice, devoid of any emotion.

"That's right," Harry responded, aware that there was no sense in hiding the truth at that point.

"I get it. I won't cause any trouble, but can I ask you guys a favor first?"

"Sure. What is it?" Harry extended his hand to her, which Isabelle grabbed to help herself get up.

"I want to see Abdul one last time."

"Abdul is already dead."

"Take me to him and kill me next to him, please."

"Okay. Angela, ask Martha if she's done, please."

Angela didn't need to ask anything, as Martha came out through the door. She was already done. Harry explained Isabelle's final wish to her, and Martha grabbed her by the arm and brought her next to Abdul. Isabelle threw herself on the floor next to her husband's dead body and started to cry and say something in Arabic.

Martha put the gun to Isabelle's head and shot her. Her body fell next to Abdul's on the floor of the terrace. Angela and Harry watched from the bedroom. They could see the driver's dead body hanging from the hand cuffed to the railing, with his back to the bedroom door. His pants were down with a substantial puddle of blood around him. They weren't sure exactly what Martha had done to him, though they could imagine. Rest assured, his final minutes of life were most likely not very pleasant. The point was that they had now finished the first part of the mission. It was seven in the morning, already Monday.

"Piotr, first part of the operation complete. Bring the van with the materials for the second part. And bring coffee and croissants for everyone," Harry ordered on the phone.

"Okay, boss. Melinda is with me. She insists on helping more. What should I do?" Piotr asked.

Harry was afraid of that. That girl had a strong desire to help, but that didn't remove the fact that she didn't have training and could make mistakes. Not to mention that seeing the scene in the villa—with a pile of dead bodies and almost certainly including an unwilling eunuch, straight out of a Kill Bill movie—probably wasn't the best thing for her mental health. The mission wasn't over. Their lives were no longer in danger, but they had to leave everything spotless to avoid raising suspicions, and she had to know how to do that.

"I don't care what she says. Convince her to go rest and tell her that we'll call her when we're done. I guess tonight. If she doesn't listen, give her a sleepy. That's the end of it. We don't have time for nonsense."

A sleepy was a maneuver that they learned during training for the Conglomerate: it stuns a person to the point of leaving them unconscious and asleep for several hours. It involved squeezing a specific point on the neck with substantial strength, but not in excess. As long as it was executed correctly, it wasn't dangerous. The person recovered consciousness after some time as though nothing happened. It was quite useful for the cases in which a mission asset tried to stray from the plan. However, if executed wrong, it could kill the person, so it was only used in extreme cases.

"Great, will do. I'll be there in fifteen minutes. *Żegnajcie przyjaciele*."

Now the boring part of the mission awaited them, which wasn't going to be so easy. It had to look like an accident or a suicide, which, with so many dead bodies, would be complicated, especially because of the eunuch. "*Let's see what cop believes that someone committed suicide by shooting themselves in the balls*," Harry thought. Piotr quickly arrived with breakfast. The four of them took ten minutes to drink coffee and eat some croissants at the edge of the pool to get some energy. Around 8 a.m., the second part of the operation commenced. Right then, Harry's phone vibrated. It was a text from Sofia:

*"I'm taking a plane to London. Call me later at noon if you can."* Great. Something was probably wrong. But one thing at a time.

The mission consisted of killing Abdul and Isabelle, but making it look like a suicide or an accident, such that any police investigation would reach one of those conclusions, preventing any implication of FAI or any trail leading back to a foreign intelligence agency. It was important that the death of Abdul and Isabelle was made public and that all countries found out about it. Many probably wouldn't believe the official version, but there would be no way of proving it was an assassination to stop Abdul, nor those who had been responsible.

Given the scene of the dead bodies that they had before them, it wouldn't be an easy task, especially given how tired they were from having gone so long without sleep. But it was unlikely that someone would go to the villa to bother them, and there wasn't the risk of someone catching them in the act. In fact, they would most likely have to leave an anonymous tip for the police afterwards, otherwise no one would ever go to the villa. Thus, they could take their time. Harry gave the pertinent instructions.

"Alright, guys, let's unload the bleach, the mops, and everything that Piotr brought and leave it at the entrance. We have two dead bodies in the living room, another in the surveillance room, another two in the yard, another on the stairs, two more in the main bedroom, and then Abdul and Isabelle. As we discussed, the plan is to fake Abdul and Isabelle's suicide which is relatively easy. As for the others, there are five that we can also make to look like a group suicide. But then we have the patrol who died outside with bullets from a weapon that isn't theirs, and a eunuch who no one in their right mind would buy as a suicide at all."

Harry, with this latter statement, didn't mean to reproach Martha. Martha had earned every right in the world to get her revenge, and if she had wanted it, it was because something serious had happened to her. It was obvious that if it had put the mission at risk, it wouldn't have happened, and Martha herself would have been the first to accept it. However, even though it was true that it entailed a slight delay, it was nothing insurmountable. They were a team, and they would sort it out together without much trouble.

"Okay, then," Harry continued. "Once we unload all the cleaning material, we'll put the three dead bodies that are causing us problems in the car. Sound good? We'll take them away from here. Then we'll take all the others to the main bedroom. We'll put Abdul and Isabelle lying on the bed holding hands and the others on the floor around the bed. Then, we'll clean everything as if we were Mister fucking Clean himself. Angela, write up a farewell note acting as Abdul and print it out. We'll leave it on the nightstand. Send it to the Conglomerate first so someone translates it to Arabic. Okay, guys, let's get to work."

They got to it, and around 1 p.m., they had everything in place. The dead bodies were in their place with their weapons in hand, a letter in which Abdul illustrated his God-complex delusion and how he had decided that collective suicide was the path to paradise, and the entire house cleaned with no trace of blood where it shouldn't have been, nor any fingerprints. As was reasonable, Martha had to take care of the bloodiest part for obvious reasons, but she willingly accepted it.

They left the villa with the doors and windows open to get the smell of bleach out and avoid making it seem like someone had cleaned it thoroughly. Then, they got in the car.

"Boss, what should we do with the three dead bodies back there?" Piotr asked.

"For now, we're going home to sleep for a bit, then we'll figure it out," Harry responded, who was exhausted. "They aren't going to go run off anywhere, so it doesn't matter if we wait a bit." They got to the house, and everyone went to sleep for a bit. Since it was already 2 p.m. and he was too tired, Harry decided not to call Sofia. He needed to rest. He sent her a message telling her, "*We're finishing up the job. I can't talk now, I'll call you later tonight.*" He turned his phone off and lay down.

Around 7 p.m., everyone started waking up. Then, at 7:30, they put pizzas in the oven to regain some energy. Now they had to decide what to do with the dead bodies. The typical move of dissolving the bodies in acid was off the table because it would take too long. Three dead bodies would take days to dissolve. Plus, they didn't have a bathtub at the house. Burning them might be an option, but the smell could travel several miles around the area, which was a risk that Harry wasn't willing to take. Suddenly, Piotr thought of something, and without swallowing his pizza, he exclaimed, "I GOT I...," and started choking. At first, everyone laughed and didn't make a big deal of it. But after six or seven seconds, they saw his face turning purple and quickly got up from their seats, alarmed. Martha grabbed Piotr, lifted him, and started doing the Heimlich maneuver. After the fourth thrust, a bit of pizza came flying out of Piotr's mouth, then Martha stopped. Piotr sat down, and Harry gave him a glass of water.

"I hope your idea is worth it after all that. The debriefing should definitely be good," Angela said, to which everyone laughed. Piotr smiled, still with the fright in his body.

"It's because of the idiot that bought pepperoni pizza."

"Are you going to tell us your idea now or what?"

"Okay, okay, okay."

Piotr's idea, broadly speaking, was a copy of a CSI episode or some other show of the type; he couldn't remember then. It was to look for a junkyard with a pressing machine, put the dead bodies in Abdul's C15, and crush it to the size of a washing machine.

When he heard Piotr's idea, Harry thought for a moment how they could have let him keep choking. When, a second after, that darkly humorous thought left his head, he said:

"We don't have a junkyard, and we don't know how to operate the pressing machine, and we can't leave the remains there afterwards either. Plus, if someone reorganizes the remains to separate the metals, they could find a remain from the dead body, and we can't take the risk. I bet that the episode where they do that they get caught, don't they?"

In the end, they opted for sneaking out past midnight to a nearby cemetery where there was a mass grave with unclaimed or unidentified dead bodies and burying them there. It seemed like a solid option. Dead bodies in a cemetery sounded like the natural solution. They located a cemetery about fifty miles from the house. A little-known cemetery like that one wouldn't have more than one security guard at night patrolling the graves, and the part with the mass grave especially was most likely not well monitored for obvious reasons. So, for a few elite mercenaries like FAI, it should be a piece of cake. They finished eating and went to sleep. Around 10 p.m., they would go to the cemetery, which would probably be closed to the public. Harry went out onto the porch at 9:30, lit a cigarette, and called Sofia. At the third ring, Sofia picked up.

"Hey, Harry. How are you? Did you finish the job?"

"Hey, Sofia. Almost. The negotiation has been tough, but it looks like it's almost done. I'll be back in Murcia tomorrow. Where are you?"

"I'm in London. I'm taking a flight to Murcia tomorrow morning. I have a lot to tell you. I'll be back at noon. Will you be around for lunch?"

"I think so, but I'll confirm by 1 p.m. or so. Meeting up would be nice. If I can, I'll make a reservation at El Sirena in a private section so we're alone. Or do you have to work in the afternoon?"

"No, no, I asked for today and tomorrow off. El Sirena sounds great."

"Are you okay, Sofia? You're acting strange."

"Yeah, yeah, I'm okay. I just prefer to talk in person, that's all."

"Okay, let's plan on that then. I have to let you go cause we have to finish the negotiation."

"Okay, see you tomorrow, Harry. Sending a kiss."

Harry hung up the phone, and when he turned around, he saw Martha behind him.

"Well, well, well. Good old Harry is in love, huh?"

"It's nothing." Harry tried to change the topic. Martha smiled.

"I'll let you know again that you're not the only one who doesn't like being lied to, Harry. I wish you the best. You deserve it. You're a good guy."

"We should get ready to head out soon."

"Okay, boss," Martha responded as she put her hand on her head, doing the typical military salute.

In truth, the conversation with Sofia had left him intrigued. A spontaneous trip to London? What could she be doing? He tried not to assume anything without having all the information. He knew all too well that reality is stranger than fiction. And it's also stranger than what one can imagine has actually happened. He didn't know to what extent that would be the case.

# CHAPTER XVIII

On the way to the cemetery, as Piotr drove, Harry called Ronald to give him the green light to get Melinda's father to safety. In the meantime, Angela called Melinda and confirmed that they were about to finish everything and that she no longer had to fear for herself or her father. She told her that the following morning, with her dad safe, they would talk about what they would do from there.

Melinda had been very brave, despite the obvious deviations from the standard protocol. In the end, if all turned out well, it would be in large part thanks to the information she provided and her bold attitude. Harry thought about recommending her to the Conglomerate training program, as he had already told her, if she wanted that.

The Conglomerate mainly recruited in two ways. Operating in the dark made it so they couldn't put an ad in the paper or on a job search website, but they had the most powerful department of human resources in the world, hands down. They always paid attention to the men and women that stood out in various police or military roles, given that they usually had networks of internal informants. The only thing these informants knew was that someone paid them very well to tell them who were the best in the respective unit or department, or who had stood out in some important operation. That was the main way they recruited new members. But there was another way, which was to follow the recommendations of the members themselves from different divisions of the Conglomerate. If a member noticed that someone may be "interesting," they could suggest them. And that's what happened in this case, though the Conglomerate always had the final say.

As Piotr drove, now about to arrive at the cemetery, Harry reflected: did he want this to be his final mission and retire? Certainly, with what he already had and the pretty penny he'd get from this mission, he had plenty to live comfortably for the rest of his life. But the rest of his life was too much time, and he didn't want to dedicate forty, fifty years to a contemplative life. Indeed, his work at FAI was a dangerous job where he put his life on the line, but it was also true that he liked it and was good at it. Although Sofia was there.... He wanted to try a different way of life. He was all out of sorts.

There was the middle ground of taking a long vacation. The Conglomerate gave the option of taking a six-month sabbatical to the most successful team leaders. The trick was that "the most successful" was a subjective criterion, and nobody knew what basis it was decided on. But after this mission, Harry believed he had the chance to request and be granted that long vacation. *"Well, better to focus on getting this mission fully over with first, and tomorrow will be a new day,"* he said to himself.

They parked near the cemetery and hid the car as much as they could. The cemetery had stone walls about six feet tall and an iron gate. They approached the gate and could see a flashlight in the distance through the dark, which they figured belonged to the guard. Next to the gate, there was a small office where they would have to enter to open the gate, since it was difficult to get the dead bodies over the walls. The office lights were off, so it was clear that only the guard with the flashlight was on the grounds patrolling. It wasn't a very big cemetery, as they had expected. They saw a camera at the entrance to the office and nothing else. When they saw that the guard's light was far enough away, Piotr used his hands to help with pushing, as Harry, Martha, and Angela jumped over the walls. Angela went to the office. She saw a conventional alarm above the door, nothing that the signal jammer she had couldn't block. That's what she did, and in five minutes, the alarm and the camera were rendered completely useless. She opened the door without much trouble, using a picklock she had, and then entered the office. Then, she sat in the dark and notified through the communicator that she was inside and awaited instructions.

Harry and Martha were stealthily approaching the guard in the dark. It was quite dark that night, and even though the moon was slightly out, it didn't give off much light. They grabbed the guard from the back by surprise and put him to sleep with a needle jab. He didn't even see him. They gave Angela the green light and saw the office lights turn on. A minute later, the cemetery gate started opening, and Piotr entered the grounds with the van. They all went to the office to meet up again. Angela told them where the mass grave was after having seen the cemetery plan in the office, then said that she had already opened it with the remote control in the office. They went all the way to the end of the grounds, and there was an open door to the left that led underground where there were various niches with no names and only one reference. They were unidentified bodies, illegal immigrants without identities, vagabonds, who, after no one had claimed their body, were buried in the mass grave at the cemetery that belonged to the corresponding city council. They were bodies which, unfortunately, no one would ever ask about or visit, so it was the perfect place to leave three dead bodies. In truth, the place exuded an atmosphere of sorrow and neglect. The people there were abandoned like an old pair of shoes. But that's how life went, and at that point, they didn't have much time to dwell on that.

They opened three niches with references and put a dead body in each one. There was enough space in each niche to fit more than one body; one was even a pile of bones, leaving plenty of room for another guest. They wouldn't put the bodies in empty niches since, if someone went to put a body there, they would find it already occupied and start asking questions, be it within a week, a month, or four years. They finished in just over an hour and a half and then left. Angela stayed inside to close the gate, then jumped over the wall with the help of a rope that her colleagues threw to her from the other side. Around midnight, they were on their way back to the house. The guard would wake up a couple of hours later in the middle of the graveyard and not remember anything. Since nothing was missing from the office and no grave was looted, he would choose not to make much of it to avoid getting fired for sleeping on the job, and no one would ever find out anything.

Now the mission was finally completely over. Had it been Harry's last one? Perhaps, but he was too tired to think about that. They arrived at the house, and Harry immediately went to bed. The others hung out on the porch to have a drink to celebrate the successful mission, but Harry didn't have the energy. The only thing he wanted was to sleep for three days straight. They had agreed to pack and head back home the following morning at 10 a.m. without any hurry. Harry fell asleep right away and woke up at 11:15 a.m. His colleagues didn't want to wake him up; they knew how much stress he had accumulated and that he needed to rest. It was a beautiful Tuesday morning, with a gorgeous sun and a cloudless sky. The FAI team already had their bags packed and everything tidy, waiting for Harry.

"Good morning, sleepyhead," Martha greeted him.

"Holy shit, is it Christmas already?" Harry responded as he stretched.

"Yes, Santa Claus. Get ready," Piotr replied as everyone laughed.

He prepared himself some coffee and took a bite of a muffin. He told Martha to talk to Ronald, and Angela to Melinda, to organize their reunion. He texted Sofia while he ate breakfast, confirming that they could meet for lunch that day, and then Alfonso to let him know that he was coming back home and suggested having a beer that day or the next to catch up. He finished breakfast, showered, and packed his bags in approximately three minutes. Then, he went out for a moment to make a call.

"Good morning, El Sirena restaurant. How can I help you?"

"Good morning. I'd like a table for two for lunch today in the private section, please."

"Is this Mr. Harry?"

"Yes. Hi, Ana. And just call me Harry. Come on, I'm not that old."

"Okay, your reservation's all set, Harry. Anything else?"

"Nope. I'll see you later around 2:30 or so. Thank you."

"See you then, Harry."

Another task done. Damn, what a good day so far. He had slept as though it had been a while since he'd done it, masturbated (but not to get rid of his stress as usual, just for pleasure), went back home (home sweet home), and had a reservation at his favorite restaurant in Murcia where, with a little luck, he would resolve everything with Sofia. He was certainly happy.

Around noon, they began their trip back to Murcia. Harry texted Sofia confirming the reservation, to which Sofia responded with a thumbs up and a smiley face. Since the mission was already over, Martha took back the reins as boss and took the floor on the trip back.

"Congratulations, everyone. We've successfully overcome a very complicated mission. You guys did great. Take the rest of the week off. I don't want to see you guys for months, got it?" This last sentence provoked some laughter. "No, really, you guys are amazing partners in crime. I loved being back in action with you guys."

"What's going to happen with Melinda?" Angela asked.

"I'll take care of that. You'll find out soon," Martha replied, closing the conversation.

It was evident that Martha had enjoyed actively participating in an on-the-ground mission again. And even though Harry knew that what had happened with the "eunuch" had affected her, as it would anyone else (she didn't know what had happened but could imagine), he also knew that wasn't going to stop her if there was another mission in the future. She was strong and had seen and suffered first-hand plenty of things in her career.  That wouldn't be an obstacle, if Harry decided to leave, for her to occupy his position if she preferred it over her current one. But that remained to be seen. Right now, he wanted to leave work aside. The week off would undoubtedly be great for him to disconnect and recharge. He would think later about whether it would be worth it to continue. They took Harry all the way to his apartment. He dropped his bags, opened some windows, got changed, and walked unhurriedly to the restaurant. He got there first, and Ana, the waitress that called Harry "mister," took him to his table. It was in one of the private rooms, the one with the smallest table which was for four. The restaurant had various rooms that served as private areas. Harry hadn't been in one, but he knew that politicians, businessman, and others of the sort usually met there to close deals. The private areas provided them with discretion, and the food and drinks were delicious, so it was the perfect spot.

Harry sat at the table and ordered a beer while he waited. Five minutes later, Sofia arrived. She smiled at Harry and sat down. Harry reciprocated the smile.

"Well, hello there. How are you?"

"Good, Harry, and you? You look cute. I've never been here in the private area."

"Well, thank you. So do you. I thought here would be best for us to talk about everything without anyone bothering us or eavesdropping."

"Yes, I agree. Excuse me?" She looked at Ana, who was inside the room putting an extra small table next to the one they were seated at. "Could I also have a beer, please? Thank you."

Ana brought her a beer and gave them menus to look through.

"Hey, Harry, do you want to order a bottle of white wine?"

"Sure, but you already know that I don't know much about wine."

"Leave that to me."

The room where they were both at a table for four wasn't too big, but for the two of them, it was perfect. It had a glass door with a sensor, so they were alone and had a guarantee of privacy at all times. The table had a button that, when pushed, notified the waiter to come, making it so the waiters didn't interrupt, except to bring food or drinks. Music with relaxing sounds softly played in the background, and the walls were painted white and navy blue with details of beaches, fishers, etc.—all sea related. Harry had never loved fish or seafood until he found that spot. Martha was the one who took him there for the first time when he was new to Murcia.

"Okay, Harry, before anything, the last time we saw each other was horrible. I said it then, but now with some time behind us, I'll say it again. I'm so sorry for what happened with Loretta. I'm sorry for what I did, and I regret it. It wasn't right. If we said that we wanted to try getting serious, what I did that night wasn't appropriate. I got carried away, and that isn't an excuse. But I can't be asking for forgiveness every ten minutes either. What I mean is that even though it was wrong, it's not like we were married or had a totally serious relationship. So, I need to know if you've forgiven me before going on, because I won't be going around downtown Murcia flogging myself with a whip." Sofia took a sip of her beer after saying this.

Harry responded:

"I've forgiven you, Sofia. I didn't like what happened and I'll try to forget it, but I've forgiven you. We all make mistakes, and all I know is I missed you and, despite what happened, I want to be with you. And that's not something I decided just because; it's how I feel, that's it. So, yes, I don't want you to flog yourself all throughout Murcia."

"I also missed you, if I'm being honest. Do you want to start over?" Sofia asked, placing her hand palm-up on the table.

"Yes, I do," Harry replied, laughing and taking her hand.

Sofia got up from the table, went towards Harry, and gave him a kiss.

Fantastic: a clean slate. Perhaps if this had happened to Alfonso or any other person, and they had asked him for advice, Harry probably would have advised them to be cautious and not trust her. But, in the end, it's one thing to say it and another thing to do it. And a lot of times Harry knew that they didn't have to coincide. Moreover, he frankly didn't care what other people thought. He didn't have to justify his decision to anyone, not even a bit.

Sofia also felt relieved. She felt that she had messed up, but she could ask for forgiveness and show remorse an infinite number of times. No one is perfect, and having truly regretted it, she had decided to love herself a bit and accept her actions. Whoever was with her would have to accept that that had happened and move on. It was up to her to promise that it wouldn't happen again, that's all. If Harry was willing to start over, great. And, if not, life goes on, as they tend to say; she would have messed up, end of story. In all honesty, she was happy that Harry was willing to start over. She was very happy.

Sofia sat back down.

"Hey, we should ask if they have a fresh appetizer today," Sofia suggested.

"Sounds great," Harry responded as he pressed the button.

Thirty seconds later, Ana showed up. They asked her for the fresh catch of the day as an appetizer and a bottle of Albariño to pair, which Sofia chose as a wine expert. As they waited, Sofia continued talking:

"So, I think, to start off on the right foot, we should be honest, don't you think? I'd also like to tell you everything that's happened these past few days."

Harry thought she was right, and that perhaps he should start being honest about his job. The Conglomerate didn't expressly demand you keep what your job entailed a secret. They understood that a proper mercenary or spy, as in any other job, performs better if they're happy. And hiding what they do from their partner is an element of added stress that can make the person eventually snap, or the relationship to end and the person snap. And if someone snaps, they become useless. That's why, at the beginning of the training, they said that there was total freedom to talk to their partner about the job, when they reached the point that they wanted to. Of course, if someone outside their partner or close family circle (adult children were the only exception) found out, apart from the immediate dismissal of the mercenary and the discrediting of all those involved, could lead to some terrible "accident" in extreme cases. When they explained that to you, they gave (supposedly) real examples of such accidents that had happened to people that had let their tongue slip in the past. This, combined with the generous pay from the Conglomerate, made the system function and kept anyone from talking about the job with people they shouldn't.

If the couple broke up at a given time, the person who wasn't the mercenary had to sign a lifelong confidentiality agreement (they called it "friends forever"). Otherwise, they risked being left with nothing legally, and who knows what illegally. The members and their partners also signed it when they retired from the Conglomerate. But as long as no one spoke, there was no issue at all.

It was prohibited to talk to any other family member about the subject; they made that plenty clear before the training. If there were people that wanted to quit then, they had the opportunity to leave, which many, in fact, did. If you stayed, you began the training.

Harry believed that Sofia was someone who could handle Harry being a mercenary and not some fake office Indiana Jones. But, damn, maybe it was too soon. "Listen, Sofia, I'm glad that we're giving each other another opportunity. By the way, I'm a mercenary and I just killed several jihadists. How was your English class today?"

He would tell her, but it was too soon; it wasn't the right time.

"Sounds good, Sofia. What happened these past few days?" Harry answered.

Sofia told him how the day after she had spoken to Loretta (she decided to omit the rest of the night with the cars since it wouldn't add anything) and how Loretta had left, as well as the whole week-end with her parents. She explained how she tried to see if she was okay through one of her friends on social media, but nothing. Harry didn't notice anything out of the ordinary in the story. Then, right when Ana brought them some fresh oysters and red shrimp that looked amazing, they got to the point where Sofia had received the call from the police on Sunday at noon. Sofia started from there, and after listening to her, Harry nearly choked on a shrimp.

# CHAPTER XIX

"Listen, Ms. Lombardi, you were at the police station last night reporting a missing person by the name of Loretta, according to what my colleague told me. Well, here's the situation: a lifeless body of a woman has just been found. I'm sorry to tell you this, but it fits the description of your friend that you gave. It doesn't have documentation, and since you said that her family lives abroad, could you come and identify the body, please?"

Sofia was speechless.

"Ma'am, are you there?"

She finally reacted:

"Yes, yes, sorry. Of course I'll go. Where is it?"

"At the Institute of Legal Medicine, next to Reina Sofia hospital."

"Okay. I'll be there. Officer?"

"Yes?"

"What happened? Did she suffer?"

"Don't worry about that, Ms. Lombardi. She didn't suffer. Please understand that I can't say anything else right now. I'll see you soon. Ask for Sergeant Augusto Gambín."

"Thank you, see you soon."

Sofia hung up and ran to her car. Was Loretta dead? How could that be? She was anxious to get answers, to say the least. She quickly got to the car and then to the morgue in record time. She walked into the entrance of the building where there was a security guard at a desk that served as reception. She said who she was, and that Sergeant Gambín expected her, and the guard informed his colleagues on the walkie talkie. A minute later, a person who Sofia assumed was Sergeant Augusto Gambín appeared at the door. He was a tall man of strong complexion with a beard, around forty-five to fifty years old. He shook Sofia's hand and asked her to come with him. After three or four minutes, which to Sofia seemed like three or four hours of walking through never-ending hallways, they got to a room with four exam tables covered with sheets, presumably with dead bodies underneath. The room was just like in the movies: cold, with metal door compartments, and tables with forensic instruments. There was one person in the room with a white lab coat, who Sofia imagined was the forensic doctor or perhaps an assistant, who waved at her.

"Are you ready? We can take however much time you need," the sergeant asked.

"I'm ready, sergeant. Let's get this over with, please," Sofia replied, thinking that if the sergeant didn't remove the sheet in five seconds, she would.

It wasn't necessary. He lowered the sheet, and the face of a young girl was exposed. Her eyes were closed, and anyone who didn't know might think that she was sleeping peacefully. Sofia felt sorry for her, but at the same time relief. It wasn't Loretta.

"It isn't her, sergeant. She looks a lot like her, but it's not her. I've never seen this poor girl in my life."

A slight grimace of displeasure appeared on the sergeant's face, almost unnoticeable. Not identifying the dead body meant that he still had work to do, and that it may take a while to identify the murderer and, by extension, catch him.

"Are you sure? Take a good look, please," the sergeant insisted.

"One hundred percent, sergeant. I've known Loretta for a while. It's not her. I'm sorry I couldn't be of help."

"Okay, then. I'm glad for you that it isn't your friend. I'll walk you out," the sergeant responded, opening the room door.

As they walked through the labyrinth of hallways in the morgue, Sofia asked the sergeant, "It's normal to feel relief, right?"

"You mean you're happy that it isn't your friend? Of course. What society considers correct is one thing, but reality is a different thing. And, unless we were hypocrites, we would all think the same. Better someone else's friend than mine. Don't feel bad about that."

"I mean, I feel sorry for that poor girl, but..."

"Don't explain yourself. I completely understand," the sergeant responded right when they got to the door that led to the reception.

Sofia wished him good luck, shook his hand, and walked out. When she left the building, she hoped to never have to return, at least not while being aware of it.

She got back to her car. She was happy. A moment prior, she thought she was about to die from anxiety, but the relief had now made her quite happy. She was still worried about Loretta, but at least the dead body she had just seen wasn't her, which wasn't nothing. She went home, ordered Chinese food for delivery, and lay down to take a nap. When she got up around 5 p.m., she saw a forty-two second voice message on her phone from an unknown number. She thought it might be Barbara, to whom she had given her number. She was right. The message was a bit difficult to hear because of the wind in the background, but it said the following:

*"Hey, it's Barbara. You gave me your number online. Look, Loretta told me to tell you that she doesn't want to hear from you anymore and to forget about her. And I prefer not to repeat what she told me to tell you because I don't know you and I have nothing against you. She says that she'll come to the apartment tomorrow with someone to get her things and that she'd prefer it if you weren't there. Please let me know if that's possible."*

Sofia texted back: "Okay, I won't be here tomorrow. And I'm changing the lock the day after. Goodbye."

Her anger started to overcome her. So, she was worried that something had happened to her, since she had missed work without calling, had to identify a fucking dead body to rule out that it wasn't her.... And now she had to forget about her forever?

Okay, then, no worries, because that's absolutely what she would do. Fucking bitch. Who the fuck did she think she was? She lit a cigarette as she stared into the distance. She only felt anger at that moment. Little by little, she started to relax as the cigarette burned down. She truly didn't expect this from Loretta. She didn't imagine her relationship with her would end like this. But life is ultimately a succession of sometimes unpredictable events that determine subsequent events, and so on and so forth. Not everything turns out the way you want, and it doesn't make sense to despair or hold grudges. Even though she felt angry, she had to consider that perhaps all of this was ultimately for the best. And perhaps in the future everything will change, and they can be friends again. No one knew.

In any case, she had no intention of being at home the next day. She preferred not to be in the same city as Loretta, not even in the same country. The further away, the better. In fact, that's what occurred to her to do.

Sofia's parents had a small apartment in London. Years ago, they had opened an important line of business in the United Kingdom, where they obtained very important clients. Consequently, they started traveling there often. Sofia remembered that as a little girl her father or mother (one of them always stayed with her; they never left her in the care of anyone else) made recurring trips to London. Since that situation went on for some time, and the business was going great, Francesco and Arianna decided to invest in an apartment in London when they saw a good opportunity. They found a good deal in Earl's Court: a small, two-floor apartment, of just six-hundred and fifty square feet, but enough to be considered a home they could go to after a day of work or a place to go to on a weekend or holiday to visit London and disconnect. Years ago, they used it plenty, but less so now. Francesco and Arianna had more and more meetings online, and though every now and then they went, it was more for pleasure than for work. And they hadn't been there since before the COVID-19 pandemic. The pandemic was what they needed to become less inclined, with age, to get on a plane.

They thought about selling the apartment, but Sofia convinced them not to, since they didn't need the money, and it was nice to have it. Sofia quite liked it because she had decorated it to her taste, and she also had keys and could go any time she wanted. She went from time to time, at least two or three times a year. In fact, the last time had been to spend a weekend with Loretta—such is life. The apartment had a cleaning service contracted by Sofia's parents that went in and ventilated the apartment every week they went there. If you notified twenty-four hours before going, they prepared it for your arrival; they cleaned everything, prepared the bed, and even bought whatever you wanted at the supermarket.

She saw online that there was a flight to London early the following morning at a good price. She bought it with a return flight for the day after. Then, she called the cleaning service, which was available seven days a week, and let them know that she was coming so that they would have everything ready for her. On Monday she would call the Language School and take a couple of personal days that she was entitled to by contract, and that would take care of that matter.

And that's what she did: she spent the day in London. She went around Harrods, ate at her favorite restaurant in Covent Garden, walked around Camden Town in the evening, and went back to the apartment to order Thai food for delivery and drink a beer she had asked for the day before. The following morning, she went back to Murcia. Then, later that day, she was having lunch at El Sirena restaurant with Harry, where she had just told him all this.

"What a story," Harry said with a face of shock.

"I know it seems like a TV show or something made up, but that's what happened," Sofia replied. "I'm sure that your antique dealer stories are more boring," she added, slightly joking.

"You have no idea," Harry responded. "But are you okay, then? All of this must have affected you. And it's obvious that you knew that girl for a while and shared things with her."

"Yeah, yeah, I'm okay. Hey, let's order something else, what do you think? I'm hungry."

"Yeah, sure, but don't change the subject on me."

"I'm not changing the subject. I'm hungry, damn. Let's order our main dishes and keep talking. Sound good? Plus, if we don't eat something else, we're going to end up like Las Grecas with this wine."

"What was that? End up like who?"

"Hahaha. It's an expression here in Spain. Some of my coworkers told me about it the other day and I thought it was funny. It means to be wasted. I think they were a couple of Spanish singers who apparently..., you can imagine," Sofia clarified, laughing at poor Harry.

"Las Grecas...." Harry sat there pensively. "And you said this knowing that I wouldn't know what you were talking about so you could laugh at me, right?"

Sofia blew him a kiss in a joking way.

Harry was also hungry, so he didn't put up any more resistance, though he made a mental note of the Las Grecas expression to look it up later. They both ordered the dish with the fresh catch of the day, following the recommendation that Ana gave them. It was one of the few situations in which Harry could trust people: at a restaurant. He knew that it benefitted the waiter to recommend something good. So, since she, in reality, knew more about food than he did, he usually let her choose. With the right incentives, people could indeed be trusted.

"Are you sure you're okay? You can tell me anything, don't worry," Harry insisted.

"Yes, I am, really. It was a shock to have to go identify a dead body that could have been Loretta, that's for sure. And then getting a message from a friend of hers telling me she didn't want to hear from me at all…. It was a rough Sunday, Harry, I won't lie to you," Sofia replied as she started to choke up. Harry grabbed her hand, then Sofia went on: "But there's nothing else I can do. There are things that are out of my control, like, for instance, how other people feel. The same thing I told you before. I can ask for forgiveness and be sorry, but that's it. If you're not willing, or if she isn't, in this case, I have to accept it. I'm not going to beg. Do whatever you want, end of story. So, I'm okay and I'm moving on. That's why we're here, right?"

"That's great, Sofia. Hey, here comes our food." Ana came to the table to give them their food, which smelled amazing to Harry.

"Enjoy," Ana said before leaving them, to which they both made a gesture of thanks in response, as was natural. The meal went on amid laughter. Sofia told him about her encounter with Alfonso the other night and the weekend with her parents, though she decided to omit the part about the invitation to the Tuscan villa and leave it for later. Harry told her stories about his birthplace of Arkansas, how his father had a motorcycle repair shop, but that he didn't like motorcycles at all. He also told her about the conversation from the other day with Carlos, the supposed movie producer, since he hadn't gotten to tell Sofia.

"But, this guy…, do you trust him?" Sofia asked. "I know that weird things happen to me, but a guy recruiting someone he sees on the street to be the star in a Star Wars-type movie filmed in Murcia?"

"I mean, I'm still not sure, to be honest. It sounds a little strange to me, but I'm not sure."

"Harry Fernández, come on, please. Are you sure it's not just cause you want it to be true?" Sofia asked in an ironic tone.

"Maybe. I'm not saying you're wrong. It would be nice, right?"

"I mean, it sounds fun, more fun than being an antique dealer," Sofia replied as she laughed.

They finished lunch, ate vanilla ice cream for dessert, and decided to stay a bit longer for a coffee and a drink. When Ana brought the drink, Harry asked, "Ana, we can smoke, right?"

"Yes, of course. No one else besides me is coming in here. I'll just open this window here a little for you guys. If you need anything, just press the button and I'll come."

"Thank you."

Sofia was amazed, as Harry smiled at her, took out a cigarette, and extended the pack to Sofia, who also took one. Ana left the room and closed the door behind her. Legally, smoking inside wasn't allowed in any restaurant in Spain for years. However, by being in a private room without anyone else at another table, and given that it didn't bother anyone, nor would anyone find out, Harry's request was granted. The generous tip that he always left certainly helped as well, of course.

"So, you haven't told me anything about your trip," Sofia inquired with a face of curiosity. "What kind of antique required you to go away for a few days with your whole team?"

Harry knew that moment of the date was coming, but, for some reason, it caught him by surprise. He figured that, given that the date was almost over, and the subject hadn't already come up, it wouldn't come up now. But it turned out it did, and now he had to figure out what to say. It was too early to tell her the truth. She may run away and, at the same time, be in possession of information that could be dangerous for her. But he knew that if things were serious, he would have to tell her at some point. And the less lies he told her now, the better. What to do, then? Tell her the truth? Tell her some made-up lie? Tell her half the truth?

"Hey, don't ignore me, Harry."

He had to say something, and fast.

"Well, Sofia, you see..."

# CHAPTER XX

"Well, Sofia, you see, we closed the deal with a buyer for the antique, and this buyer requested discretion and anonymity, not just about who he is, but also the antique itself. I can't tell you anything since we signed a confidentiality agreement. If I tell you, I'd be breaching it, even if you didn't tell anyone. And, if you let it slip out by chance, they would sue me for everything I've got plus the clothes on my back." Harry didn't like lying at all, but that's what came out. He would have time later to regret it. It was a temporary lie.

"Well, I don't want that to happen. I don't need you to get sued to see you without your clothes," Sofia replied.

Around 6:30, they asked for the check and split the bill (Harry left her a generous tip), then left the restaurant.

"Alright, Harry, I'm going to head home."

"Do you want me to come with you?"

"I want it, but I'd prefer it if we took things slow for now. Is that okay? Plus, I should get ready for a class tomorrow, even though I might do it tomorrow morning."

"Great, we'll talk tomorrow, then. I had a great time."

"Me too, Harry." Sofia went up to him, and they gave each other a kiss goodbye that reinforced that last statement.

"Bye, handsome."

"Bye, *bambina.*"

They went their separate ways from the entrance of El Sirena; Sofia started walking towards her car, while Harry went the other way to his apartment. Harry was exhausted, so on the way home he texted Alfonso to tell him that he was going home to relax and asked if they would meet up for lunch the next day, to which Alfonso immediately replied with, "Great, meet me somewhere in Plaza de las Flores. I'll call you when I leave work." Harry loved that about Alfonso: how easy it was to make plans with him. There were people who, to confirm or make plans with, seemingly had to first consult the Oracle of Delphi, check the alignment of the planets that day, or file a court order. Alfonso wasn't like that. If he couldn't, he couldn't, but if he was free, he would sign up for a bombing[20], as they say in Spain. And since Harry was a bit similar in that regard, they complimented each other well. He got home, and the exhaustion he already had multiplied two- or three-fold as soon as he lay down on the couch. Some sex would have certainly been nice, but who was he kidding? He wouldn't have traded his time on the couch then for nearly anything. He turned on the TV and looked for a movie. He selected shuffle mode because he didn't want to think about what movie to watch. He preferred to have the TV do it for him. The movie didn't matter much, as ten minutes later, Harry was sound asleep, snoring away, and wouldn't wake up until 5 a.m., by then Wednesday.

Sofia, for her part, was also tired. She had gotten up early to catch her return flight to London, and after being at the restaurant for so long, she didn't feel like preparing for her class the following day. But she liked her job and took it seriously, so she intended to prepare soon. She got home and checked if Loretta's things were gone. Her room was empty, apart from the bed and the mattress without its sheets, an empty closet, and a desk with a table and a chair. Given the circumstances, she couldn't trust anything at that point, so she

---

20 Translator's note: "He would sign up for a bombing" is the literal translation of the original *"se apuntaba a un bombardeo,"* a Spanish saying that implies that someone is always up to do anything.

opened her drawers to check that all her things were still there and that nothing important was missing. At first glance, that seemed to be the case, so she felt at ease.

She sat down to prepare for tomorrow's class, and in forty-five minutes, she had it ready. A couple of grammar activities and a group speaking exercise consisting of a debate about public transportation in the city of Murcia would be enough to fill the class time. And if time remained, she would do a round of questions or the trick of ending class five minutes early. Afterwards, she watched a bit of TV, spoke on the phone with her dad to tell her how the apartment in London was, ate something quick for dinner, then went to bed. Truth be told, she'd been wanting sex, so she masturbated in bed before going to sleep to satisfy herself. In any case, she thought she had done the right thing earlier by going home. If she wanted to start over and try for a serious relationship, she preferred to take it slowly and not run the risk of it becoming nothing more than a sexual relationship. Evidently, that didn't mean that she didn't have sexual needs to attend to, and that's what she had done. Fully satisfied, she slept the whole night.

It was five in the morning, and Harry was awake and activated, ready to go. What could he do? He wasn't that hungry, but he knew how to "fabricate" it. He put on an old Simpsons T-shirt and some shorts and went for a run. There was a path along the shore of the river near his apartment which people often used for running or biking—a nice spot. Perhaps it could use a few more trees, though there were some planted along the shore of the river. From time to time, you would cross paths with a duck, which Harry liked. Even though it was dark, Harry wasn't afraid. There was news of a girl that had been attacked once, or a junkie that had robbed a jogger who had gone out when it was still mostly dark, but Harry wasn't afraid of any of that. He had just carried out a mission where they had killed the most wanted terrorist in the world; he wouldn't worry now about getting robbed by a couple of dimwits while he did some exercise. Harry ran along the shore of the river for an hour with the light from the city streetlamps. He only came across a couple of brave souls like himself, no sign of junkies or rapists. He got back home around 6:30, showered, and was hungry by then, so he made himself his American breakfast, this time in massive proportions. The morning passed by with nothing remarkable occurring, spending most of it writing a small report recommending Melinda for the training program so that Martha would send it to the bigwigs of the Conglomerate. In the recommendation, though he of course didn't lie, he tried not to get Angela in trouble for having broken the protocol, and, consequently, not to get himself in trouble as the person in charge of FAI, since he was her direct superior. Although, on the other hand, if they fired him, he could avoid deciding whether to quit or not; they would make the decision for him. *"Harry, what the hell are you saying, man? If you want to leave, leave; don't wait for them to kick you out,"* he thought then. He indeed had to think long and hard about whether or not he wanted to quit, but he had to be a professional and a colleague until the end.

He finished it, sent it to Martha, and surfed the internet a bit until it was time to go. It was a cloudy day, but he decided not to bring an umbrella. He sat in one of the bars in the Plaza de las Flores and waited there for Alfonso, who showed up at the table ten minutes later.

"Man, Harry, it's been a while. What's up? How are you?"

"Great, man. I'm back."

"Yeah, you are. How was your trip?"

"Good, good. We closed a good deal, and the client was really happy."

"That's awesome, man. Hey, I wanted to talk about that movie you told me about."

"Yeah, that's what I wanted to talk to you about. What should we do about that? I personally still don't believe it's real."

"I mean, I don't know, Harry. Why don't you call the guy and see what he says? Tell him that we accept, and let's see what happens then."

"Should we accept it?"

"I mean, are you going to say no to filming a movie? And that type of movie, too? Fuck, man, you got to live a little." Alfonso raised his glass of beer, and Harry toasted with him, though with a look of not quite knowing what to do.

"I mean, I'm not a civil servant, Alfonso. I can't just ask for a leave of absence." Quite an awful excuse Harry had just given to his friend to avoid admitting that he was mentally out of sorts.

"You're right, Harry. I mean, I'm not really sure how I would do it either. But, anyways, if I'm an extra, I don't think I'd have to be filming for four months. I'm sure I could take a few days off. But if you're the star, you'd definitely have to figure something out."

"I know, that's what I'm saying."

"But if you want to, then do it, Harry. If not, you'll regret it forever. At the end of the day, work is kind of a necessary evil to try to live as good a life as possible. But if you really like something, or if it could be a once-in-a-lifetime experience, don't waste the opportunity. If it doesn't turn out well, you can always find another necessary evil after if you have to."

"Alfonso, did you suddenly turn into Nietzsche or something?"

"That was fucking awesome, wasn't it?" Alfonso responded as they both laughed.

However, after that moment of laughter, Harry realized that Alfonso was right, and he got to thinking about when he lived in the US and had a friend named Richard. Richard was a plumber and made quite a lot of money. His dream was to open a shop that specialized in music to sell concert tickets, instruments, records, objects from artists he would acquire at auctions, miscellaneous merchandise, in addition to importing records of less popular music from other countries to make it more popular. And, above all, to chat about music with whoever went to his store to ask him something or recommend bands, etc. To be a sort of "music advisor," so to speak. Internet competency didn't matter to him; making enough money to live was more than enough for him. It was the dream he wanted to fulfill to be happy. He tried to save a bit to get it underway, but one day while crossing the street, a drunk driver ran him over, and his dream and his life vanished. Harry, days after, reflected a lot and swore to himself that he would try to never let what happened to Richard happen to him. And right now, he was remembering that moment.

It's not like being an actor was his dream, but it was true that, if the opportunity presented itself, it didn't sound bad, especially keeping in mind that it could be an upgrade compared to the missions. It was less dangerous for his integrity and had the bonus of not having to kill people and lie to his girlfriend about it, which was no small thing.

"Alright, yeah. I'm going to call him and see what he tells me," Harry concluded. "After we eat, we'll grab a coffee at the café next door, and I'll make the call there.

"Awesome," Alfonso responded.

They ate, and, now at the café, the moment of truth arrived. Harry dialed the number that was on the card that Carlos had given him and put it on speaker so Alfonso could listen. They were at a table apart from the café, and no one else was there then.

The phone rang several times, but no one answered. Harry had a look of disappointment.

"Now what do we...." Before Harry could finish his sentence, his phone rang. The number he had called was returning the call. Harry picked up with the speaker on:

"Hello? I got a missed call from this number. Who is this?" a voice asked from the other end of the phone.

"Hey, Carlos? It's Harry. Do you remember me?"

"Ah, Harry Fernández, right? Yeah, man, of course I do. You're calling about the movie, aren't you?"

"Yes, I am. I wanted to tell you that, on paper, it sounds good, but I want to know more."

"Well, look, here's what's going on. Since we talked last week, we've had some issues with a few things, some permit from the government. My director is also giving me the roundabout.... Anyways, some bullshit that isn't relevant." Carlos spoke quite fast, but they could understand him. "So, everything is going to get delayed, including the casting with the audition you'd have to do. I'm—well, my team and I are working to speed everything up, but to be honest, casting is the least of my worries right now, Harry."

Harry looked disappointed. He had already started imagining taking his first steps as an actor, then suddenly it seemed as if the world was telling him, "Stay in your lane." He wasn't quite sure what to say, so, after a few seconds of silence, Carlos started talking again:

"Look, I'm sorry, really, but this is still on the table, okay? Here's what we'll do. Next week or the week after, at the latest, I expect to have everything all sorted out. This is your number, right? At the beginning of June, the first or the second, at the latest, I'll give you a call, sound good? Then we'll figure it out. But this is still on the table, Harry. It'll move forward as sure as my name is Carlos Timoteo."

"Carlos Timoteo?" Harry asked.

"Good, I see you're still there, since you didn't say anything..., you made me have to turn to telling you my last name so you would say something. You're a tough dude, Harry," Carlos responded in a playful tone.

"Ah, sorry. To be honest, I was kind of crushed at first. But yes, okay, let's do as you say. Sounds good. We'll talk in June."

"Great, Harry. Let's plan on that."

"Thanks, Carlos."

"Thank *you*. Talk later." And the conversation ended.

"Now what, Alfonso?" Harry couldn't hide the disappointment in his voice.

"Well, another week of you not becoming famous, Harry. That's all. Don't worry, man," Alfonso replied as he paused to take a sip of his coffee, then continued. "Look, that's how these things are. There might be delays. Or maybe he's a scammer or a con artist, I don't know. But the worst that could happen is that you go on as normal. I mean, with your job, Sofia…. It's not like it's that bad, right? Plus, you can always consider doing other things, man. The movie thing is cool, but, if it doesn't work out, start an online business, open a blog about whatever, learn to play guitar…. There are tons of things."

Alfonso was right. He had to think about what to do. If he was tired of putting his life on the line and wanted to quit, he would have to look for a "hobby." It wasn't a question of money, so he wouldn't do just anything for work; he would do something he liked. Or perhaps he was still stressed from the last mission, and in a few days, it would disappear, and he would continue on at FAI for longer. At any rate, the week off would be good for him to think.

That night, Sofia went to Harry's place to have some pizza for dinner and watch a movie. During dinner, Harry told her he would go away for the rest of the week to relax and think, after telling her about the call with Carlos. With money not being a problem, that evening he had reserved a room in a hotel with a spa in the Alps for the following day. They watched the first ten minutes of the movie, given that lust had taken hold of both of them, and they had no desire to contain it.

They spent the night together. Sofia left the next day, and Harry left for the airport mid-morning. He spent his time until that Sunday between the spa, the terraces of the resort complex looking at the mountains, the jacuzzi in his suite, morning jogs, and in-room massages. His only contact with the external world was a call he made to Sofia on Friday. He had a bunch of messages on his phone, but he ignored all of them. From what he did see, they had apparently already given the tip-off to the authorities about Abdul's death, and all the news agencies and international media had picked it up. If it was on BBC news, which he had glimpsed on Thursday night when he had dinner in the hotel bar, then the information was already in circulation.

And with the mission complete, and once Martha had informed the Conglomerate so that they, in turn, informed the client, an anonymous message would have been left to the local police in the area. Harry didn't know the details, but it was probably something innocent: "There's a strange smell coming from the property in the area, and no one is answering the door. Can you check it out?" And they would hang up. A couple of local police officers would go and see that it was true, and then they would go in and see why.

Harry, in any case, didn't pay much attention to the report. He had gone to disconnect, and that's precisely what he would do. Thus, that day he finished his dinner and went to his room to have some whiskey from the minibar and watch a movie so he wouldn't have to think too much. He went back home on Sunday recharged, as they say, but still without any clarity about his future. He decided to continue with the flow of his life a little longer to see where it would lead.

The following month and a half went by without anything special happening. They had a week of training at FAI on new technology that the Conglomerate was incorporating into the team—specifically, drones with certain artificial intelligence, and some sort of highly effective "truth serum." Apart from that, just a couple of missions of little importance, covering expenses and not much else. It was a calm period.

Carlos didn't call, and Harry didn't worry about calling him either. The most likely case was that he was a charlatan, a con, and whatever he had planned fell apart. Harry decided to forget the matter entirely. Alfonso didn't insist either, as he knew Harry and probably thought that it wasn't worth it to give his friend false hope. Harry, meanwhile, continued on with his job without making any decision about his future. That period for Harry was a bit apathetic in his professional life.

His relationship with Sofia continued its course, the normal course of a relationship. They would meet up, go to the movies, have lunch, dinner, have regular sex.... They even spent a weekend together at a beach resort. They were both quite happy and well. They still lived in their apartments for the time being. Sofia had decided not to look for a roommate and would take on the extra expense. She didn't want to bring strangers in at that point, and money wasn't a problem for her either. Her salary was good, but what she received every month from the family business without having to do anything granted her certain luxuries. And, though she had always tried not to touch that money and live off what she made herself, at that point, she decided that, if she was lucky enough to have that financial benefit, she would take advantage of it. It's not as though she had made a vow of poverty or was guilty of the evils of the world.

On Thursday, July 15th, they ordered some food for dinner, and as they ate at Sofia's place, she told Harry about the invitation to the Tuscan villa for her mother's birthday. Truth be told, she was sure that Harry would say yes, but ninety-nine percent sure. When he received Sofia's verbal invitation, Harry was interested in knowing more about the Tuscan villa and loved the idea, but he couldn't help but feel bad. He felt that their relationship was taking a significant step then, as it meant meeting his partner's parents and spending an entire birthday weekend with them. And, if he was taking that step, perhaps the moment had come to tell Sofia the truth about his work, and that she had the right to decide whether she wanted to move forward or not.

"Okay, Sofia, listen carefully. I haven't been honest with you about my job up until now. But seeing that our relationship is moving forward, I'm going to tell you exactly what my job is before we take any more steps. If you want me to leave after hearing this, I'd understand," Harry said.

He told her everything, as Sofia was left astonished.

# CHAPTER XXI

Harry told her what he did for work, from when he started in the US to what he did now at FAI. Of course, before doing so, he warned her that she couldn't talk about it with anyone else, and that if she wasn't willing to do that, he couldn't tell her anything, to which Sofia accepted.

"Well, that's everything. I know it's hard to believe, but it's the truth." Sofia didn't say anything, so Harry got up. "If you want me to leave, I'd understand."

Sofia got up as well.

"Where do you think you're going? Don't move. Let me see if I got this right," she said as she got closer to him. Then, she put her arms around him and said, "So, my boyfriend is some sort of tough guy who goes around selling himself to the highest bidder, huh?"

"Something like that. Are you okay with that? It doesn't worry you?"

"Didn't you say you don't kill innocent people?"

"No, never, but…"

"With that in mind, if it's your work, you like it, and you make money, why would I worry? Who am I to lecture anyone or tell them what they should do or what job they should have?" Sofia responded, interrupting him.

Harry stood there in thought for a couple of seconds, then Sofia said, "We all have skeletons in the closet."

"Yeah, but mine are real."

"You think too much, Harry Fernández. There's nothing wrong with what you guys do. Sometimes, you guys even make the world better by getting rid of terrorists from it." Then, she whispered in his ear, "Plus, it's actually pretty hot. Fuck me, Harry." She started kissing him on the neck.

Harry was taken aback for a second as he didn't expect that reaction, but it was nothing more than that—a second. Then, he surrendered to the moment with a smile from ear to ear and ripped off Sofia's shirt, breaking several buttons, as they went to the bedroom.

After sex, Sofia fell asleep immediately. Harry stayed in bed thinking for a bit longer. Truth be told, their dinner hadn't at all gone as he had initially thought; he had been invited to meet his girlfriend's parents at a luxurious villa in Tuscany for a weekend, he had revealed to Sofia what he did for work, and, the most surprising of all, she hadn't told him to go back where he came from, but rather, she was okay with everything—more than okay, even, except for her shirt that he had ripped to shreds, which she probably wouldn't be as okay with once she saw it. In any case, he would buy her a new one, problem solved.

*"Harry, listen to Sofia for once and stop thinking, man. It went well—end of story,"* his inner voice told him then. It was true. It was already over with and had gone well. Harry fell asleep.

The following morning, Sofia woke up early, while Harry still snored away next to her, sleeping like a log. She lay there for a bit, looking at the ceiling as she thought about what had been revealed to her last night. Evidently, she didn't imagine that when she proposed the trip to Tuscany for him to meet her parents, her boyfriend's response would be, *"Yeah, sounds great. But before anything, you should know that I'm actually a mercenary and I carry out missions robbing, kidnapping, torturing, and killing people. Do you want some more wine, babe?"*

She had been left in shock and even thought it was a joke at one point. But seeing that it was true and that, knowing Harry, it was likely a moment of high stress for him, she decided to ease the tension and not make a huge deal about it. In fact, for her, it really wasn't a huge deal. She knew Harry well and that he was a good person. So, what, he killed a few scum bags? Great, there were fewer left in this world. As long as he was happy and at peace with himself and his work, who was she to judge what he did? Today, people are quite prone to constantly judge others. That wasn't the case with her at all, and she had no intention to start judging her boyfriend. For her, it was good enough that he swore he didn't kill innocent people. Plus, as she had said, she didn't have a perfect record either.

She perfectly understood why he hadn't told her about it before. It wasn't something to reveal on the first date, nor on the second, either. And he had done it right when some time had already gone by in the relationship and before taking an important step, which meant that he was sure and resolute about moving forward with the relationship in a serious way.

Harry woke up shortly after, at 8 a.m.

"Shit, I'm late," he exclaimed as he jumped out of bed.

"Do you have a spy meeting today?" Sofia asked from the bed.

"Sofia, please, don't joke about that. You could let it slip anywhere. Please, promise me," Harry said very seriously.

Sofia saw the serious expression on Harry's face and replied:

"Okay, sorry, you're right. But only if you buy me a new shirt, Mr. Tough Guy."

For a moment, Harry thought that it may have been a mistake to tell Sofia. If she didn't take it seriously, she could cause him problems. But what's done is done; there was no turning back. He hoped he wouldn't regret it. He smiled at Sofia's comment about the shirt and gave her a thumbs up.

"I don't have time for breakfast," Harry said as he got out of the shower. "We'll talk later, okay?"

He said goodbye to Sofia and left. He got to work at record time (luckily, he had a couple of changes of clothes at Sofia's apartment, so he didn't have to stop at his place), greeted Pepe, who said that they were waiting for him as Harry ran upstairs. *"As if I didn't know,"* Harry thought as he got to the third floor. It was an important day. Martha, who they hadn't seen since the Abdul Akhbar mission, had called for a meeting, which meant that something was going on.

He opened the door to the third floor where Martha, Angela, and Piotr were there waiting.

"You're late," Martha said.

"It's good to see you too, Martha. How are you? You look thinner," Harry replied as he smiled.

"You're late."

"I know. I'm sorry."

"Sit down."

Harry sat down, greeted Angela and Piotr with a look, who returned the gesture, then Martha started to speak.

"You guys remember Melinda, right? Well, with our recommendations, she started the training with the Conglomerate a few days after we finished the mission in Almería, and it seems like she's doing pretty well despite the short time she's been there. So, I've been asked to make one of you her mentor before she starts working on the ground, and I recommended Angela," she said, looking directly at her. "Given the trust you built in her and your excellent skillset, I think you're the right person. All this despite your disrespect for the protocol, a behavior that will, without a doubt, be corrected soon, right?"

"Yes, Martha, don't worry. It'll be an honor for me to serve as Melinda's mentor," Angela responded.

"Good. All set, then," Martha continued. "Tomorrow afternoon you'll take a flight to New York where you'll be taken to the training center where Melinda is. You'll be there for three months. Afterwards, we'll talk, but you can come back here if you'd like to."

Harry knew that Angela would be a great mentor. And perhaps this was what she needed to fully mature. It was a good decision all around, though he was upset that he couldn't have her on the team. She was a fundamental member.

"Congratulations, Angela. You deserve it. You'll make Melinda a fantastic mercenary." Harry got up and gave Angela a hug. "So, then, Martha, will it just be me and Piotr left?" Harry added, guessing what the response would be.

"No, that's another thing I wanted to tell you guys. I've asked and been granted to officially come back as a field agent. And I'll be here with you guys tentatively in Angela's absence if that sounds good to you."

"What if it doesn't sound good?"

"Well, Harry, it doesn't matter; I'll be here either way." It was a fancy way of saying, "*Don't be a jerk, come on.*"

"That's the Martha I know, yessir," Harry exclaimed as he laughed, getting a laugh from the others as well.

"Well, then, dinner and drinks tonight, on me," Angela said. "I won't take no as an answer. I'll go home to pack my bags and then text you guys with a time and a place, sound good?"

Everyone agreed, and Angela went home, seemingly quite happy. They had a small mission to do that day. Angela wouldn't participate, so Harry thought it could be a good opportunity for Martha to make a "debut." So, Martha explained the mission, and Harry replied:

"Is it okay with you if you do it, and we observe you? That way you can start getting back in the swing of things."

"Sure, Harry. What you say goes; you're the team leader. In fact, the missions will come to you from now on. I'm at your service. However, if you're okay with it, since I have contact with the higher ups, I'll still do the mission reports," Martha responded.

Harry loved hearing that, so he agreed. He had no particular interest in doing bureaucratic work. Regarding Martha's compliance, he didn't expect anything else. She had already demonstrated during the Almería mission that she respected the chain of command and, above all, Harry.

The mission itself was nothing complex. A man in Cartagena[21] had proposed to his girlfriend, and she had accepted. A couple of months later, he found out that she was cheating on him and cut off the engagement, but asked her to return the ring, to which she said she wouldn't return anything. The ring had diamonds worth twenty thousand euros, so her fiancée wasn't willing to lose it like that, and he didn't want to follow the slow and torturous legal path, which also didn't ensure that he would get it back. The mission consisted of recovering the ring and returning it to its buyer. One of the easy missions—six thousand euros for very little work. They went to Cartagena by car and arrived around 11 a.m. The woman with the ring always had breakfast at a café around 11:30. Martha posed as a customer and waited as she drank a coffee, while Piotr and Harry waited outside in the car near the café. They alerted Martha when they saw the woman with the ring appear. The only thing that Martha had to do was follow her into the bathroom when she went, wait for her to come out, put her back inside, hold her at knifepoint, and force her to give her the ring.

When she gave it to her, Martha said:

"I recommend you don't say anything to anyone about this. If you don't say anything, nothing will happen to you or anyone around you; that's a promise. I only want the ring. However, if you say something, you'll regret it. Got it, Rebeca?"

"How do you know my name?" Rebeca said, sobbing.

"Got it, Rebeca?" Martha repeated. Rebeca nodded her head. "Good. Now, when I leave, lock the stall and count to thirty, and then leave. And then you can enjoy your breakfast. Don't worry, nothing will happen to you," Martha declared.

Martha walked out of the restaurant, got in the car, and they went back to Murcia. Mission accomplished. Martha had shown that she hadn't forgotten how to be a field agent since Almería, though Harry didn't have any doubt about that.

---

21  Port city in the southeast of Spain, about thirty miles south of Murcia.

He was truly happy to have Martha on the team in a more permanent role. The Almería mission would hardly have been carried out successfully without her, both for her ideas and her performance on the ground. Perhaps having Martha on the team would make her consider staying at FAI longer. They complemented each other well.

They got a text from Angela with the address of the place for dinner, a restaurant in downtown Murcia that Harry had never been to: El Gigante. They got to Murcia and planned on meeting at the restaurant at 8 p.m. On the way home, Harry called Sofia.

"Hey, I'm done work for the day. How are you?"

"Wow, what a nice life. That's great. How was the meeting?"

"Good. Angela is leaving tomorrow for a few months for a job she got assigned to and she's inviting us for dinner and drinks tonight."

"Okay, cool. I'll see if I can also meet up with some coworkers for dinner, since it's Friday."

"Wait, Sofia, do you want to stop by El Gigante around 8:30 or so? I can introduce you to my colleagues."

"Really? Of course."

Harry had talked to her about all of them when he told her about his work. He hadn't gone into detail about the mission or anything specific, but it was only natural that he told her about who he worked with. It wouldn't hurt for her to meet them in person. In fact, he knew Martha's husband Tom, for example. He was a friendly guy, director of marketing at a vegetable export company in Murcia, who had been living there for more than fifteen years. Martha had introduced him to Harry in El Paso, and they had run into each other three or four times since then, though still not in Murcia, interestingly enough.

"Great, then I'll see you then, *bambina*."

"Okay, handsome. *Ciao*."

Harry ate lunch at Chema, then went back home to rest. He spent the entire afternoon reading. At 8 p.m., he was at El Gigante, on time as always. He asked for the table reserved under Angela, then they took him to a private room in the restaurant. He was the first one to get there, but a few minutes later Piotr, Martha, and Angela arrived.

"Looking great, ladies" Harry said. "And you look handsome yourself," he added, looking at Piotr, who laughed and gave him a friendly jab on the shoulder.

Indeed, they were quite well dressed. Martha had on a short, light green dress with a round neckline, with a matching handbag of the same color, and white heels. Angela, for her part, was wearing a short-sleeved black top with an asymmetrical neckline, and a matching dark miniskirt. And Piotr had dark jeans, a white dress shirt, and a navy-blue blazer. Harry didn't like dressing up much, but for this occasion, since it was a special one, he had put on a purple dress shirt with matching chinos.

"Thanks, Harry. Good thing you don't lie," Martha replied, as everyone laughed.

"Hey, Angela, I told Sofia to stop by here soon to say hi; that way I can introduce you to her before you leave, if you don't mind," Harry inquired.

"Great, Harry, of course. She should stay for dinner if she wants to. We'd love to get to know her," Angela responded.

At 8:30, Sofia texted Harry that she was at the entrance, and Harry told her to come to the private room. Sofia showed up a minute later and introduced herself to everyone. Everyone greeted her and insisted that she stay for dinner.

"Come on, stay. You're invited," Angela said.

"Thank you, really, but I'm meeting up with some friends."

"Okay, then, but come for a drink afterwards. I reserved a booth at the Lobo Marrón for eleven o'clock."

"Yeah, come for some drinks later. We'll give you the dirt on Harry," Piotr insisted.

"In that case, I'll definitely come by later," Sofia responded.

"Hey, I'm right here; plus, I'm the boss," Harry said as everyone laughed. "You see the respect these fuckers have for me?" he asked Sofia as he laughed as well.

"Well, it was great meeting you all. I'll come by later. Thank you guys," Sofia said before she left.

As soon as she left the room, Angela said, "I really like her, Harry. She's so nice."

"Yeah, she is. I'm glad you guys like her."

"I'm really happy for you, Harry," Martha said as she poured some wine in her glass, then added, "A toast to Angela. FAI will miss you."

Everyone toasted, then Angela got up from her chair and said, "Thanks, Martha. Thanks to all of you for coming. I know that some of us haven't known each other for too long, others do, but for me, you guys are like family. We've shared heavy moments, and that creates a tie that's really hard to understand from the outside. I don't want to talk a lot because I don't want to cry right off the bat." A tear fell down her cheek. "So, I'll just say that this isn't 'goodbye'; it's 'until next time.' Now, let's enjoy the damn night."

Everyone clapped, then the food started coming in right after. Dinner went quite well. Everyone liked the food, the wine and beer flowed freely, and the conversations revolved around anecdotes from the missions they had done together over those past few months. What struck Harry the most was when Angela talked about how she had a boyfriend in college who wanted to be a professional RPG[22] player, but whose parents made him study computer science "in case his plan didn't work out—to have a plan B." He was the one who told her one day about a group of mercenaries through a friend of a friend who had hired them for a job. At first, Ángela thought it was one of his RPGs that he usually made up and that he was crazy, but it piqued her curiosity. Then, when she finished college and her PhD

---

22 Translator's note: Role-playing game.

(and her relationship with that guy, incidentally), unsure about what to do, she decided to get in touch with them.

"I had to call that ex, ask him for his friend's number, and that friend told me to go to the north park on campus at 7 p.m. and sit on the third bench to the left. He couldn't tell me anything else. At that point I didn't know if it was a movie or something, but I went. I sat down where he told me to, and a girl who was jogging came up and sat on the same bench to rest. I remember she said, 'Are you here for any particular reason or are you just hanging out?' I told her that I was told to sit there if I wanted to talk to a group of elites and try to join them. She said she didn't know what I was talking about and left. I sat there for another hour, and no one else showed up. I went home, and the next morning they called me and said to go to a particular street and get in a blue van that would be parked there. I kept wondering if it was a joke or a movie or something, but me being me, I went. And, well, I talked to a recruiter who already had all my information, and now, here I am, my friends. Damn, finally, I could tell that story—what a relief." Everyone laughed. "Man, I've had to make up so many lies when telling people about my job."

Angela paid the bill, and then around eleven they went to the booth they had reserved at the Lobo Marrón. The booth (in reality, it wasn't exactly a booth, but an area elevated four steps above the floor) was quite nice in Harry's opinion. There was a security guard there so that no one who wasn't invited by the members of the group would come up, and a restroom exclusively for the booth. They let a waiter know to bring the drinks. The rest of the bar was visible from up there, and the same music played. Around 11:30, after having a glass of champagne that they gave the booth as a "welcome gift", Harry went out to smoke alongside Martha.

"How's Tom?" Harry asked, initiating the conversation.

"Tom left, Harry. He left last month."

"He left? What do you mean?" Harry asked, intrigued.

"He left home with his secretary."

"What the…That son of a…"

"I don't blame him, Harry."

"Can I ask what happened?"

"Well, he says that I stopped being married to him a long time ago and that I was married to work. It's true that I've been traveling a lot this past year, and when I was home, I thought about work. He told me that several times, but I didn't pay attention," Martha explained as she finished her cigarette.

"Damn. I'm sorry, Martha."

"I guess that his new secretary showing up a few months ago, who's twenty years younger than me, was what made him ultimately decide," Martha went on in an ironic tone. Harry didn't know what to say. He didn't expect that his cigarette break and innocent and trivial question would turn into a whole drama. "It doesn't matter, Harry, whether he cheated on me or not, but Tom does have a point in what he told me. It's too late for me now, Harry, but let me give you some advice. Don't let this job take up all your mental space, or you'll regret it, truly. Should we go back in?"

Harry nodded, then they both went back to the booth. Harry was left a bit astonished at what Martha had told him, but he tried not to think about it then. Around 12:15, Sofia showed up with a couple of coworkers. Angela brought them up to the booth, and Sofia introduced her coworkers, Martín and Luis. Sofia told them that her boyfriend and his colleagues were high-end antique dealers who searched, bought, and sold antiques across the world. They both found it quite interesting. They both bought a round of drinks for everyone to thank them for letting them in the booth without having known them, which started them off on the right foot. They were all laughing and chatting until around 1:30 in the morning. Martha had hit it off with Luis that night, and they both said goodbye and left at that time. Sofia told Harry that Luis had recently become single and was in the mood to have some fun. *Well, he'll do just that,* Harry thought. Martín left ten minutes later, leaving Piotr, Angela, Sofia, and Harry. They ordered another round, and after they finished, Harry and Sofia said they were heading out. Harry gave Angela a warm goodbye.

"Angela, it's been a pleasure to have you on the team. I want you to know that if I was ever mean to you, it wasn't anything personal, it was for your own good, and that I think you're an excellent agent and you'll do great as a mentor. And I really hope you come back."

"Thank you, Harry. I know. You were the best boss I could have ever had. Of course I'll come back."

"Tell Melinda I say hi and that I hope to see her too. And thank you for tonight."

"Will do. Thank you for coming." Right after, she added, whispering in his ear, "And take care of this girl."

They left the bar, at that point quite tired and with a substantial amount of alcohol in them. In a display of clarity, they thought it would be best for Sofia to stay the night at Harry's, since it wasn't worth it to get a taxi at that point, much less for her to drive in that state.

Along the way, they laughed as they talked about Martha and Luis, and Harry told her that the two who had gone out for some fun would of course end up together, given their recent events.

"Shit, good for them," Harry said.

"Of course," Sofia replied. They were approaching the entrance to Harry's building when she added, "Hey, I enjoyed meeting your fellow mercenaries. They're good people, and fun. Next time, you'll have to come out with my coworkers.

"Of course. It's a plan."

Harry opened the door, and they went inside the apartment. Sofia fell asleep right as she got in bed. It took Harry a few more minutes. Up until that moment, he had been thinking about the advice that Martha had given him. He thought that she was completely right, though it was also true that it didn't have to happen to him. Before work destroyed his personal life, he would leave it. At least that's what Harry thought then.

# CHAPTER XXII

Harry's phone went off at six in the morning—an urgent notice from FAI with the message "luggage." "*No fucking way*," Harry thought, with his massive hangover. It was as if a dozen hammers were hitting his head all at the same time. He got up and had to lie back down for a few seconds because of the dizziness he had. Then, once he could finally get up, he packed as best as he could and woke Sofia up.

"I have to go. I'll be gone for a few days."

"What? What do you mean?" Sofia responded with her eyes closed.

"Yeah, I don't know when I'll be back. I'll let you know as soon as I know. Go back to sleep. I'll leave you a pair of keys here so you can lock up when you leave. Bye." Harry gave her a kiss and then left.

"Harry, be careful, okay? I love you," Sofia said from the bed.

Harry stopped dead in his tracks and turned around.

"I will. I love you too." Then, he left.

"*Damn, what just happened? This is serious now, Harry*," he said to himself as he went downstairs and ordered a taxi on his phone. He could walk, but he didn't want to with his suitcase, not to mention that he wasn't in the best physical state to do so.

He arrived at the FAI offices, and Martha and Piotr were already there. They both seemed to be in a particularly good mood for how early it was and having gone out the night before. "*They must have had a good end to the night*," Harry thought.

"Good morning. What well-timed mission do we have, Martha?" Harry greeted them without much enthusiasm.

"No clue. I already told you that you'll receive the missions now," Martha answered as she shrugged her shoulders. "But I hope it's worth it, cause I had to kick out the hot guy I was hooking up with before morning sex."

"Thanks for the information, Martha," Harry responded with a smile, as Piotr laughed.

Ten minutes later, as they were finishing their coffee, Harry got a text that he read out loud: "Go to the airport, private terminal. You guys have a flight to Amsterdam waiting. We'll inform you on the plane."

They grabbed the keys to a vehicle and went to the airport. The airport wasn't too far, and at that time on a Saturday, there was no traffic, so they got there within twenty minutes. They parked and went to the private terminal where there was a small plane with its doors open and the engine on. A guy with a yellow vest was waiting on the runway. As soon as he saw them, he gestured with his hand for them to board the plane. They quickly boarded the plane where the pilot was waiting for them.

"Good morning. You three are the ones they told me about, right? Alright, well, we're going to Amsterdam. Take a seat and put on your seatbelts. There's no on-board service. You guys have a fridge in the back and a coffee maker. Grab whatever you want. We'll leave in five minutes," the pilot said as he closed the doors as Harry walked in, who was the last to enter. "Ah, I'm Captain Castaño and I'll be your pilot. If you need anything, press the intercom on the tables; otherwise, I won't be able to hear you. And when the seatbelt lights are on, everyone fasten their seatbelts. Any questions?"

Everyone shook their heads no, then Captain Castaño went into the cabin and left the three FAI members alone in the plane.

Harry wondered what type of mission it would be that they chartered a private plane for to leave as soon as possible. Moreover, at first sight, it was the best plane he had ever been on as far as comfort went. It had two rows of couches instead of seats, one across from the other, with an aisle in the middle, a restroom in the back, and the fridge and the coffee maker that the pilot had mentioned. The couches had arms that could be raised and some small foldable tables on them, like the ones on school desks.

"Come on, Harry, it's not like this is Air Force One. Sit down, man," Martha said when she saw that Harry was somewhat amazed.

"Have you been in Air Force One, by chance?" Harry responded as he sat down and fastened his seatbelt.

"One day, I'll tell you the story," Martha replied with a smile.

They quickly took off, and as soon as they could, they all got up to go to the coffee machine.

"These coffee capsules are like water," Piotr said as he grabbed his. "I'm going to have to make fifteen of these for it to have an effect on me."

"Alright, guys, I think the mission briefing has arrived. Shall we take a look?" Martha suggested as she sat on a couch and took out her tablet. Harry and Piotr did the same, as an instructional message started playing on their devices with a gallery of images regarding the mission. The explanation lasted about ten minutes. Apparently, the great-granddaughter of an old German Nazi general named Tess lived on the outskirts of Amsterdam, born Dutch and now without the German surname of her great-grandfather. She had been discovered by accident by the nephew of Jewish survivors from the Second World War named Hans. After looking at Tess's social media profile, he saw in a few of her pictures some paintings that his father had often talked to him about in the living room of her villa. Tess, even though she was Dutch, spoke German quite fluently and liked to practice it on social media by talking to people from Germany. And Hans liked to meet girls from other countries, so a group called "Non-Germans in German" was tempting for him. And while looking at the profiles of the members (female members to be exact), he came across a surprise. In one of the girls' living rooms, there were some paintings identical to the ones from the old photographs that his father had shown him. He investigated a bit on social media, checking the information and the dates that she had posted, and everything fit.

Upon realizing this, Hans contacted the Conglomerate. He did quite well financially in life, so money wasn't an issue. He wanted to recover his family paintings and knew that going to the authorities could turn into an exasperating and perhaps useless labyrinth. Moreover, he didn't know what Tess's reaction might be; she could very well destroy the paintings instead of returning them to a Jewish dog or hide them never to be found again. So, he decided to turn to professionals to carefully remove the paintings and make sure by any means necessary that Tess would keep her mouth shut about it.

After the Conglomerate's investigations, they had the location of Tess's villa and all the information on her routine. Initially, it was a mission for the Cork section, but since they were at full capacity, they had subcontracted between divisions and ultimately concluded that FAI was the best option. It was a good mission—Hans would pay some eight hundred thousand euros—so the airfare wasn't a huge problem.

"So? It doesn't seem like an overly complex mission, right?" Harry asked his colleagues.

"On paper, no. A thirty-something-year-old woman who lives alone in a villa, single and childless—it won't be very hard to subdue her and persuade her to let us take her paintings," Martha replied.

"It seems too easy," Piotr contributed to the conversation as he continued looking over the file on Tess. "Here it says that the villa has an alarm that's always activated. We can try to deactivate it, but I'd need time to study it," he concluded.

"Or we can do what we did in Almería and have the door unlocked for us, which would be quicker and get us home sooner," Martha responded.

"True. Look at page eighteen in the dossier," Piotr exclaimed.

Harry went to page eighteen of the document and began reading to himself. *"She usually plays badminton once a week in the city and goes by bike. She likes to go to various coffee shops[23] in the area, but there's no record of her consuming drugs. She usually meets with a couple of friends a couple times per week, Julia and Lily. On Saturday nights, she normally calls a gigolo service, and two of them always go to the villa and stay the whole night, then leave in the morning..."*

Harry stopped reading. "No, no fucking way," Harry said.

"Wait, I'm sorry, should I remind you what I had to do in Almería? What's wrong? Just cause you're a guy and you have a girlfriend you can't pose as a gigolo to get in that nazi's house?" Martha responded, furious.

"Harry, she's right. And it's the best way to get in without drawing the neighbors' attention," Piotr concluded the conversation.

Harry remained silent for a few seconds. He didn't at all like the idea of having to act as a gigolo. He didn't care if he had to shoot the nazi, but acting as a prostitute.... Although, on the other hand, if it was just to have an excuse to enter the house, it wouldn't be that big of a deal.

"Well, in reality, it's only to get in, right?" he said a bit timidly.

"And if you have to do something inside, what then?" Martha asked menacingly.

Martha was right. *"Damn, Harry, don't be a jerk. She had to suck a terrorist's dick, and here you are with this bullshit,"* his internal voice said. Indeed, he had never had to turn to doing anything sexual in any mission. Perhaps that's why he didn't feel comfortable. Plus,

---

23  Translator's note: "Coffee shop" in Amsterdam refers to an establishment where you can buy and consume marihuana—as well as coffee and other food and non-alcoholic drinks—hence the mention of drugs right after. In Spanish, they use the English "coffee shop" which carries this connotation.

he had just told his girlfriend that he loved her, so now the thought of being a gigolo made him squirm, even though it would only be a front. But that's how this job was. The mission was above everything else. He most definitely wanted to quit at that moment more than ever. But whether he quit or not, the mission had to be done, and he had to be professional. Plus, Martha deserved his respect.

"You're right, Martha. I apologize. It's the best idea, the most discreet. Piotr and I will pose as the gigolos that she requests and go inside, get the paintings, and complete the mission," Harry admitted.

Martha looked at him and shot him a subtle smile of approval.

They checked Tess's credit card statement and saw that there was a payment from the previous day with an item tagged as "House party, reservation." It was the payment for gigolo services that day, made the day before. Therefore, that very Saturday, they had the opportunity to carry out the mission. Harry thought it was great; the sooner they finished, the sooner they'd go back home. They arrived at the airport and went to the hotel booked for them by the Cork delegation. It was a suite bigger than Harry's own apartment, with three rooms. They had a bottle of quality champagne in the bar cabinet with a thank you note from their Cork colleagues, a thoughtful detail. They ate something, then went to rent a car and head to Tess's villa. Given that there was only one route to the villa, they parked the car at a certain distance, hidden within the vegetation. According to the information they had, the car labeled "House Party" would show up in approximately two hours, so they went over the plan. The plan was to stop the car, put the real gigolos to sleep with the "sleepy" maneuver, and hide them in the trunk of the car. Then, Piotr and Harry would head towards Tess's villa and would knock on the door posing as the service requested. Tess spoke English perfectly, so that would be the language they would address her in, given that neither Harry nor Piotr spoke Dutch or German. They didn't think that would matter much to Tess, given the nature of the service she required. Once she let them in, they would immobilize her, get the paintings, "suggest" to her that it's best not to report anything, and mission accomplished. Whether she was a nazi or not didn't concern them. It wasn't part of the mission, so even if they found that she had a tablecloth with a black swastika against a red background and an altar for the one and only Hitler, they wouldn't do anything about it. In theory, it shouldn't take long. Martha, in the meantime, would be in the rental car waiting, watching, and listening to everything with a hidden camera inside a ring that Harry would wear.

The time passed, and around 7:30 p.m. they saw the gigolo car in the distance. Martha got in the middle of the road to raise her arms so that they would stop. The car stopped, then Martha said to them in English if they could take a look at her car that suddenly wouldn't start. The gigolos parked to the side and walked towards the car. As they got closer, Harry and Piotr came out from where they were hiding and gave them a sleepy, making them instantly pass out. Then, they continued with the plan.  Luckily, the gigolos' car had a large trunk where the two sleeping angels could fit without much trouble. To get them in, however, they had to take out a briefcase with the company's logo, which they assumed were the outfits necessary to provide the service.

The moment of truth arrived. Harry and Piotr knocked on the door, and Tess opened it.

"Hello," Harry said. "We're from the House Party."

"Yes, I was expecting you guys. You don't speak Dutch?" Tess asked, also in perfect English, without fully opening the door.

"No, I'm sorry. We hope that isn't a problem," Piotr replied.

"Not at all, handsome," Tess responded, who then opened the door a bit more, revealing her other hand gripping a gun.

"Come on in, guys," she added as she pointed the gun at them.

They seemed to have no other option, so they went inside, as Tess closed the door behind them.

# CHAPTER XXIII

Sofia woke up three hours after Harry left and stayed in bed for a bit with a substantial hangover—in no hurry to get up. She liked Harry's apartment and realized that she had never been there alone. Harry had left with a suitcase, so, in reality, if she wanted to, she could stay there the entire weekend. She didn't have to decide right then and there, so she would think about it. What she was sure of was that she liked Harry's apartment more than hers, and that if she was going to move in with him, she would definitely move to his place before he moved to hers.

She slowly began the process of getting herself "vertical" as she thought about how hungry she was. She made herself breakfast with what was there, seeing what Harry had in the refrigerator and the pantry. As she ate, besides rejoicing in how well the scrambled eggs had turned out, she thought about what she would do that weekend. She had a hangover, and her boyfriend unexpectedly had to leave, so anyone in their right mind would more or less take it easy on such a Saturday.

But Sofia wasn't just anyone, and, moreover, she was in the mood for "activity." She had been feeling happy as of late—everything was going well. And when she was in such good spirits, she didn't like sitting around watching TV or reading. Once she finished breakfast, she showered then lay down on the couch for a bit. She grabbed her phone to see what plans she could make, but a couple of minutes later, Harry's doorbell rang. She looked through the peephole and saw Alfonso. She opened the door—he was surprised to see her.

"Shit, hey, Sofia. What's up?"

"Morning, Alfonso. I'm good. Harry left this morning for a trip. I don't know when he'll be back, but he took his suitcase."

"Another thrilling search for the lost ark?" Alfonso asked, laughing.

"Yep, that's what it looks like," Sofia responded, laughing as well, thinking about how right at that moment Harry could very well be slitting the throat of the leader of the Albanian mafia in Madrid, and how Alfonso was probably imagining him in Hellín[24] looking at the cutlery of an eighteenth-century family. "Do you want to come in?"

"Oh, no. Don't worry. I just came to see if Harry would grab a beer with me at the bar downstairs."

"How about me instead?" Sofia asked.

Alfonso wasn't quite sure what to say for a couple of seconds—he didn't expect that response.

"Oh, well, sure—of course. Great."

"Okay, you can go down there if you want, and I'll meet you in five minutes, or come in and wait while I get changed," Sofia said, realizing she had a plan at least for a little while.

"Okay, I'll wait for you at the bar, Sofia. I'll sit on the terrace if that's okay with you. It's a nice day out."

"Great, see you there, Alfonso," Sofia replied as she closed the door.

Sofia put on what she could, given that she didn't have many clothes at Harry's place. When she went down there, Alfonso was on the terrace of Bar Chema as he had said, with a beer and some olives. She sat next to him at the same table, and they started chatting. Truth be told, Sofia thought that he was a fun person, a good companion through thick and thin. With the second round of beer, Alfonso commented:

"Well, I was going to tell Harry, but since he's not here, and you're already at his apartment alone, which makes you relevant in his life, I'll tell you instead."

---

24 Translator's note: Town in the southeast of Spain.

"Sure, what is it?" Sofia asked, intrigued.

"Well, I'm going out with this girl, and it seems like it's serious," Alfonso responded with a smile.

"Wow, that's great, Alfonso. I'm glad. Who is it?" Sofia asked, though right after she added, "I mean, it's none of my business either. You don't have to tell me anything."

"Well, it's a girl that I knew from before. Let's just say we had something, but because of some irrelevant things, it all crashed and burned. Harry knows who it is."

Sofia nodded, but she didn't quite know what Alfonso was referring to. He had been a bit scarce on details. Alfonso realized this, then immediately added in a lower tone of voice:

"What I mean is we had slept together before, but I let it all go to shit, because I should have done something beforehand that I didn't do."

"I get it. You don't have to explain yourself to me, Alfonso. Don't worry. So, are you guys back together, then?"

"Well, yeah, we are. And as I said, it's heading toward something serious. Later today we're going to the movies, for example. It's been years since I've gone to the movies with a girl." Alfonso was glowing, like a kid with new shoes, or at least that's how he seemed to Sofia.

"No way, tell me more!"

"I was happy being single. I was only interested in sex these past few years and doing my thing without having to explain myself or commit to anything, I won't lie," Alfonso responded.

"That's awesome. Everyone has different wants and interests at different times. There's nothing wrong with it. And I think it's happened to all of us."

"That's what I think. Cheers, Sofia," Alfonso said, raising his beer.

Afterwards, Alfonso went home, and Sofia decided to stay at Harry's place, order Chinese food for delivery, and take a nap before seeing what she would do with the rest of her Saturday. Truth be told, Harry's surprise trip had thrown her off a bit, but she would find something. After waking up from her nap, she called her friend Rebeca, who also happened to be free, and they met up for a coffee in downtown Murcia. Rebeca was from Murcia whom Sofia had met right after having moved to the city in the first apartment she stayed in. She was her first roommate, and they got along quite well. At first, she worked as a waitress at a pizzeria, and it was all going well. She got paid well and had a good schedule, too. She had plenty of fun with Sofia, and she was someone whose friends and coworkers all loved.

But one night, everything went to ruin. As she opened the door to her apartment building, after coming back from her late-night shift at work past midnight, some bastard put a razor to her neck and forced her inside. Once inside, he raped her and then ran away, leaving her at the elevator door with her skirt ripped and her underwear down. It took her two more hours to go up to her apartment and wake Sofia up to tell her what had just happened as she cried. Sofia called the police and didn't let Rebecca shower to avoid eliminating evidence. She had seen it on TV, and, indeed, it ended up being crucial. They took her to the hospital where they identified her and took a DNA sample, which allowed them to identify the bastard that had assaulted her. It was a man who had been accused of rape and was out on bail pending trial. The police arrested him within a few days and sentenced him to several years in jail. Rebeca was going to therapy for quite a while. For a few years, she was unable to have any relationship and was even afraid to talk to men. During that time, she practically lost her will to live.

Sofia was by her side the whole time and was a direct witness to the entire process, supporting her as much as she could. When she slowly but surely started feeling better, her assailant was granted parole for good behavior, and Rebeca, after consulting with her therapist, made the decision to leave Murcia. At first, Sofia insisted that she stay and not let her assailant determine her life, saying it was unjust. However, in the end, she understood her position. Rebeca wasn't willing to run into him one day on the street. So, the day after telling Sofia, Rebeca took a bus to Barcelona where her sister was living and stayed there. At first, she continued talking to Sofia, but after a couple of months, they lost contact. Sofia assumed that Rebeca needed to cut ties with her previous life and respected her decision. She hadn't heard from Rebeca until about two months ago. Rebeca called her and told her that she was coming back to Murcia to live there.

"Great, Rebeca! That's awesome, right?" Sofia responded when Rebeca told her.

"Well, yeah. I want to live in my city. And my boyfriend works there, so…"

"What? Your boyfriend? Tell me more!" Sofia exclaimed.

It turned out that Rebeca had met a guy from Murcia in Barcelona a year prior, who was there for a fun weekend with a few friends, and they instantly fell in love. They started a long-distance relationship. He went there on weekends, and since everything was going well, they had decided to live together. She told him about her experience, and how that was why she hadn't gone to Murcia for all those years, but she thought she was ready. Since she didn't have a job at that point, and he did in Murcia, they decided to live in Murcia. She told everything to Sofia when they met up one day for coffee, having just returned to Murcia, years after the last time they had seen each other. Sofia found her to be substantially recovered, even perhaps like the old Rebeca.

All of that also influenced Sofia's happiness. She had regained her friend, lost for so many years, whom she had practically given up all hope of ever speaking to again. But when they met, she realized that, luckily, it seemed as if the time hadn't passed. She talked to her about Harry (leaving out the part about him being a paid mercenary), the whole story with Loretta, her family business matters…, and she couldn't believe that it was Rebecca that she was talking to, since it had been years that she hadn't heard from her.

At that time, Rebeca was working as a hairdresser at a hair salon on the outskirts of the city from Monday to Saturday in the mornings. She had found work quickly. She had to work with a bad schedule which was why they didn't see each other much, though they did regain phone contact. They had already agreed to introduce their partners to each other one day, but they still hadn't been able to set a day due to everyone's commitments. At that point, the two of them had already agreed to meet a couple of times, and this would be the third.

Sofia left Harry's apartment and headed to the café they had agreed to meet at—a very interesting place, La Pradera Sonriente, with decoration that seemed quite original to Sofia, with rural motifs and color lighting. It was about a ten-minute walk from Harry's apartment, which she was increasingly certain she would use to sleep that night, since she had absolutely no desire to go to her car afterwards and drive back to her apartment.

She wondered how Harry was doing. Now that she knew what his work really was, Harry being away on a mission and not knowing where he was or what he had to do made her rather curious. It wasn't that she was afraid that something would happen to him. She knew, or at least she wanted to believe, that he would be okay and that he knew how to take care of himself—that wasn't her concern. In truth, she thought, with a certain degree of envy, about the possible adventures he was having. She would text him later to see how it was going and would impatiently wait for his response. Another thing was if he could answer her, since that wasn't always possible in the middle of a mission. For now, she walked into La Pradera Sonriente, and after seeing that Rebeca still wasn't there, she spotted a table next to the window and sat there. There was good eighties music in the background, and the place was half full. A few tables were several drinks deep, others were couples having a cocktail, and some were young people having coffee. She ordered a cappuccino as she waited, and three minutes later, Rebeca arrived and greeted her with a smile.

They spent the following hour laughing, telling each other about how their week had gone, why Sofia was at Harry's apartment, and how Rebeca's boyfriend always left the toilet seat up even though she repeatedly told him not to. The moment came, however, when the tone shifted, and Rebeca's facial expression transformed.

"Sofia, what if I run into the ogre on the street?"

The ogre was what Rebeca and her therapist had agreed to call the man who raped her. She had used that name to refer to him for years, and, evidently, she still used it. What was certain was that they hadn't talked about the ogre since Rebeca had been back in Murcia. Sofia knew that moment had to come sooner or later, but she didn't want to be the one to bring it up, since it didn't seem like the most appropriate or best thing for Rebeca. However, given that Rebeca had brought it up, she wasn't going to evade the conversation.

"You won't run into him, Rebeca."

"How are you so sure?"

"Because I know you won't run into him."

"But..."

"Rebeca, do you remember what I told you when you decided to go to Barcelona?"

"Yeah, of course."

"What did I say?"

"You said, verbatim, 'Go get a change of scenery, but just know that the ogre won't bother you anymore.'"

"Right, I see that you didn't forget. And you trust me, right?" Sofia asked her as she held her hands.

"Of course I do, Sofia. Of course I trust you, but he got out when they gave him parole. No one knows where he is. How do you know...?"

"Well, if you trust me, you have nothing to fear. I'll say it again: the ogre will not bother you anymore, and you won't run into him on the street. I promise, okay?" Sofia looked at her intently and saw how her facial expression slowly but surely changed into one of more fortitude.

"Okay, Sofia. The ogre won't bother me."

"The ogre isn't here."

"The ogre isn't here," Rebeca repeated.

"The ogre is gone."

"The ogre is gone."

"And I will be happy."

"And I will be happy." Rebeca started gradually smiling.

Sofia, meanwhile, remembered the moment when she had told Harry that everyone had skeletons in the closet. And even though Rebeca didn't see her, Sofia smiled as well.

# CHAPTER XXIV

After Rebeca's brief emotional slump, the situation returned to normal. They left the café smiling and went to take a walk around town, doing some window shopping to see the latest items in the local stores. Rebeca had planned to meet with her boyfriend soon and had to take the tram that ran through a part of the city. So, Sofia went with her to the stop, and they gave each other a warm goodbye, arranging to have dinner one day with their partners as soon as the antique dealer was back (that's how Rebeca referred to Harry). Then, Sofia walked back to Harry's apartment, which was about a half hour away. She was already tired; she had started the day with energy, but it was dragging on for her. Her hangover from the previous day hadn't fully gone away, so she decided to stop and buy cigarettes, since she didn't have any, and then lounge on Harry's couch for a bit.

She got there and lay down to smoke a cigarette with a little wine that Harry had in the fridge. She thought about poor Rebeca, wondering if something like what had happened to her could ever be overcome. Even now, after so many years, with a partner that adored her—in her own words (despite the toilet seat issue)—having returned to her city with her life essentially put back together, Sofia had just seen that the trauma Rebeca had had since that night was still quite present in her head. It may be something that could never be fully overcome. Sofia knew her quite well and knew that this whole time she had never given up on working to be okay, on fighting to feel better. She was by no means a cowardly person and had tried not to let herself get dragged down to the depths of despair, to the abyss of madness and sorrow, but she had suffered a harrowing incident that was greater than her. For that very reason, the day the ogre was released, and she saw that bastard smiling from ear to ear, Sofia knew she wouldn't allow the possibility for Rebeca to run into him on the street again, or for him to call her, or something worse. So, she did what she thought she had to do.

...

(*Several years ago…*). Thanks to the media, she knew that the ogre was a local from Murcia, and based on the images of the plaza and the streets shown on TV that day, she essentially knew which specific area. Even if he managed to escape unnoticed and settle somewhere else, his parents, who she had seen at the trial, would probably continue to live there. Thus, as soon as she heard the news that the ogre was given parole, she went to that area in the mornings to see if she could find something out. It was an area of the city with plenty of drug dealing and a significant level of crime, but that didn't matter to Sofia. The first day, she approached a few young people that were sitting in a park, took out a twenty-euro bill, and they immediately told her where the family lived.

"But he isn't here, right?" the guy who took the twenty euros asked her. "After what he did, we don't want him around here anymore."

"Do you know where he is, by chance?" Sofia asked.

"No fucking clue, but if he shows up around here, he'll get fucked up," the young man replied.

"Damn right, man—we'd fuck that piece of shit up. You don't do that—we're honest here. His family are good people, but that guy can't come around here. Ma'am, if you give me another one of those bills, I'll tell you where they say he is," one of the other young men said who was sitting on the same bench.

Sofia took out another twenty and put her hand out to him, but when he went to grab it, she pulled it back.

"But don't lie to me, okay?"

"No, ma'am, I'm going to tell you what I've heard, that's it," the young man responded, as Sofia extended her hand again, allowing him to grab the bill. "He's working at his parents' restaurant, washing dishes where no one can see him. And he sleeps at an old house his parents had out in the country, close to the restaurant. He bikes there."

"Okay, great. Thanks," Sofia replied as she took out a one-hundred-euro bill and gave it to her new friends, winking at them. Then, she added, "You guys didn't see me."

Sofia had researched a bit online, and with parole, he was required to have a job and a fixed address where he had to be monitored by the authorities at certain hours of the day. Thus, he would go from home to work and from work to home, which meant that he would have a routine. This would facilitate Sofia in what she was thinking about doing. She didn't know which restaurant was his parents', but since she knew where his parents lived, she only had to follow their car one day. And that's exactly what she did the next day.

Around 6 a.m., Sofia was across from the ogre's parents' house. At seven, they walked out (Sofia recognized them—she hadn't forgotten their faces) and got in an old maroon Peugeot 207. Sofia followed them at a safe distance, and they quickly arrived at a farm-to-table restaurant, near some houses and stores. In Murcia, there's quite a rich and varied market gardening culture, and along with it, there are plenty of restaurants that tend to offer local products, grilled meat, rice…. They're usually modest yet quite successful places, and the ogre's parents had one that was very well known in the area. She parked at a distance and grabbed the binoculars that she had bought. She saw a man on a bike waiting at the entrance, and upon seeing him, a chill ran up her spine. There was the ogre, dressed in a white dress shirt and black pants without a belt. Smoking a cigarette, he waited for them to open the door to go in for work. Anyone who didn't know him and saw him then would think that he was an ordinary waiter or cook, waiting for them to open the door so he could go to his place of work and earn an honest living. But it couldn't be further from reality. And as the ogre threw the butt on the ground and stepped on it, totally carefree thanks to his "reintegration," her friend Rebeca was in psychological treatment. How unfair it all was. Sofia squeezed her hands in anger around the steering wheel for a microsecond. In any case, she had him located and had accomplished an important step.

Since she didn't want to get any closer than necessary to the restaurant in case the ogre or his family saw her, she looked at the place's hours online and saw that it closed at 5 p.m. Thus, she imagined that if the ogre worked full time, he would leave at that hour or shortly after. She used an excuse to ask for the evening off at work, and after lunch, she parked in the same spot where she had parked that morning and waited. Around 5:15 p.m., the ogre walked out of the restaurant, pushing his bike with the handlebars. He got on it and started pedaling in the opposite direction of Sofia, who started her car and followed him, again at a careful distance. About ten minutes later, after she had to stop a couple of times so he wouldn't suspect that a car was following him, the ogre stopped and got off his bike next to an old farmhouse in the middle of nowhere. "*Okay,*" Sofia thought, "*no neighbors nearby.*"

At that point, Sofia would have knocked on his door and shot him if she could, with no consideration or remorse. She believed in reintegration, but not for all types of crimes, and this certainly wasn't one of them. But she hadn't gone there. Something as delicate as what she was thinking about doing had to be all very well organized and planned. She now knew where the house was where the ogre lived during his vacation in the form of parole, so she went home.

The following day, she asked for the day off again, and at 3 p.m., she parked her car behind the house in an area that wasn't visible from the road. She picked the lock with a safety pin and entered. She had learned to do it by watching some videos online and practicing on her own door, and truth be told, she did it quickly—she was good at it. She locked the door behind her and observed what she had in front of her. There was a dilapidated living room, with a large couch of hard plastic, and an ancient CRT television. There was also a table with two chairs, and a small butane kitchen open to the living room. She opened another door where the bathroom was, which seemed like it hadn't been cleaned for some time. It had a broken mirror as the medicine cabinet and a bath. Then, there was another door that looked like the main bedroom, but it had an old, overturned closet on top of a bed and two chairs. She assumed that the ogre slept on the old couch. The house certainly had space, and with repairs and new furniture it could look quite nice, but Sofia hadn't gone there to give her opinion as an interior decorator. By then, Sofia knew that she was getting to the point of no return and that it still wasn't too late. She could leave right then and there, and no one would know anything. And for a moment, she considered leaving the house. But something kept her from definitively changing her mind. She stared at the table and saw that there were several magazines with pictures of naked women on it. She had nothing against porn—she even liked it from time to time—but the porn combined with a released rapist perhaps didn't foreshadow anything good, she thought. The pig was obsessed with women and was on the loose. Yes, he was on parole and had to be monitored—all the stuff that Sofia and all of society had heard many times. But she had also heard about reoffending rapists plenty of times. And even though she didn't know how a person could think that way, she believed that soon the magazines wouldn't be enough for him, and that he would end up looking for the next Rebeca in line. Maybe he'll get caught before he can do anything, or perhaps not, and a new victim will emerge. So, she removed the idea from her head of abandoning her plan and continued on.

She grabbed some of the ogre's clothes that she found and stuff that she thought someone who wanted to run away would take. She put it all in a trash bag and placed it in her car. Then, she went back to the house and waited patiently. Two hours later, she saw the ogre approaching her on his bike from the window. She put on a ski mask and went behind the door with a knife in hand. The ogre opened the door, and right when he turned around and closed it, Sofia grabbed him from behind, twisting his arm with one hand and putting the knife to his neck with the other.

"You're going to open the door again now, got it?"

"Agh!" The ogre was groaning in pain. "What do you want, you bitch?"

Sofia twisted his arm a little more and pressed the knife against his neck slightly harder. "Got it?" she repeated.

"Yes, okay, okay." The ogre opened the door, and with his hands behind his back, Sofia put him in handcuffs that she had brought.

"Good. Walk towards the back," Sofia ordered as she took him by the arms with one hand and pressed the knife on his back with the other.

They went around the house and got to Sofia's car, where she opened the trunk.

"Get in," Sofia ordered the ogre.

"I'm not getting in there, you bitch. Who the fuck are you?" the ogre replied, trying to free himself.

Sofia hit him on the head with the knife handle and shoved him into the trunk. Then, she put duct tape over his mouth.

"Let's see if this keeps you quiet for a while," she said before closing the trunk.

She got in the car and drove off. She had the first part of the plan executed. Now she had the second and most difficult part, but she was steadfast in making sure that her friend or any other girl didn't have to run into the ogre ever again. She had to make a call, so she parked the car in an empty open field.

The field was a five-minute drive away from the closest road. She stayed there until it got dark, patiently reading and smoking in her car. Once it was dark enough, Sofia got out, opened the trunk, and looked at the ogre, handcuffed and muzzled. She didn't have the ski mask on anymore. She wanted him to know who she was.

"You remember me, right?" Sofia started talking to him. "I was at the trial when they sentenced you for raping my friend. My friend has never been the same since she ran into you, you know? I don't even think she'll ever go back to normal. The day they sentenced you was a happy day for me, but I'd say it was just another day for her. Nothing can alleviate her pain, not even revenge or justice, however you want to call it. In fact, the situation might get worse with you free. It might get worse if she sees you on the street, if she starts hearing about you, or even if, when you get sick of jacking off to those magazines, you rape another girl, and she sees you again on TV. Because that'll happen, won't it? Soon, you won't be satisfied and you'll be on the prowl again. Maybe not tomorrow or the day after. You may even wait for your sentence to end. But you'll do it. Or, better yet, you would do it, because I'm not going to let you do it. You understand, right?"

The ogre looked at her and made sounds as if he wanted to speak but couldn't because he still had the duct tape over his mouth.

"Oh, do you want to say something? Darn, I'm so sorry. That's not going to happen," Sofia said as she grabbed him by the arm and helped him out of the trunk.

As soon as his feet touched the ground, she kicked him in the ankle and pushed his head against the ground to put him on his knees. Once she did, she put her foot on his calves and grabbed him by the hair. Then, she leaned a bit forward and started to whisper in his ear.

"Shh, I don't want to hear you, so I'm not going to let you say anything. Don't waste your energy. Or, well, waste it if you want. It won't matter in the end."

Sofia noticed that the ogre started to cry. He tried to twist his way free and remove the handcuffs. For a fraction of a second, she even felt bad. But that fraction of a second vanished when she remembered Rebeca's face knocking on the apartment door late at night, drenched in tears, in despair and half naked.

"Goodbye. You won't hurt anyone ever again," Sofia said as she slit his neck with the knife. The ogre quickly bled out and died.

After making sure he was in fact dead, Sofia put the ogre back in the trunk, this time lifeless. The ogre wasn't too big, and Sofia was in good shape, so she managed to lift the dead body from the ground and place it in the trunk, although with some difficulty. She closed the trunk and leaned on the car for a minute to catch her breath. Then, she got in and headed to her destination. Along the way, she turned on the radio at high volume and started singing as she smiled in a way that she hadn't in a long time.

Half an hour later, she arrived at the destination. She stopped the car in front of a closed door in a small industrial area. She took out her phone and called the same number as before.

"It's me. I'm here. You're alone, right? Can you open the door?"

"Yeah, I'm alone. I'm coming," a voice said from the other end of the line.

The door opened mechanically, and Sofia went in. She drove on a small dirt road for thirty seconds, then arrived at the door of a building with a sign that said "PAQUI INCINERATIONS LLC." The door opened, and she saw someone signaling to her to drive forward. Sofia followed and left the car where she was told to. Then, she got out and went to greet her friend.

"Paqui, thank you so much. How are you?"

Paqui was Sofia's friend from university. She studied teacher education with her, but her parents had a business they founded when she was quite young (in fact, they named it after her), so she decided to work there. However. Sofia and Paqui were still very good friends after university. They had shared important moments together, and Paqui felt indebted to her. What happened was that one day, Sofia saved Paqui from a pill overdose, during a rough period. If Sofia hadn't been worried about her and hadn't shown up at her apartment, unlocking it with the key she had for emergencies, Paqui would be dead. Only the two of them knew that story, and the doctors at the hospital, so Paqui, who settled down and moved on, promised she would do anything for her.  And the moment to "even the score" had arrived, given that, coincidentally, Paqui's business was animal incineration services, a good metaphor for the ogre.

"Sofia, how are you? It's so good to see you. So, what favor am I doing for you?" Paqui asked, whom Sofia hadn't given any details to on the phone. The only thing she had said was that she needed a favor from her company that same night.

Sofia didn't respond but instead opened the trunk.

Paqui put her hand over her mouth in a sign of shock. "Sofia, what did you do? Who is this?"

"It's the motherfucker that raped Rebeca."

"And did you…?"

"Yes," Sofia interrupted. "I need his remains gone. I know I'm putting you in a tough situation, and I wouldn't do it unless it was truly necessary."

Paqui looked at her and said, "Nonsense. Come on, I'll help you get him out of the car. Wait, let me get the forklift."

Paqui brought a sort of electric forklift for transporting animal bodies. It was a bit small, but the ogre fit. They both took him out of the trunk and threw him on the forklift with his clothes and everything that Sofia had taken from his house. They threw it all into the massive crematory oven that Paqui had in the building, along with some dead goats.

"Well, there you go. With the heat output from this thing, there won't be a trace left of him within a couple of hours," Paqui said.

Sofia then started to cry, seemingly inconsolable. Paqui hugged her, and they stood there holding each other for a few minutes.

"Hey, how about I make you a coffee and you hang out with me for this thrilling night shift?" Paqui asked.

Sofia smiled as she dried her tears and nodded her head.

For the next two hours, Sofia told her how she had planned everything and how she had carried it out.

Paqui listened attentively, a bit astonished, to be fair.

"Do you think I'm a monster?" Sofia said after finishing.

"Absolutely not. Do you think you're a monster?" Paqui asked.

"No. I don't know. I kidnapped and killed a person in cold blood."

"Do you think that guy deserved to be considered a person?" Sofia didn't know what to say, as Paqui continued to speak:

"Look, I understand how you feel, but it's already done, and maybe the world is a better place now than it was a few hours ago. And no one will find out about what happened. I'm not going to tell you to forget about it because you won't forget about it, but I will tell you to learn to forgive yourself and to live with it."

Paqui's words, along with her way of saying them, were reassuring. Sofia, now calmer, nodded her head. Soon, there was no trace of the ogre left, and she went back home. Paqui insisted that she stay with her—she had a comfortable couch in her office—but Sofia preferred to go home, though she was very grateful. That night and the following one she couldn't sleep, but the third night she slept like a baby.

Everyone thought the ogre had run away. There were no signs of a struggle at his house, and his clothing and belongings had disappeared. It wouldn't be the first prisoner on parole that ran away, so a search and arrest warrant was issued, but with no success. The order was still in effect as of the current date, though as it happens with everything, people had forgotten about it.

...

(*Back to the present...*). Sofia finished her cigarette on Harry's couch as she recalled all of that. She had lost contact with Paqui a bit in recent months, with whom she had never talked about what happened since that night. Perhaps it was time to revisit it. She also remembered that she felt strange for a few days, but then quickly went back to normal. Of course, she had never done any harm to anyone else since then and was at peace with herself and the skeletons in her closet. Would she tell Harry about it? Perhaps she should. Given the circumstances, she didn't think it would scare him. *"Ugh, Harry, I wonder what you're doing right now,"* she thought at that moment.

# CHAPTER XXV

Over a thousand miles away from Sofia, Harry and Piotr walked into the house, as Tess pointed her gun at them. She closed the door and kept the gun pointed at them.

"Well, you guys are new. They've never sent you here before. I'll explain how this works. You do everything I say until eight in the morning when the service ends, got it?"

"Yes, ma'am."

"Oh, call me Tess."

"Yes, Tess."

"Great. Now take your shirts off. Let's go," Tess concluded as she kept the gun pointed at them.

Harry and Piotr complied and took off their shirts. Tess stood there watching them with a certain lustful air.

"Great job, guys. Don't be afraid of the gun—it's simply to remind you who's boss. I didn't get your names, but since I'm the boss, you'll be Mark (looking at Harry), and you're Robert (looking at Piotr). Mark, Robert, follow me into the living room, please."

The newly named Mark and Robert followed Tess into the living room. As they did, Harry looked at Tess's gun which seemed to him to be real, though, without examining it more closely, he couldn't be sure. Thus, caution called for him to assume that it was real for the moment and to be careful about what they did as long as Tess was the one who was armed.

They walked into a massive living room, with a table and chairs in one corner, the biggest chaise lounge couch that Harry had ever seen facing an enormous TV, and in the other corner, visible from the couch, something that wasn't normally found in a living room: a small, elevated stage—a step with a stripper pole like the ones in strip clubs. Apart from that, the living room was decorated in a rather gaudy way and perhaps somewhat excessively ornamented. There were many silver picture frames, several vases, candelabras, a large fish tank with fish inside…. There wasn't much free space. At first glance, they didn't see any nazi symbols, though they couldn't observe in detail.

Piotr nudged Harry with his elbow and pointed with his head to one of the walls. The paintings that they had gone to get were hanging there. "*Perfect. Now we just have to free ourselves from this insane woman with a gun,*" Harry thought.

"Robert, open that cabinet over there and grab two glasses and the bottle of vodka, if you don't mind," Tess said. "Mark, come here and sit on the couch."

Piotr was heading to the cabinet as Tess had told him to when, raising her voice a bit, she said:

"Hey, Robert." He then stopped and heard the sound of her removing the safety on the gun as she pointed it at him. "If I speak to you, you answer me, got it?"

Piotr immediately got it and responded:

"Yes, Tess. I'm sorry. It won't happen again."

"That's what I like to hear. Grab the glasses and the vodka and bring them here."

Harry had already sat on the couch and watched the whole scene from there. Tess seemed to be a bit unstable, so they had to be cautious if they didn't want the mission to get complicated, especially while she had a gun in her hand. Everything seemed to indicate that they may have underestimated the difficulty of the mission.

Piotr left the glasses and the bottle of vodka on the table next to the couch. It was a brand that Harry had never seen, with

Cyrillic characters all over it. Then, Tess, still with the gun in hand, said:

"Thanks, Robert. Now run to the pole and dance for us." Tess pressed a button on a controller that was on the couch, and soft music started playing in the background.

"Yes, Tess," Piotr responded, having already learned his lesson, as he headed to the pole.

Then, Tess addressed Harry.

"This is a unique and exclusive vodka. They only make ten bottles a year in Russia. Don't ask me how I get it because I won't tell you. Go ahead, Mark, pour a couple of glasses and give one to me."

"Yes, Tess." Harry poured two glasses, keeping one and giving Tess the other.

"Chug it all and pour another," Tess ordered him. Harry obeyed. Truth be told, he usually didn't drink vodka that much, but this one had a great taste, even though it burned his throat.

"You like it, don't you?"

"Yes, Tess. It was good."

"I'm glad," Tess said as she snuggled up to Harry on the couch.

Tess was quite attractive. She was wearing a white T-shirt and a miniskirt that barely covered her. Plus, a black bra could be seen through her T-shirt. Tess then put the gun to Harry's neck and grabbed his private parts with her other hand. Harry was unsettled and caught by surprise. Attempting to take the gun away was risky at that point. If Tess had quick reflexes, or even if she didn't, he could end up getting shot deliberately or accidentally. For the moment, he couldn't do anything other than go with the flow and hope that her guard would come down. Tess got on top of Harry. The gun was still pointed at his neck.

"Do I get you hard, Mark?"

"Yes, Tess, really hard."

"That's how I like it."

Tess started moving on top of Harry, and though it was biologically inevitable that his body part started to get aroused, Harry wasn't comfortable at all. Suddenly, the doorbell rang, as if someone was responding to Harry's mental call for help. "*Who is it?*" he thought. "*Could it be Martha? She was watching everything and probably came up with some plan, since nothing is turning out as expected. Yeah, it's got to be her.*"

Tess "got off" of Harry, who still had a substantial erection, and headed to the door.

"Be right back, darling. Don't miss me too much," she said, looking at Harry as she kept the gun pointed at him and winked at him. Then, she turned towards Piotr and pointed the gun at him. "Robert, you keep dancing, honey, got it?"

"Yes, Tess," Piotr responded as he continued to dance.

Tess left the room and headed towards the door. Piotr looked at Harry and shrugged his shoulders in a gesture that seemed to say, "What do we do? This lunatic has a loose screw in her head. She's going to shoot us and bury us out back." Harry, in turn, gestured to him with his hands as if to tell him to relax. But the person who wasn't relaxed at all was Harry himself, so that gesture to calm his colleague down was to convince himself that they would make it out of this.

He wondered what Sofia was doing then. Since it was Saturday night, she was either relaxing at his apartment (he knew her—with her hangover she was probably too lazy to go to her house) or she was having a drink with a friend at some bar. That girl was invincible.

What would she think if she saw Harry right now with a supposed nazi on top of his private parts, most likely having to take it even further for the sake of the mission? If this wasn't his last mission, he certainly didn't have many left in him. And all this for a few paintings.

"*Harry, stop thinking about Sofia. Focus on figuring out how to get out of this,*" his inner voice told him then. It was indeed best to concentrate on how to get out of the house alive.

They heard Tess talking to someone in Dutch for a moment, followed by the door closing. A few seconds later, Tess reappeared with the gun still pointed at them.

Another girl was with her. Tess said something to her in Dutch, then added in English, "Here they are, as I said. They only speak English. Their names are Mark and Robert. Guys, this is Dita. She's joining us tonight. You'll submit to her just like to me, got it?"

"Yes, Tess," Harry and Piotr responded almost in unison.

Just what they needed—another girl. The newly arrived Dita didn't seem to have a gun, at least, but another person could complicate the mission even more.

"Okay, I was with Mark, so you go with Robert for now, Dita," Tess said.

"Okay. I assure you, it's no problem for me at all," Dita replied, walking towards the stage where Piotr was dancing.

Dita didn't have a gun and didn't seem too big, so it shouldn't be difficult for Piotr to subdue her. If Harry managed to subdue Tess, they would have the situation under control, at least in theory. But the gun seemed like an extension of Tess's arm, and she still had it pointed at Harry. For Tess to let her guard down with the gun, Harry knew what he had to do. It wasn't what he wanted to do, but he had no other choice.

Tess took off her shirt and got back on top of Harry.

"Where did we leave off, Mark?" Tess asked as she began to move on top of Harry's private part.

"Right here, Tess," Harry responded, unhooking her bra.

Tess then smiled and whispered in Harry's ear, "That's how I like it. We're going to have a real good time."

Tess kept the gun pointed at Harry's neck for the next minute, but she got to the point where she left the gun on the couch and started unbuttoning Harry's pants.

"*Bingo*," Harry thought then. He grabbed Tess by the waist and threw her towards the opposite end of the couch where the gun was. He quickly went towards her, twisted her arm, and immobilized her by getting behind her. Tess screamed as he twisted her arm, and then Dita, who was watching Piotr dance in underwear and putting money inside, turned around. Piotr took advantage of that moment to subdue her quite easily.

They tied Dita and Tess to chairs and gagged them. Then, a few minutes later, Martha appeared with a box, left at the hotel by their colleagues from the Cork delegation, to store the paintings.

"It's about damn time, don't you think?" Harry said to her as he finished putting his clothes back on.

"Did you want me to come in here Rambo-style? You guys had the situation under control, Harry. If I had interrupted, it would have added an unpredictable element to the situation. A gun in the hands of a slightly unstable mind—we don't know what could have happened," Martha replied, then added, "and you know that perfectly well."

It was true. Martha was right. Though they hadn't considered the possibility of Tess's gun, it was most likely that what happened would happen—that at some point, she would let her guard down, and they could subdue her without much trouble, and that they could even subdue Dita too, as long as she wasn't armed. Would they have perhaps had to carry their gigolo role to the extreme before that happened? Possibly, but those were "occupational hazards." The most prudent and objective thing for the success of the mission was to not intervene in order to avoid that, as Martha had done. And it's not like they were in the wild west. They couldn't go through life shooting and killing people to complete missions. Harry not being thrilled about having to have sex with a stranger didn't outweigh the importance of successfully completing the mission. And deep down, Harry knew that. That didn't mean that he had to like it.

"Alright, let's grab the paintings so we can go home asap," Martha said.

The three of them took the paintings off the wall and carefully placed them in the box to avoid damaging them. As they did so, they looked around at the décor of the house. Everything seemed normal relative to the extravagance, except for perhaps the dance stage in the living room with the stripper pole. They wondered if one of the pieces of decor distributed around the house was also inherited from her nazi family, stolen from their rightful owner. They had no way of knowing.

Once they had the paintings put away, around 11 p.m., they opened the drawers and searched the house until they found what they wanted. Then, they went back to the living room and removed the gags from Dita and Tess. Since the three of them were speaking in Spanish, Dita and Tess hadn't understood anything that Harry, Martha, and Piotr were saying as they searched the house.

"Alright, Tess, you've probably already inferred that my colleague and I aren't from the gigolo company, right?" Harry started speaking in English, to which Tess responded by spitting in his face. "You should go to the doctor to get that cough checked out," Harry responded as he cleaned himself with a tissue.

"What do you guys want? Why are you doing this to us? Tess and I didn't do anything wrong," Dita asked. By the tone of voice she asked the question in, it seemed to Harry that Dita, in reality, didn't know anything about who Tess was and that she had gotten trapped in the situation purely by bad luck.

"You don't know who your friend is, do you? Your friend is a nazi," Piotr said to Dita. Speaking skills were not Piotr's most noteworthy ability, though there was no need to overthink it or sugarcoat it either.

"That's right" Martha confirmed.

"Dita, don't listen to these people," Tess exclaimed.

"Shut up for a second, damn," Harry said as he put the gag back on Tess.

Dita looked around with a face of incredulity. Then, Harry pointed to a box that said *"arbeit macht frei.*[25]*"* He opened it, and

---

25 "Work will set you free," a German phrase written on the entrance of several nazi concentration and extermination camps.

there was everything from gold teeth to rings, necklaces, and diamonds inside. There was also an envelope with a letter written in German and seemingly signed by Tess's grandfather. Martha spoke German, so she could translate it, and they realized what it was about.

"You don't speak German, right, Dita?" Martha asked her, to which Dita responded by nodding her head no. "Well, I'll tell you what it essentially says in English."

Martha started to translate the letter out loud:

"Dear Tess, by now, you must be a young lady. I'm writing to you because I know that I don't have much time left in this world and I want you to have a good memory of me. I know you probably don't remember me. You were very young when I last saw you, and you didn't even speak German. Your mother did what she had to do by going to Holland, but you have to be proud of your roots, and your roots are in Germany. Specifically, in the greatest Germany in history, and not in what it's become now, kneeling before its decadent enemies.

I'll just tell you to be proud of your roots but be careful in showing it. I hope you live to see better days when you can freely express it, but for the time being, listen to your mother and go unnoticed. I'll send you a box with gifts that your great grandfather, my father, collected during his great work cleaning and purifying society. Keep it forever and open the box whenever you have questions about who you are so you see the important work that your family did it Auschwitz.

With love, your grandfather Jürgen."

Martha then lifted her gaze and saw that Dita was looking at Tess with an infuriated face. She started reprimanding her in Dutch, then addressed her captors:

"I had no idea, I swear."

"We believe you—don't worry. Either way, we'll give you the opportunity to explain yourself," Martha replied as she removed the gag from Tess and asked her if she had anything to say, to which she said yes.

"Yes, it's true that I have nazi roots, and that my grandfather gave me that box with the letter when I was little. I see that you guys took some paintings. I inherited those paintings from my parents. I have no idea where they bought them or where they got them from. But I can infer that if you guys have taken them it's because they didn't buy them, right? Even if you don't believe me, I'm telling you I had no idea. I couldn't care less what you guys think, but Dita, listen to me: I'm not a nazi. My family was nazi, but I'm not responsible for the actions of my family."

"Why did you keep that box with stuff stolen from people in extermination camps?" Harry asked.

"Because it was a gift. Who am I going to return their gold teeth to? They've probably been dead for eighty years. It's helped me to try and understand why my family participated in supporting the nazis."

"And have you accomplished that?"

"No, not yet. But I'll keep trying."

Harry, Piotr, and Martha all looked at each other, then Harry said:

"That's quite a story you just told. She convinced you, Dita, didn't she? With that whole thing about not being responsible for the actions of your family and blah, blah, blah. I mean, she's right about that, don't you think? Of course. Well, in the end, we don't care whether you're a nazi or not. We're going to take the paintings, that's it. We won't do anything to you guys, nor will we report you. That's not our job. Although, just for the record, I'll let you know that we don't buy your story at all."

They grabbed the paintings and put them in their rental car. Before that, they took the sleeping gigolos and put them back in their car. In a couple of hours or so they would wake up dazed, not having any idea about what had happened. Tess and Dita were still tied up, and the moment had arrived to make sure they wouldn't tell anyone about what had happened.

"Alright, ladies," Martha began to say, "here's what's going to happen. We're going to leave you tied up back-to-back. You shouldn't have any issue untying yourselves within a few minutes. We're going to take the paintings and return them to the heir of their rightful owners. Apart from that, Tess, we're going to take your grandfather's box, including the letter. If it by chance occurred to you to report us for stealing the paintings, everything would come to light, and your public and social life would end. You'd have to move away. And wherever you'd go, we'd make sure that they know as well. And, of course, you could tell them that thing about not being responsible for what your family did. We'd see how many people believe you're not a nazi. Maybe you'd be lucky, and everyone believes you. But if I were you, I wouldn't try. If you don't report it and you let it go, you have my word that nothing will come to light—it's none of our business. What do you say?"

Tess responded:

"I won't say anything. I promise."

"Good, that's how I like it. As for you, Dita, your presence wasn't expected. We have nothing against you. We trust that you won't say anything about what happened here tonight, right?"

"No, no, absolutely not."

"Either way, as a precaution, we have a picture of your ID, and we know your full name and address. If something about this came to light, I'm very sorry to tell you that you might have some problems. But we won't get there, right?"

"No, no, I won't say anything. Nothing happened."

"Excellent. Just so you see that we aren't bad people, here's a thousand euros for the inconvenience caused." Martha put ten one-hundred-euro bills in her purse.

"Ah, by the way, ladies, the two gigolos that were supposed to come instead of us are outside sleeping. They have no idea about what happened, and soon they'll wake up dazed. They're all yours, okay? Make up whatever story you want and do with them whatever you want to do. It's none of our business," Harry added.

It was one in the morning on Sunday, July 18th when they left the house with the paintings. They let the high command know that the mission was complete, and then went to the hotel. They ordered the gourmet room service that came included: some lobsters and oysters for dinner, then they drank the champagne they were given as a gift. As they sat at the table polishing off the last of the champagne, Martha said:

"You guys did great. Harry, I know that it was especially hard for you, but you faced it with plenty of professionalism and put the mission above everything else. Congratulations."

Harry raised his glass enthusiastically.

Around 3 a.m., they went to sleep. Another mission successfully completed. Today, Harry was a little better off than he was yesterday, financially speaking. His professionalism in the mission had been impeccable, and Martha praised him for it. Was he happy? That was a different question.

# CHAPTER XXVI

Around 11a.m., Harry, Piotr, and Martha arrived at the airport to board the same private plane that had brought them. Before getting on, Harry called Sofia.

"Hey, *bambina*, how are you?"

"Good, just hanging out here at your apartment. How about you?"

"Good. We're heading back; I'll be at the airport around two or so. You want to have lunch at El Sirena?"

"Sure, of course. Should I make a reservation and we meet there or do you have to stop by the house?"

"Let's meet there. I'll come right from the airport. I have to go—we're leaving. I love you." Harry wanted to say that to her.

"I love you, too, Harry. *Ciao*."

The flight went smoothly. Taking advantage of the comfort of the plane, each of them slept on a couch for nearly the whole flight. Right after landing, Piotr received a text that said that he, and only he, had another mission.

"*Damn, that poor guy has some bad luck—Sunday at noon, having just gotten back from another mission*," Harry thought, but didn't say it to him. He imagined that his knowledge of engineering and architecture was needed for some mission. "*Maybe sometimes it's best not to know so many things*," Harry thought to himself, smiling. Piotr took a taxi with Martha to the FAI building, and Harry took one to El Sirena. Martha wasn't called upon for the mission, but she wanted to finish preparing the mission report so that FAI would get paid as soon as possible, and she preferred to do it there rather than at her house. Harry thought that she must have really wanted to, as it could just as easily be done the next day, but he didn't say anything. He thought that perhaps she didn't want to spend more time alone at home than was absolutely necessary.

Harry arrived at El Sirena, where Sofia was already waiting at a table in a private area like last time. Ana wasn't there this time, but the waiter they got turned out to be just as good.

"So, how was the mission?" Sofia asked as they ate.

"Good. Mission accomplished."

"Is that all you're going to tell me?"

"I mean, Sofia, I don't think it's a good idea for me to go into specific details about the missions."

"Okay, as you wish, but as I said, I don't care about the skeletons you have in your closet. You told me they're never innocent, and that's good enough for me. I don't think it's good to keep all that inside, Harry, but I respect your wish. You can tell me anything whenever you want."

"You're right, Sofia, but I need some time for that, okay? I don't really feel like talking about work right now."

"Yeah, of course. Can you pass me the wine, please?"

"Of course. Hey, it's good, isn't it?"

"Do you think I would just pick any wine?"

"What about you? What did you do, *bambina*? Besides occupying my apartment, of course."

"Hahaha. Well, Saturday I had a drink with your friend Alfonso, and he told me some very interesting things, just so you know."

"Don't believe half of what that fucker tells you." They both laughed.

"He's nice. He was looking for you because he wanted to tell you something, but since you weren't here, he told me. He says he's dating a girl seriously."

"What the fuck? My Alfonso?" Harry nearly choked.

"Your Alfonso, yes. And he said you know the girl."

"Oh yeah? Who is it?"

"He didn't tell me much—just that they had slept together before, but he didn't do something he should have, and then it all went downhill."

"Jeez, based on what you're saying, it could be any girl." They laughed again, then Harry added, "I'll ask him."

"Ask him and then tell me. I'm intrigued."

"Of course. Damn, this turbot is amazing."

"Don't even get me started on this lobster."

"So, what else did you do?"

"Well, I was also with my friend Rebeca. Do you remember what I told you about her? And about meeting up with her and her boyfriend? She was living in Barcelona and..."

"Yes," Harry interrupted, "that poor girl who had that thing happen to her. How is she?"

"Good. She looks good, but she still has her moments even after all these years."

"Damn, that's awful. Well, whenever you want, we can hang out with them, of course. I like meeting your friends."

"Okay. I'll see if I can organize something this week, unless they send you off somewhere."

"Yeah, you never know. But for now, I'm free."

They finished eating and didn't want coffee or dessert. They went to Harry's apartment and took a nap, after which they had sex. At first, Harry wasn't very receptive, but he quickly got over it and ended up getting into it. He realized how much Sofia turned him on. After the recent episode with Tess, he couldn't avoid the comparison in his head, even though he hadn't had actual sex with Tess until the end. And even though Tess was a very attractive woman objectively, and he of course liked it and had gotten aroused, the difference compared to Sofia was enormous for him on a mental level.

He wouldn't be able to put it into words, but it must have been that Sofia was THE PERSON, all uppercase, for him, and that affected sex and everything else. Although the fact that Tess was pointing a gun at him and that everything was forced made the comparison a bit absurd.

After they finished and were relaxing in bed, Harry said to Sofia, "Why don't you come live with me?"

Sofia looked at him incredulously.

"Was the sex today *that good*?"

They both burst out laughing for a few seconds.

"I'm serious, *bambina*."

"Well, I hadn't considered it, honestly, but I think it's a good idea. Yeah, I'd like that, Harry," Sofia responded.

It hadn't been premeditated, but it had come out of Harry from within, and he had decided to ask it then. He felt it was the natural next step given the circumstances. They talked for a bit and decided that, since money wasn't an issue for either of them, they would look for a house they liked without worrying about whether it was for sale or rent. Once they found their ideal home, they would then buy it or rent it and simply split the cost in half. What they were sure of was that they would live in the city of Murcia, since they both loved the city. Harry, in particular, quickly fell in love with its historic center, its bars, its walking areas, its people. At that point, he didn't see himself living anywhere else, whether he worked at FAI or not. And Sofia had already been there for several years, so for her, it was already home.

"Either way, Harry, if it's okay with you, let's wait until we get back from Tuscany to start looking for a place. If you survive that weekend with my family and still want us to live together, then we'll start the search. Does that sound good?" Sofia said as she got up from the bed to get dressed.

"Do you think I'll be able to?"

"I can assure you it'll be harder than any of your missions."

"Hey, where are you going?"

"I have to go to my place, Harry. I don't have any clean clothes to put on, plus I have food I don't want to waste and all that."

"Ah, true. You're right," Harry said, then added, "Either way, even if we start looking for a place after Tuscany, grab the spare key to the apartment from the second drawer of the thing at the entrance. For you, so you can come whenever you want."

"Okay, handsome, of course. Here's what we'll do. Tomorrow morning I'll pack a suitcase and come here, does that sound good?"

"Sounds great."

Sofia went home, and Harry got up to read some Agatha Christie on the couch for a bit. Around 8 p.m. or so, he texted Alfonso: "*I heard you have something to tell me.*" Alfonso replied, "Come on over." Harry didn't much feel like it, but curiosity got the best of him, so he got dressed and went down to Alfonso's place.

"Well, well, look who it is. Indiana Jones! Did you find the lost ark?" Alfonso greeted him upon opening the door.

"Yeah, it was up your ass, moron," Harry responded. They laughed and gave each other a hug. Harry went to the living room and sat on the couch.

Alfonso's place was very tidy, which wasn't normal at all. The couch cover was in its place, the remotes for the different devices weren't scattered on the table or spread around the living room, but rather were all in the box he had next to the couch that was specifically for the remotes. And not only that, but even all the dishes were washed. Without a doubt, something important was going on.

"Beer?" Alfonso asked from the kitchen.

"No, just water. Thanks," Harry responded.

Alfonso came and sat down with an obvious smile.

"So," Harry started talking, "a little bird told me that you have something to tell me."

"Oh yeah? Well, I don't know who would have told you that," Alfonso responded ironically.

"Come on, cut it out, man."

"Okay. Well, exactly that, Harry, I'm dating a girl. Seriously dating. Her name is Maria."

"That's awesome, man. Maria…" Harry thought for a moment. "Sofia said that you said I already know her, but that name doesn't ring a bell right now."

"You say *'no me suena,'* not the bell thing."[26] Harry still had some issues with some expressions in Spanish, and Alfonso corrected him before explaining. "Do you remember Barbara, the one from the supermarket? Her sister."

"Her sister? The sister I'm thinking of?"

"That very one," Alfonso declared.

"The one that slapped you because…?"

"The same one."

"Damn, man. How did that happen?"

"Well, she called me one day and asked if I wanted to get a coffee with her—she said she wanted to. I was surprised, but I said yes. I figured I had nothing to lose, plus my curiosity was piqued. And the coffee went well—it was nice. Before, as far as talking goes, I hadn't talked to her too much, you know…"

"Right, right, I imagine."

"But we got along well. Plus, the girl is gorgeous. You've seen her before…"

"I mean, yeah, she's nice on the eyes."

"So then the next day we met up again, this time for a beer and then dinner. And it went really, really well. We finished dinner and then spent the night here. And, yeah, I mean, you could say we're officially boyfriend and girlfriend," Alfonso concluded.

---

26 Translator's note: In the original in Spanish, Harry directly translates the saying "It doesn't ring a bell" to Spanish, to which Alfonso corrects him with the appropriate saying in Spanish, i.e., *"no me suena."*

"That's great, man. If she's the reason your dishes are clean, she's worth it just for that." They both laughed at Harry's joke. "Wait, what about Barbara?" Harry was interested.

"Well, it's strange, because apparently they don't talk now," Alfonso replied.

It didn't surprise Harry all that much. He didn't quite understand why Alfonso found it strange. In his mind, it was reasonable that if, after finding out your sister was sleeping with the guy you were sleeping with at the same time, and after he sent both of you packing, you discover that she started dating him, maybe you would want to stop talking to your sister.

"I mean, Alfonso, it makes sense that Barbara doesn't want to talk to her sister after finding out about this, don't you think?"

"No, no, Harry. That has nothing to do with it. Maria says that she fell off the map. From what she told me, the last thing she heard is that her friend was going to stay with her for a few days. After that, she got a text one day saying she was leaving and to not look for her, because she needed a change of scenery and to clear her mind. And she hasn't heard anything since. She went to her apartment, and it was empty. She'd turned in her irrevocable resignation at work."

"Damn, bro, what a story."

"I know. She told me last week. She went to the police to report it, but they told her that she was an adult who said herself she was leaving, and that unless she could prove that something happened to her, they couldn't do anything."

Harry listened closely. He wasn't the only one who experienced strange things. He thought to himself then that maybe everyone wasn't a mercenary pretending to be an antique dealer, but each person certainly had enough stories to write a book, each more extravagant than the other. Alfonso continued:

"So, in the end, Maria convinced herself that the police were right, and she stopped worrying. She said if her sister Barbara needs anything, she'll call her, because, after all, she's the one who left.

Plus, she said that her text ended by saying that she would call her when the time came, so that was good enough for her."

"You're a heartbreaker, huh?"

"No way. I didn't do anything, man."

"Well, Alfonso, I also have something to tell you. Sofia and I are going to look for a place to live together."

"Really? Shit, that's great, man. I'm glad. But in Murcia, right? Don't run away to New Hampshire on me."

"Yeah, here. I have no intention of moving out of this city. We'll look for options, but around here. Don't worry, you won't get away from me that easily. By the way, you name a random state in the US and that's good enough for you, huh?" Harry asked, laughing.

"The first that came to my mind in the moment. That's how dumb I am," Alfonso replied, giving him a slap on the shoulder as he laughed. They chatted for a while, and Alfonso told him about how Maria had created her own marketing and social media consulting company that was going quite well for her then. Truth be told, those things didn't interest Harry much at all, but he understood that it was quite a modern thing that he couldn't do anything to avoid, and that more and more people worked in that field. The future was in social media and not in antique dealers. And his friend was telling him something about the girl he had just started dating, so he had to fake a bit of interest.

Harry and Alfonso agreed to meet one day for dinner with their girlfriends and have Maria officially meet Harry and Sofia. Harry went back to his apartment and ordered a pizza for dinner. *"That story about Maria and Barbara was so weird,"* Harry thought while he ate the pizza. Suddenly, she disappears without a trace, resigning from her job and telling her sister not to look for her and that she'll call her. The story was clearly far from ordinary. But he wasn't one to judge anyone either, apart from the fact that everyone's circumstances are different, and that he couldn't know those of Barbara in this case. Either way, despite how curious the story was, he would let it be. At the end of the day, her own sister seemed to have moved on, so he wasn't going to investigate who her friend was or where Barbara might be, especially after the police hadn't even done so. Plus, he already had enough to think about. He was about to live with another person, and soon he would meet her parents and have to decide whether he wanted to continue as a mercenary at FAI or not. However, he had already almost fully made up his mind on that.

# CHAPTER XXVII

Friday July 30ᵗʰ had finally arrived, and Sofia was quite nervous. She was sure that when she packed, she had forgotten to pack half of the stuff that she wanted to bring to Tuscany for the weekend. But there was no turning back. They were at the airport waiting for the boarding gate for their flight to Florence, and if she had forgotten to pack her panties, bra, or toothbrush, it would have been too late.

"Sofia, relax. Everything will be okay," Harry said as he touched her leg to calm her down.

"Okay, you're right. I'm just not sure if I have everything. I probably forgot something and…"

"Well," Harry interrupted her, "if you forgot your underwear, then you'll be colder, and if you forgot your bikini, then you'll just go skinny dipping. Who cares?"

"You're silly, aren't you?"

"You know it." Harry smiled at her, grabbed her hand, then added, "Your parents are going to love me, and I'm sure I'll love them too. Plus, we're on vacation. Cheer up."

Indeed, they both had an entire month of vacation ahead of them. It was always possible that Harry would get called for an urgent mission, but the Conglomerate initially gave FAI the entire month, and anything that might come up would be handled by other delegations. Spain practically came to a standstill in August, which Harry found remarkable, but FAI wasn't going to be an exception.

Apart from the weekend in Tuscany, they had nothing planned, which wasn't necessarily a bad thing. Neither of them thought it was bad, nor did they get too overwhelmed by going with the flow of everything. They had to live in the moment.

Sofia was already living with Harry at his apartment for the last few days, and she had told her landlord that she was leaving hers. At first, he wasn't too thrilled, given that it would be difficult for him to find a new tenant in August, but with a couple of months of extra rent that Sofia had given him, it was all resolved without much trouble. She had opted to do that rather than tell Harry to break his legs like a proper mercenary.

Living together during those first few days went quite well. Since Sofia liked to cook and practically had the mornings free, she took care of making food most days. Harry's schedule was more chaotic for obvious reasons, but he tried to take care of dinners, much less elaborate than Sofia's meals. Besides that, a person came twice a week to clean and organize the house, so everything on that front was going smoothly. They were in the phase of getting used to each other in their day-to-day lives, and everything was going well for the moment. All the sex they were having those first few days of living together also helped.

On the third day of them living together, Sofia told Harry in full detail about the episode with the ogre years ago and how it had ended. Harry was shocked listening to her, but without any type of reproach, as was only natural, keeping in mind how understanding she had been when he told her about his actual work duties. He didn't ask for any type of explanation and had no problem with the fact that his girlfriend had gotten rid of a rapist from the face of the earth. She assured him that she was okay, so for Harry, that was good enough. He understood that the expression about skeletons in the closet that she had told him was more real than figurative.

Apart from that, Harry had finally made up his mind and, after talking about it with Sofia and receiving her unconditional support, sent an email to the corresponding department with his resignation. If all went well, they would respond with a "friends forever" for him and Sofia, and once both their signatures were sent, his relationship with FAI and the Conglomerate would end. That said, the Conglomerate didn't exactly abide by the Workers Statute or the labor regulations of the country, so they could answer whenever they felt like it. It could take three days, two weeks, four months…. But Harry had now taken that step. He had already fully decided that he wanted to leave that life behind and dedicate himself to something more "normal" and compatible with a romantic relationship. He still didn't know what, but he had all the time in the world to think about it.

Before formally requesting his resignation, he had talked about it with Martha. He thought he owed it to her for professional and personal courtesy. He could have waited until they responded to him, but he preferred to tell her before, and so he did. He invited her for a coffee and told her. Martha said that she had already imagined, and that, knowing he had plenty of money, he was doing the right thing. She, for her part, told him that she had taken about a year-long vacation that they had granted her. She would go back to the US for some time, and then she didn't know what she would do. Harry was happy for her. She deserved a break. She didn't seem to him to be in bad spirits. Martha was a strong person and would move past the situation with Tom. Harry had no doubt about it. He asked her if she knew, then, what would happen with FAI, but she didn't know anything. They would both find out soon, probably after August.

And there they were now, in an airport packed with people as would be the case on a Friday, July 30th, like any other normal couple leaving for vacation. The flight left on time and landed in Florence a couple of hours later without incident, besides a bit of turbulence that had caught Harry while he was in the bathroom, who ended up hitting his head on the door, but nothing serious. There was a chauffeur waiting at the airport with a sign in hand that said "Sofia Lombardi." An hour-long journey to the villa awaited them.

Sofia seemed to have relaxed a bit, or at least that's what Harry thought. He was, for his part, a bit eager, but relaxed. He was turning over in his head (still aching from the bump in the airplane) much more about when and how the Conglomerate would respond to his resignation request than wondering if Sofia's parents would like him or not. He was quite confident in himself.

Harry had never been to Italy, and the scenery from the car looked quite beautiful to him. There was plenty of grass and green pasture, though not many trees—that's for sure. And old, small towns of stone could be seen along the road. The bad part was that it was quite hot, which he didn't fare very well with.

"Perfect temperature, isn't it? You guys came at a good time," the chauffer said to them in perfect English at one point during the journey shortly before arriving.

"*Yeah, yeah, great weather. We'll see if I don't melt between now and Sunday,*" Harry thought without saying anything.

A few minutes later, they arrived at the villa, and Francesco and Arianna came out to greet them. They hugged their daughter and greeted her in Italian, who replied with something in Italian that Harry didn't understand. Then, she introduced them to Harry.

"*Piacere di conoscervi*[27]" Harry said to them in the best Italian he could to try and gain some points in his favor.

"Sofia already told us that you don't speak Italian, don't worry. But thank you, it's very kind. It's a pleasure, Harry," Francesco greeted him.

"What a relief, sir, because I don't know how to say anything else," Harry responded, to which everyone laughed. It seemed like they had gotten off on the right foot.

"Do you guys want to get in the pool? It's hot, isn't it?" Arianna asked.

"That would be great, ma'am. And yes, it is," Harry replied.

------------

27  "Nice to meet you" in Italian.

"Take a dip if you'd like. And don't call me ma'am; Arianna is just fine. And my husband is Francesco; no need to say 'sir.' We're Italian, but not mafiosos. Please, don't perpetuate stereotypes." Everyone laughed.

Harry found them to be quite pleasant from the start—a great sense of humor and very hospitable. He didn't understand why Sofia was nervous. Sofia took him to her room, which was on the second floor and quite big. Her window faced the pool and an all-green landscape with mountains in the distance. There were certainly more trees there than along the road they had taken.

"Look, Harry, look out there," Sofia pointed out the window toward the horizon.

Harry stuck his head out of the window and saw a group of deer grazing without any worry whatsoever. There were about eight to ten of them, some three hundred feet from the pool, near the fence that demarcated the property. It was indeed a beautiful landscape.

They put on their bathing suits and went down to get in the pool for a bit before dinner. Sofia's parents loved Harry's swimming trunks, which were from the movie Back to the Future.

Harry felt that he had already won them over. The birthday celebration would be the following day, and during dinner (the best wood-oven pizzas that Harry had ever eaten), apart from asking Harry about his job as an antique dealer, they talked about the plan for the next day. There would be about one hundred and fifty guests, with some of Sofia's cousins, her uncles and aunts, and many family friends and company employees. The attire would be informal, given the heat and the fact that people would swim in the pool. There would also be a group of servers and a hired chef that would come to prepare and serve barbecue meat and hors d'oeuvres (or as they call it in Italy, *antipasti*) for all the guests. And after the cake, drinks for everyone who wanted them, and later in the evening, a light cold dinner. What most surprised Harry was that they had also contracted a service to decorate the villa early in the morning and who, apparently, would remove the decoration on Monday. It seemed curious to him, to say the least. The birthday would undoubtedly be celebrated to the nth degree and be quite the event.

Around 11 p.m., Sofia's parents went to bed, and the two of them stayed at the table next to the pool digesting the pizzas a bit with decaf espresso.

"I'm doing a lot of Italian things, aren't I? Pizzas, espresso, the Aperol[28] I had before…You can't complain, *bambina*," Harry said.

"Hahaha. Absolutely—as if you were born and raised in Milan."

"Hey, you have nothing to worry about. I like your parents a lot."

"Yeah, I can tell. You won them over right away. It's probably because they're older and they're letting their guard down."

"Or because I'm undeniably charming." They both laughed.

"Well, don't get too confident. Tomorrow is key," Sofia said as she got up from her seat, then added, "I'm going to bed, Harry. I'm tired. Are you coming?"

Harry nodded his head and got up as well. It had been a long day, and it was time to sleep.

The next day, the party went great. Harry met Giancarlo and Manuela, who were Sofia's uncle and aunt, and several male and female cousins whose names he didn't remember. Besides Sofia's parents, few people spoke English or Spanish, so he couldn't socialize too much. Arianna, for her part, got excited when they brought her the cake and gave a short speech that Harry didn't understand, but it seemed quite moving judging by the guests' faces. Sofia gave her mother a gold choker as a gift that she loved, or at least that's what she said. And the key moment for Harry was when, at one point in the evening, Francesco approached him and told him that his daughter looked very happy, which he thanked him for.

"I'm also very happy, Francesco. She's great. You two raised a wonderful daughter."

---

28  A popular Italian drink.

"I don't need to tell you that if you hurt my daughter, I'll kill you, right?" Francesco responded with a face that seemed to Harry like a mix between sarcastic and sincere.

"No need at all," Harry replied, trying to smile. Francesco gave him a pat on the shoulder and walked away, satisfied with the conversation.

Harry didn't make a huge deal of it. It must have been the local sense of humor or Francesco's in particular. He figured that Francesco didn't know to what extent his daughter could defend herself alone.

Truth be told, Harry was comfortable, but not entirely. On the one hand, it was a beautiful day which always raised morale. Even though it was exceedingly hot for him, the pool was quite nice, especially when the servers came by and offered beer. And though he couldn't talk much with everyone because of the language barrier, it didn't make him uncomfortable either. He was with Sofia, her parents, and a cousin who did speak English, and that was all he needed. Moreover, the food was incredible; he didn't need anything else. However, at the same time, he couldn't stop thinking about his requested resignation and how he increasingly wanted the moment of an affirmative response to arrive so he could start his new life, without having to be tied to that necessary evil, as his friend Alfonso had called work. And that made him somewhat uneasy when, in normal circumstances, he would be enjoying a day like this quite a lot.

"Harry, are you okay? Come back to earth!" Arianna said to him at one point in the evening.

"Oh, yeah, sorry. I got lost in my dumb thoughts," Harry replied as his face turned as red as a tomato, which made Sofia laugh.

"Harry, are you okay, babe?" Sofia asked him without anyone hearing them as they leaned on the edge of the pool.

"Yeah, *bambina*, I'm okay, I was just in my own world a bit, but I'm okay. I'm having a really good time. It's all so nice, and the people are great."

"That's because you don't understand anything they're saying."

"Well, sometimes, it's better that way, don't you think?" They both laughed and continued the conversation.

"Hey, the return flight tomorrow is at 6 p.m., right? Or is it at seven? Do you remember?" Harry asked.

"At 5:30. Wait, that's what I was going to say. What are we going to do? We're on vacation and we have nothing planned. You've never seen Murcia in summer, but a lot of things close right away and, as you saw these past few days, you can't hang out outside. Everyone leaves. It's like a ghost town."

"Well, I'm not sure. We can go wherever we want, really."

"Well, we can think on it."

"Yeah, I'll see if I think of something after another gin tonic and a trip to the bathroom, okay?" Harry said, then gave Sofia a kiss and got out of the pool, concluding the conversation about planning their next several days of vacation.

Around 11 p.m., people started heading out, and at 12:30, everyone had already left. Then, Harry and Sofia went to their bedroom.

"So, did you have a good time? What did you think?" Sofia asked him, now in bed.

"Good, really good. Your family really went all-out. It was a top-of-the-line celebration, don't you think?" Harry replied as he caressed her affectionately.

"Yeah, that's how my parents are. We're Mediterranean, Harry; we like parties. Hey, by the way, I thought about something. How about we think about what to do this month in London instead of Murcia? There's a flight leaving the day after tomorrow at 9:30 a.m. from Murcia. We get back tomorrow, pack up, and the next morning we leave, and I'll show you our apartment there. Then we can plan whatever we want and go wherever we want. How does that sound?"

"Hey, that might be nice."

"I'm glad you like the idea. Either way, I already bought the tickets, so…," Sofia responded, laughing.

"What? When?"

"Earlier when I went to the bathroom at one point. I thought of it, looked on my phone, and bought them. That's how I am, Harry Fernández, so get used to it," Sofia replied as she got closer to Harry.

"So, London—another city where we'll have sex."

"We still haven't had it here."

"There's a simple solution to that."

The next day, with a considerable hangover, after having lunch and thanking Francesco and Arianna for everything, Harry and Sofia went to the airport to return to Murcia. Sofia told Harry that her parents had told her that they loved him, which boosted Harry's confidence in a certain way, though he didn't have the energy to express it then. They had drunk a lot the previous day. Plus, in the end, the night had been full of partying, and he had just recently eaten, so he felt like sleeping for three consecutive days. And Sofia essentially felt the same way at that point, too.

They slept the whole flight. They arrived at Harry's apartment around 9:30 p.m. It was Sunday, August 1ˢᵗ, and most things were closed, but the Chinese restaurants didn't fail, so they ordered dinner for delivery which arrived quickly, around ten. They ate dinner and barely said anything to each other because of how tired they were, and at 10:30, they were sound asleep. They got up at seven, had breakfast, packed up in record time, and forty-five minutes later, they ordered a taxi to take them to the airport to catch their flight to London.

London greeted them with rain, as was foreseeable given what they had seen in the weather report. With their raincoats on, they got a taxi at Stansted Airport to Sofia's apartment in Earl's Court. Harry was fascinated by the fact that they drove in the left lane, as well as all things British in general, given how different it was from Spain or even the US in many ways. There was a traffic jam going into London, so they took a bit longer than expected, with the consequent increase in price for the trip.

They finally arrived. Sofia had taken care of letting the cleaning service know the day before, and they got everything ready. Harry was impressed.

"So, you call, and they clean it all for you? They make your bed and stock your fridge with whatever you want?" he asked, incredulous.

"That's right. Impressed? Do you think you mercenaries are the only ones that know how to live it up?" Sofia replied, smiling.

It certainly seemed amazing to Harry to have an apartment right in London available and ready to be used at any moment, living in a city like Murcia where there were daily flights to London. "*This woman is, without a doubt, the love of my life*," Harry thought to himself in a humorous tone.

If he didn't have a job like the one at FAI, where he never knew when he might be in some part of the world and where his life could be in danger, then on any of Sofia's days off or holidays, they could go to London, to "her house." It wasn't like going to a hotel; it was a proper house. He loved the idea.

How long would they take to respond to his resignation? They couldn't deny it to him. In the past few months, he had led successful missions worth millions of dollars. They had eliminated the most wanted terrorist, recovered artwork stolen by nazis. Obviously, he had been paid for it, but he deserved to be free to live his life. They had already profited enough from him. It was just a matter of time; he had said so a few days prior. Plus, he was on vacation—there was no reason to worry. That same day in the evening, they went to Picadilly Circus to drink some pints and talk about their next vacation destination. Harry thought that it would be good for him, to avoid thinking about his resignation, to immerse himself in the atmosphere of a British pub, with soccer in the background, drunk people playing darts, and décor featuring dark wood-paneled walls and pillars.

They both felt like going to a beach, so they quickly came to an agreement. Money wasn't a problem, but places being fully booked might be. The philosophy of not planning and living in the moment had those minor issues. But with just a quick search, which lasted approximately three fourths of a pint of Guinness, they booked a resort with everything included on the island of Tortola in the British Virgin Islands. They would fly at night the next day from London to San Juan, Puerto Rico, and from there to their destination, where they would spend three weeks lying on a beach, drinking mojitos, riding jet skis, and trying not to get stressed or even think about the next day. They booked everything with trip cancellation insurance, since, with FAI, Harry could never be sure if he had days off.

They didn't have beachwear in London, so they decided to go to a department store the following morning to get swimsuits, towels, and bikinis. Then, everything would be planned and ready, quick and easy. That night, they went to a pub on Carnaby Street for dinner, which was a very lively area. However, they soon went back to the apartment to sleep, since the next day they had to get up early to go shopping and then spend several hours in the airport and the plane. Harry read a bit of a book that he had read halfway, but just a couple of pages were enough for him to decide to put the book on the nightstand and try to sleep with Sofia, who had already succumbed to sleep a while ago.

He truly wanted to go to the beach, especially because he wouldn't have to worry about anything besides making sure the waiter was close to the deckchairs to order as many mojitos as he wanted. It would be nice to relax and not think about anything. He fell asleep peacefully, imagining himself already lying on a hammock on an idyllic beach.

They arrived at the airport with plenty of time to spare, as Harry liked. They checked their bags and got in line to go through security. Heathrow Airport was filled to the brim with people, as was to be expected, so they figured that it would take a while, but it wasn't a problem; that's why they had arrived early. They got through smoothly, then headed to immigration control. After showing his passport, the police officer looked at Harry, looked at the passport photo, and put it through a machine that emitted a red light and a rather harsh sound.

"Sir, this passport isn't valid," the officer told him.

"What do you mean? Just yesterday they validated it here when we came from Spain," Harry responded.

The officer got on his walkie talkie, and a few seconds later, a pair of officers, a man and a woman, showed up.

"Please, follow my colleagues. Your companion can wait here if she'd like."

"Okay, *bambina*, wait here. I'll see what's going on with my passport," Harry told Sofia, as she showed a face of acceptance (she had no choice) and sat down on one of the seats there.

Harry followed the officers to a room with a desk, a laptop, and a couple of chairs. The female officer sat at the desk with the laptop in front of her, while the male officer stood behind Harry.

"Please, sit down, mister...Fernández, correct?" the officer said to Harry.

"Yes, Fernández."

"Where are you from?"

"I'm American, but my father is Spanish."

"I see. Your native language is English, then? You understand it and speak it well from what I can tell, correct?"

"Yes, it's my native language. Don't worry."

"Okay, brilliant. And what brings you here to the UK, Mr. Fernández?"

"Well, my partner..., the girl that was with me out there, her family has an apartment here, and we're on vacation. Now we're going to the British Virgin Islands for a few weeks."

"I see."

"Is there are problem, officer?"

"This trip you're telling me about must not be cheap, isn't that right?"

"I mean, you can imagine for yourself, but, excuse me for saying this, but I don't think that's any of your business. Is there a problem with my passport?"

"Well, Mr. Fernández, rest assured, your passport is perfectly valid and there's no issue with it. We'll let you go soon. We received orders from our superiors to bring you in here. Now that we've finished our security questions, they've now told us to leave and that you stay here for a moment, understood?"

Harry didn't understand what was going on. They had pretended that there was a problem with his passport to take him to an isolated room, where they had asked him security-related questions, and now they were going to leave him alone? Why? Since he couldn't do much about it either way, he said, "*Okay, then,*" and stayed seated, but alert.

The officers left the room with the laptop in hand, and Harry was left alone. He got up from the chair and stood facing the door. A couple of minutes later, a man with dark pants and a pink shirt showed up, about the same age and height as Harry. He didn't greet him. The man had a tablet that he turned on after entering the room and turned it around so Harry could see it. A video started playing on the screen of an older man sitting in an office. Harry instantly recognized him. It was the one and only King of England.

# CHAPTER XXVIII

The video was quite short, barely reaching a minute. In it, the King of England thanked Harry on behalf of the entire British public for having recovered the Royal Game of Ur for the British Museum, and also asked him to extend his praise to his colleagues. Truth be told, Harry didn't quite know what to say at that moment. He was speechless. When the video ended, the man turned off the tablet and finally spoke to Harry:

"Sorry for all the fuss, Mr. Fernández, but when we learned that you were in England, His Majesty wanted to send you his praises. He hadn't been able to do it publicly because, as you already know, it's a secret that it'd been stolen from the museum. That's why I had to show you this video in secret, and from here it will disappear. We hope we haven't caused you any trouble. You won't miss your flight, will you?"

"Oh, no, no. I have plenty of time. Well, send my thanks to the King for his praise. To be honest, it was all quite unexpected," Harry responded.

Harry didn't have much esteem for the King of England or for any monarchy in general. In the US, it was seen as something quite strange, foreign, in some sense, and a bit antiquated. But he also believed that he wasn't one to impose that belief on anyone, and that if there were countries where they were happy with that form of government or that symbolic institution, why not. And now that a king, who was still the leader of the state, "personally" praised him for a job, of course it gave him great satisfaction. Was receiving royal praises a reason not to quit FAI? Well, it wasn't that big of a deal, either—or was it, perhaps?

Harry shook the hand of the man with the tablet, who then left the room. He told Harry to count to fifteen before leaving, and Harry complied. He was probably an officer from the government secret service and didn't want to be seen with Harry for security reasons.

Sofia stood up when she saw Harry, and Harry gave her a thumbs up.

"What happened, Harry?"

"I'll tell you later. You're not going to believe it."

They went through passport control, now without any issues, and boarded the plane. Despite Sofia's insistence, Harry didn't tell her anything right away. He didn't trust that someone on the plane might hear him, and it was something that could put his identity at risk.

They slept through the whole flight and landed in Puerto Rico at dawn. They transferred there and flew to Tortola, where they arrived a couple of hours later, exhausted.

Once they were in the bungalow at the resort that they had booked, Harry finally told Sofia about the King of England praising him, and Sofia was amazed.

"Are you joking?"

"Whether you believe it or not, that's what happened."

"You are the fucking man, Harry. Do you realize that?"

"To be honest, I liked it. I won't lie."

"It's incredible. Damn, the worst part is not being able to tell anyone."

"That's right—don't even think about it, okay?"

"Of course, but it would be nice to brag a bit.

"Well, I don't know about you, but I'm going to the water," Harry concluded the subject.

The bungalow was right on the beach, so they only had to open the door, go down three steps on the porch, and they were on the sand. It had a double bedroom, a living room with a dining table, four chairs, and a couch facing a TV, which was the most comfortable couch that Harry had ever sat on. Moreover, there was a small kitchen with a refrigerator, a couple of burners, and a large bathroom with a jacuzzi bathtub. It was indeed very well equipped and quite spacious, although, after what it had cost them, they didn't expect anything less. There was a stand with drinks and another with food on the beach with a person in each one and a waiter who was in charge of bringing what people ordered to their deckchairs, in the sand or on the bungalow porch, whichever they preferred. There was also another area behind with several pools, restaurants, and bars.

And that's how they spent three weeks there: from the crystalline-water beaches to the pool, from there to another pool, to a restaurant, to the bungalow to make love facing the sea, from there to the beach, and so on. They left for a couple of days on an excursion to some nearby islands, but, in general, they stayed at the resort.

The vacation certainly helped Harry disconnect. He didn't hear anything from FAI that whole time, though he didn't receive a response to his resignation request either. Three weeks after their arrival, they returned to Spain via Madrid. On Wednesday, August 18th, they were back in Murcia, still with several days of vacation ahead of them that, keeping with their trend, they didn't know how or where they would spend.

Shortly after landing, Alfonso called Harry, and they talked for a bit. He invited them to come over to his apartment for dinner the next day, and that way they could meet Maria. Harry, after consulting with Sofia, accepted the invitation. In truth, Harry was curious to see Alfonso with a formal girlfriend. It was a completely novel situation for him. And he also wanted to meet Maria, to see what the girl was like who had invited his friend Alfonso on a date and had managed to get him to give up his playboy lifestyle for her.

Around 7:30 p.m. on Thursday, they went down to Alfonso's place with a bottle of wine that Sofia had chosen at the supermarket to be proper guests and not arrive empty-handed. It was boiling hot in Murcia in August, so Harry had put on a slightly dressy T-shirt and some jean shorts with sandals, while Sofia wore a short summer dress with a colorful design. They rang the doorbell, and Alfonso opened the door a few seconds later.

"Welcome, friends. Come on in." He hugged Harry and gave Sofia two kisses on her cheeks, then added, "Damn, you guys are tan, huh? Wow, thanks for the wine. You didn't have to."

They went to the living room where Maria was sitting on the couch; when she saw them come in, she got up and approached them.

"Hi, I'm Maria. Pleasure to meet you."

"Hi, Maria. I'm Harry, and this is Sofia. The pleasure is ours." They exchanged pleasantries.

Maria was wearing a jean miniskirt and a white tank top. Harry found her quite attractive. He remembered her from the few seconds that he had seen her with her sister coming out of the elevator on that fateful night for Alfonso, but he hadn't gotten a good look at her then.

"Please, sit down. Beer, wine?" Alfonso asked as he brought a tray of several types of cold cuts and a basket of bread and left them on the table in front of the couch. The appetizer before dinner went quite well. Maria talked about how she began her marketing company and how difficult it had been for her, but that now the business was going great. She proved to be quite an easy-going and pleasant woman. She made a great impression on Harry. At one point, when the two of them were alone, Harry confirmed that Sofia felt the same way.

Around half past nine or so, they sat at the table, and Alfonso brought out a salad with cherry tomatoes, lettuce, arugula, pickles, boiled egg, and tuna. Nothing too crazy or complicated, but quite delicious and fresh for the season they were in.

As they ate the salad, a scent wafted in from the kitchen that smelled fantastic to Harry.

"Whatever you're making smells great," Sofia exclaimed.

"It's barbecue ribs, almost done baking in the oven. I made the barbecue sauce, so don't get your hopes up," Maria said, as everyone laughed.

"I'm sure it's great," Harry replied.

"By the way, Harry," Maria started inquiring, "Alfonso told me about the antique business you have, and it sounded really interesting to me. If you want, we can talk someday about how to advertise it a bit on social media and all that. It's not a very common business and it might have potential."

Harry didn't give a damn about social media and didn't give a damn about FAI's social media because they didn't need clients for antique dealers. But he had to fake it for his cover and to avoid offending Maria.

"Thank you, Maria. I'll keep it in mind," he responded.

"Okay, no pressure. By the way, I remember you met my sister Barbara from the supermarket, right?"

"Yes, I did. How is she?" Harry played dumb as though he knew nothing.

"She's great. She's in Vietnam now and says she's with a friend, but she didn't tell me much else. I don't even know her friend's name. Anyways, she says she's good and that she'll be back soon," Maria replied.

"Wow, that's great. I'm glad." Harry didn't quite know what to say.

Alfonso brought the tray from the oven with the ribs and put it in the middle of the table. The ribs cooked in the oven for several hours at a low temperature, and they fell off the bone right when he touched them with a spoon because of how tender they were. And the barbecue sauce was perfect, with just the right balance of sweet and spicy, but not too sweet or strong. Maria certainly had a talent for cooking.

They finished dinner, and after some pleasant conversation, Harry and Sofia said goodbye and agreed to return the invitation another day. Harry winked at Alfonso when leaving as if to say, "*Don't let her go, moron—she's awesome,*" to which Alfonso responded with a smile and a subtle nod of the head.

Once they were both in bed, Sofia asked Harry:

"Wait, so Maria's sister is named Barbara?"

"Yeah, it is. Why do you ask?"

"What happened? Did she just suddenly leave?"

"Yeah. Apparently, she fell off the map and left with a friend who was going to stay with her for a few days. It's a weird story, but she said she talked to her and that she's fine. I guess everyone has their moments."

"And when was that?"

"I'm not sure. A few months ago, I guess, because I saw the girl once in May, which was when Alfonso met her. And Barbara was there. What are you thinking?"

"This mysterious friend is probably Loretta."

"What?"

"Damn, Harry, I thought you were a spy. The dates fit, Loretta's friend who she was going to stay with and who texted me was named Barbara, they both fell off the map...."

What Sofia was saying made sense. It hadn't occurred to him to connect it all. Sofia certainly had the makings of a detective or an investigator. He already knew she was smart, but she also had another kind of intelligence that was scarce among the general public, in Harry's opinion: cleverness, ingenuity, common sense.

"Do you want to...?" Harry began to ask when Sofia interrupted him and cut off his chance to say more.

"No, I don't care. I don't want to know anything about Loretta. I have no interest in finding out anything. It made me curious, that's all."

"You're so smart, Sofia."

"Do you think I would have been a good mercenary?" Sofia asked as she caressed him.

"The best. And the sexiest," Harry replied, as Sofia laughed.

Harry fell asleep thinking about what Sofia would be like working at FAI. She would indeed be a great asset; he had no doubt. Sofia had already killed someone before, and though she believed she had already moved past it, and he wouldn't say anything to her about it, he knew that wasn't true. You don't forget that; once you kill, you're capable of doing it again. But it wasn't only that she had already killed someone (the guy undoubtedly deserved it), but that she had carried it out methodically and by herself, apart from the help to get rid of the body, which she got her friend to help her with, something else she had thought about. In short, she had practically carried out a mission that without a doubt could have been an FAI mission. Damn, and to think that FAI and all the divisions of the Conglomerate did much easier missions than what Sofia did to get rid of the ogre. He could name her an honorary member of FAI. Perhaps it was better to keep that a secret, now that Sofia had a "normal" life. He didn't want to make her unnecessarily remember past experiences.

Harry and Sofia spent the rest of August between Harry's apartment, a couple of excursions to see the beaches in an area that Harry still hadn't seen, and walks in nature at times during the day when the Murcia heat in August could be tolerated. During the hottest points of the day, they started looking at houses to visit in September. Sofia had no desire whatsoever to call real estate agencies, go to the houses, be on high alert to find where the catch would be in the house (there's always a catch, she believed), and put up with the typical statements from the real estate agent that are false ninety-five percent of the time. "If you're interested, you have to let me know right away, okay? This house sells itself, and I already have several interested buyers." *"Yes, of course! I'll go ahead and send you the reservation fee right now. Give me a minute to go pee just in case, you jerk."* Though she did want to have her own home with Harry, paid for by both. And Harry was noticeably excited, so she would do everything she could to put on a brave face. But she also hoped they wouldn't have to see too many homes; she wanted the process to be quick. Looking at houses and all that…it was way too boring for her.

With the nonsense from the dinner at Alfonso's, he had been thinking at certain points in the past few days, "what if she had been an FAI mercenary?" She certainly would have done well. She didn't fear anyone; he had no doubt about that.

On September 1ˢᵗ, they had their first appointment to see a house later in the day. That morning, Harry went to FAI. Vacation was over, and, since he didn't get a response to his resignation, he had to go back to work. It was the first day and it was still hotter than hell itself, so he went in shorts and a T-shirt. Martha, in theory, was on a long vacation, so it would only be Piotr and Harry there, since Angela was still in the US as an instructor.

He arrived at FAI and greeted Pepe. He talked with him for ten minutes about how his summer had gone and various trivial matters, then went up to the second floor. When he put the key in, the door opened immediately; it wasn't locked, which meant that Piotr was probably already inside waiting for him. He walked in and closed the door behind him, but he didn't see Piotr.

Martha was on the couch and looked at Harry.

"What's going on, Martha? What are you doing here?" Harry asked as he approached her, knowing that something was wrong. Martha's facial expression was between angry and even sad, Harry would say. She had bags under her eyes that she hadn't bothered to cover up with makeup.

"Sit down, Harry."

Harry complied and sat on the couch next to Martha. "Tell me what's going on. Where's Piotr? He isn't here yet?"

"Piotr died, Harry," Martha said as she grabbed his hand.

# CHAPTER XXIX

"Martha, what the hell are you saying?" Harry asked, stunned.

"Exactly what you heard, Harry. I was here in Murcia last night, coincidentally, doing some cleaning around the house, and the Conglomerate called me. Since I knew you were coming to the office today, I came to tell you in person," Martha responded.

Harry jumped up from the couch.

"But what exactly happened, Martha?"

"An accident, Harry."

"An accident? Come on, what? What do you mean an accident?"

"He was driving with his daughter on a road in Warsaw, and a truck coming towards them ran into them. He died on the spot, and his daughter Anka is in the hospital. The truck driver also died. I thought the same as you, but if it had been a murder, I don't think the murderer would have wanted to die too, so I'm taking the accident story at face value."

Harry didn't know what to think. What Martha was saying made sense, but even so…. It was hard for him to believe that after having completed elite missions, using paramilitary tactics, killing terrorists…, he could die in such a trivial way.

Harry sat on the couch, still incredulous, as Martha told him what the Conglomerate had told her and how it had all happened. Apparently, Piotr and his daughter Anka were heading to a small town near Warsaw to spend the day, where Piotr knew a great restaurant close to a natural area that he loved as a child.

Anka, Piotr's daughter, was fifteen years old and lived in Warsaw with her mother, Piotr's ex-wife. She didn't spend much time with her father, and summer was one of the few times in which she could be with him for several days in a row. Contrary to what often happens, and just as it always should be, Anka's mother didn't speak badly about her father in any way. Things between the two of them hadn't worked out, but that didn't mean that Piotr was a bad person or that he didn't love his daughter. As such, he made sure to remind her of that whenever it was necessary, so the relationship between the three of them was solid despite the separation. That's why, even though she was at a difficult age, as teenage years are, she liked to spend time with her father whenever she could.

Thus, on Monday, August 30th around 10 a.m., they were both heading to their destination in the car that Piotr had in Poland. Piotr also kept a small apartment in Warsaw, where he escaped from Murcia to be with Anka when he had time off and was on vacation.

According to the police report, when they were about to arrive at their destination, on a road with a speed limit of sixty kilometers per hour[29], a truck coming towards them went into the oncoming lane with the ill fate of Piotr and Anka driving in that lane.

Apparently, what caused the truck to go into the oncoming lane, after the initial forensic investigation, was speeding and possibly some drowsiness on the part of the driver, as he had no trace of alcohol or drugs.

Piotr turned to try and dodge the truck after seeing it coming straight at him, but he couldn't. He hit them off the road, and they ran into a tree directly on the driver's side, causing Piotr's immediate death after the airbags failed to go off and a massive blow to his head. Anka's airbags did go off, which saved her life, even though the impact wasn't on her side.

---

29  About thirty-seven miles per hour.

As for the truck driver, after he lost control, he suffered a severe blow that caused internal bleeding in his liver which led to his death in the hospital a few hours later.

The doctors told Anka that she needed another day of rest in the hospital, thus delaying the funeral. The Conglomerate had booked them a private flight to Warsaw in a couple of hours. Harry called Sofia, who immediately told him she was coming with him. Angela would fly from New York and meet them in Warsaw; in fact, she was already airborne.

That same night, Sofia, Harry, and Martha were in Warsaw. They met with Angela in a very emotional reunion. They went to the hotel, which the Conglomerate had found for them, since it was too late to see Anka in the hospital at that hour; they would see her the following day at the cemetery. In fact, they would meet her for the first time, given that they had never seen her before, except for in a picture that Piotr had shown them.

They left what little luggage they had in their rooms and went down to the hotel restaurant for dinner, at a table for four in a corner away from everyone else. No one was hungry, but they made the effort to be together at that moment, if nothing else.

They ordered something light to get something in their stomachs, and after finishing, Harry decided to order a whiskey, and everyone followed him. Up until then, the dinner had gone by in an almost deathly silence, where it seemed like each of them was reflecting upon the moment they were having. With the first sip of whiskey, Angela broke the silence, raising her glass.

"For Piotr, wherever you may be."

Everyone raised their glass for a toast, and right after, Harry said, smiling, "Do you guys remember when that fucker almost choked to death on a slice of pizza?"

"Ah, yeah, in Almería. So dumb. He couldn't swallow first and then talk," Martha responded, also smiling.

"What happened? Tell me the story," Sofia asked.

And then they spent another half hour recalling anecdotes about Piotr, even laughing at some of them. Even Angela, who seemed the most affected, ended up laughing as well.

Harry had initiated the round of anecdotes entirely on purpose; that's how he was. He knew that they all needed their moment to mourn, as anyone would, including him. But Piotr surely would have preferred, wherever he may have been, that they remembered the good times with him. And he believed that he had to cheer up Martha and especially Angela, in addition to himself. He didn't know how intense her relationship with Piotr was in terms of affection, but she was visibly quite distraught. Harry didn't generally trust people, but he did trust his colleagues. And he loved the people he could trust, and he wanted her to cheer up as much as possible.

They went up to their rooms to sleep. Harry didn't think he'd be able to sleep, but he at least had to try. He got in the bed, which looked quite uncomfortable to him, and his suspicion was confirmed as soon as his back touched the mattress.

"*Motherfucker*," Harry thought. Sofia, for her part, got in bed next to him and was snoring away two minutes later.

Harry couldn't sleep the entire night, partly because of the mattress, but also because he couldn't stop thinking and ruminating over how Piotr, with the FAI job, hadn't had the time he deserved to be with his daughter. He didn't have kids and didn't plan on it now, but the underlying idea was the same: having the time to enjoy life. Something terrible could happen to you at any moment, and the only thing you have are the times you truly enjoyed. He was more and more convinced about his significant decision to resign from FAI.

The funeral was at 10 a.m. on that Thursday, September 2nd. The ceremony was outdoors. It was a beautiful day, weather-wise, with a glowing sun and no clouds in the sky. It was all in Polish, so they didn't understand anything, but it seemed rather moving, and not understanding the words didn't keep them from getting quite emotional.

There weren't many people. Harry imagined that the fact that Piotr had lived in Murcia for quite some time meant that he no longer knew many people in his native Poland. His daughter Anka was there, whom they recognized from the pictures, with a woman that they assumed was her mother. Apart from them, there were about twenty-five other people standing at a moderate distance, since they didn't want to draw too much attention. When the ceremony ended and all the guests had given their condolences to Anka and her mother, the FAI members, along with Sofia, went up to her. Harry initiated the conversation.

"You're Anka, right? Do you speak English?"

Anka looked at him as she wiped her tears away.

"Yes, you're my father's colleagues, right?"

"Yes, we are. I'm Harry, and this is Martha and Angela, and my girlfriend Sofia, who wasn't a colleague but knew him."

Anka practically fell onto Harry, drenched in tears, as he embraced her for a moment. Then, after introducing themselves to her mother, they all sat down in some chairs that were there. Her mother spoke nothing but Polish, so Anka told her to go and that when she was done, she would call her, but that she wanted to get to know her father's colleagues a bit more. Her mother, though initially looking reluctant to leave her daughter, said something to her in Polish, waved goodbye to everyone, and walked away.

They all sat down in what looked like a sort of semicircle, with Anka in the middle. The young girl, after drying her tears again, started speaking in a rather proper English with an Eastern European accent.

"My father spoke to me a lot about you all and what he really did. I know what you actually do, what my father did."

Everyone looked at each other with a face of not quite knowing what to say, but Anka kept talking.

"I know he wasn't supposed to tell me, because it goes against the rules. But my father said that I was always very mature for my age. I don't know if it's because of my parents' separation or what, but he said I was, and that I was prepared for the real world, and that this was the real world."

Everyone could see then why Piotr thought that way about his daughter. She was, without a doubt, notably mature for her age.

"Anka, I'm not quite sure what your dad told you what we do, but...," Harry started to explain himself to Anka, but she interrupted him.

"He told me everything, Harry: how you make so much money with jobs that might include killing people, that you've killed terrorists, that you've recovered stolen things and all that."

"Your father was a good man, Anka," Martha said.

"I know. My mother always says that too, and from what my father always told me, you all are, too. He always insisted on the fact that, whether mercenaries or not, it's very important to surround yourself with good people, people willing to do anything for you, and that, luckily, he had done that." Anka started getting emotional again.

They stayed there for a while longer. Without a doubt, for how introverted and quiet Piotr was, his daughter was the complete opposite. Truth be told, everyone thought she was great, lovable, and charming. They agreed for her to come to Spain some time, whenever she was ready, to learn Spanish and see where her father worked and lived. Everyone offered their house as a place for her to stay in Murcia, however long she wanted. They exchanged phone numbers and email addresses to stay in touch. Without a doubt, they had all practically gained a sort of daughter or little sister. Before lunchtime, Anka's mother picked her up, and they said goodbye to her. The FAI group in its entirety, along with Sofia, took a taxi to the airport, since they had a flight back to Murcia and were going together. They were sad, but at the same time reassured. Having met Anka and spent such a meaningful moment with her let them leave on a good note. It was clear that that girl had innate charisma and was special; she would be a good leader at work or whatever she dedicated herself to.

On the way to the airport, Harry received a response to his resignation. In truth, with all the emotions of the moment, he had in fact forgotten about it. The response email was quite long, but Harry went directly to the end. He knew that the response would be at the end; the rest was essentially filler. And at the end, it said the following:

"Therefore, given the current circumstances, we cannot accept your resignation and would like to continue working with you, while always remaining open to hearing any suggestions to make your time at FAI as enjoyable as possible."

# EPILOGUE

After a few days of lingering anger, Harry understood the reasoning of the Conglomerate's decision, given the circumstances. FAI had just lost a member in a tragic manner, and they couldn't let go of its leader. For the next five months, Harry and Martha (whose extended vacation was annulled) were left alone as both the managers and agents of FAI at the same time. They were exhausting months, given that two people alone were sometimes insufficient for some missions, but since they worked so well together, they always managed to get them done. During that time, Harry did sometimes come home exhausted and occasionally in a bad mood, though he tried not to take it out on Sofia.

Harry lived with Sofia in a gorgeous penthouse quite close to where he lived before. They bought it three weeks after coming back from Piotr's funeral, and Alfonso, the first time he visited, was so impressed that he asked where his room was.

At the beginning of February the following year, Angela returned to FAI with an old friend who joined as a field agent, Melinda. All this helped the missions to be more manageable. Around that time, Harry and Sofia, who were happier than ever, got married in grand fashion at the Lombardi family Tuscany villa in a ceremony that the whole FAI team attended, as was only natural, as well as the young Anka, who arranged with Harry and Sofia to come to Murcia the following year to finish high school and stay at their house, where there was plenty of room.

Regarding Sofia, she continued teaching at the language school, though from time to time and always unofficially, without the Conglomerate knowing, she helped FAI in some missions when it came to providing ideas, as a sort of consultant. Everyone saw that she could easily be one of them. In fact, Angela and Martha would jokingly call her "the honorary member of FAI."

Harry gradually came to terms with the fact that he was still a mercenary and that he was still young; he would have other opportunities to retire. With the help of weekly therapy sessions, he slowly came to terms with it and eventually found peace with continuing a bit longer in his necessary evil and accumulating skeletons in the closet. At least for now.

9 788410 901841